GAT·1

J
CHE

Chetwin, Grace.

The riddle & the
rune
1395

AUG 16 1988

$13.95   g   d

DATE		

© THE BAKER & TAYLOR CO.

The Riddle and the Rune

Also by Grace Chetwin

GOM ON WINDY MOUNTAIN
ON ALL HALLOWS' EVE
OUT OF THE DARK WORLD

Grace Chetwin

THE RIDDLE
AND THE RUNE

FROM
Tales of Gom
IN THE
LEGENDS OF ULM

Bradbury Press · New York

Bradbury Press
An Affiliate of Macmillan, Inc.
866 Third Avenue, New York, N.Y. 10022
Collier Macmillan Canada, Inc.
Printed and bound in the United States of America
10 9 8 7 6 5 4 3 2 1

The text of this book is set in 12 pt. Garamond #3.

Library of Congress Cataloging-in-Publication Data

Chetwin, Grace.
The riddle & the rune.

Summary: Gom sets forth to seek his destiny,
discovering that he has new powers and a gift for making
friends such as the magnificent horse, Stormfleet, who
accompanies him through many adventures.
{1. Fantasy} I. Title. II. Title: Riddle and the
rune.
PZ7.C42555Ri 1987 {Fic} 87-10284
ISBN 0-02-718312-2

For my father, Charles William Chetwin.
In memory.

GREAT

RINGING
VALLEY

THE WILDS

DUNDERFOSSE

SUNDOR
Sundborg

SOUTHERN

KRUGK

HIGH VARGUE

Quend

Green Vale

Bragget-on-the-Edge

LONG VALLEY

Lake Langoth

Pen'langoth

SHORE

Part

1

Chapter One

WAY AHEAD, over the far mountain peaks, the sun was setting. Halfway toward them, in the middle of the high plateau, the small, solitary figure of a boy stopped, closing his eyes against the brilliant light, and leaning wearily on his staff.

Staff? It was really a walking stick: quite new, finely carved with wild animals chasing up and down and around its length, nose to tail. A pert brown sparrow perched atop it, her tiny black eyes seemingly alive and scanning the way ahead. Stig had fashioned the stick to suit his own great size, with the sparrow for handle. Now it served his son for staff, the sparrow coming level with Gom's chest.

"That's a fine stick, Father. The best you've ever made," Gom had said, not even a week before. Stout, too, to bear Stig's massive weight.

"Aye. It'll serve you well enough when I'm gone," his father had answered, as though he'd known his time had come.

Sure enough, only two days ago Gom had buried his father on Windy Mountain and, grieving, had raised a cairn of gray stones over his grave. After that, in spite of the promise Gom had made to Stig to stay safely home and become Clack's next woodcutter, Gom had left to seek Harga, his mother.

His hand strayed inside his shirt to the stone that hung about his neck from a leather thong. Harga's rune. The magic charm his mother had left with him when she'd disappeared the day of his birth. Feeling its faint vibrations under his hand, he put it to his ear, but heard nothing. All his life the stone had remained silent—save for that last moment by his father's grave when there had come from the rune such beautiful humming as had filled Gom with wonder.

His eyes still tight shut, he pictured the lonely pile of stones above the town. It would be days before anyone could get up there because of the snow. Even for him that last trip down the icy trail had been perilous and no one knew that trail as well as he—now that Stig was dead. At that thought, grief welled up afresh within him, catching at his throat.

Turning, Gom looked back to the far horizon over which night was falling fast. Even after only a few hours traveling Gom had lost sight of the peak that had been his home for all of his life. And why not? Hadn't Hoot Owl told him that Windy Mountain was but a pimple on the great face of the world?

Somewhere back in that twilight the townsfolk were drawing curtains and lighting lamps, Hoot Owl was waking up to hunt, while Stig—

His breath became a sob.

Father! Oh, Father.

He stared through a blur toward his distant home, feeling desolate and alone. Alone? Not entirely. A sudden gust reminded him of Wind, old friend of uncertain temper. Wind, who over the years had brought him whiffs of the Sea, and scents from Far Away.

Now that very Wind blew in his face, whipping his hair, snatching his breath. *Stir yourself, or freeze!* it urged. *On your way!*

Still fingering the rune, feeling the familiar lines criss-crossing the smooth black stone, and the tiny knobs and whorls that held the power of Harga's name, Gom turned away from the darkening mountains and stumbled on toward the radiant peaks ahead, over winter grass and brake until the sun set and the ground glowed with its own luminescence.

He began to look about him in the twilight for a suitable resting place. It was almost too dark to see where he trod when he finally came across a little stream beside a stand of spindly alder hung with vines.

He leaned his staff against a tree and pulled some of the vines down behind him to make a windbreak. Then he groped around for what dead and brittle branches he could find in that poor light. Some of the tinder he set aside, and piled the rest like a tiny corn stook in front of his makeshift shelter. Fishing out his tinder box, he struck a spark against the dusty kindling, where it caught, smoldering. Wind touched the spark, and fanned it lightly into flame. It was small, scarce big enough to warm his hands, but the light was welcome.

He sat, huddled into his jacket, his hands outstretched, staring into the sputtering flames. He thought with longing of Harga's old blanket worked with suns and moons and stars; a blanket small and light enough to roll up and carry on one's back—if only one had thought of it. Fool, to leave home so unprepared at the tag end of winter!

Gom Gom, dumb as a log;
His head's all wind, and his tongue's all frog!

The townschildren's old taunt might well be true, he thought bitterly.

He pictured the little hut, his bed by the far wall.

And Stig's, opposite. And the hearth, dark and cold. There'd be no songs by the fire that night. Or ever again. He doubled over, tight with grief.

Hunger stirred him, finally. He foraged in his left jacket pocket and pulled out a hunk of stale bread, a wedge of cheese, all there'd been left in the larder. The cheese was too hard and dry to break. He reached into his back pocket for his knife. It wasn't there. He felt in another pocket, then another. It wasn't in those either. Had he dropped it? No. He remembered now. He'd left it on the table in the hut. He, a woodcutter's son, had actually left home without his knife! Disgusted at himself, he settled for using his teeth. One nibble of cheese, one nibble of bread, and he stowed them away again. He well knew how to make little go far.

From his right jacket pocket, he took out Stig's ancient green glass water bottle and weighed it in his hand. Still half full. He removed the stopper and drank deep, as he could afford to, with that nearby stream.

Gom replaced the stopper and put the bottle back, guiltily thinking how it had been his father's custom every winter's evening to have them wash before going to bed. He certainly needed it. His hands were black from messing with the fire, and he was covered in grit. He glanced toward the stream and shuddered. Too cold.

Cold, and lonely. Everybody in the world that night had a roof to lie under, and someone with whom to share it, he thought miserably. Everybody—save Gom Gobblechuck.

He reached into a back pocket. His fingers encountered a tiny wooden box fitted with cunning hinges that he'd fashioned years ago under Stig's watchful eye: empty, he knew, and not what he sought. He dug deeper and pulled out a small leather pouch. Loosening the drawstring, he shook the contents onto his palm. He couldn't see them well in that feeble firelight, but he could feel his old treasures, mementos of home: seeds, the pod of a hoarbell, a honeybee's sac, the cocoon of a moon moth, and a tiny flake of gold. Lightly, lovingly, he fingered them, caressed them almost, taking comfort from each one, then restored them back to the pouch.

Gom took up the last of the kindling, placed it carefully on the little fire, then pulled his jacket around him and lay down to sleep.

After a few minutes, he was aware of the glass bottle pressing into his ribs. He rolled over, tried another way. Ah, that was better. He brought his knees up, wrapped his arms about them, and tried to let his mind drift.

As he lay there, shivering, waiting for sleep to come, his body began to tingle.

He came alert.

He'd not had a waking dream since the time he'd found the hermit Mandrik's bones in the caves under Windy Mountain and had taken them out to bury them under the stars. Ah, what a wondrous dream that had been, when the ancient skull had come to life and Mandrik had told Gom that Harga was the greatest wizard in the world and that Gom must go seek her with the rune after Stig was gone.

The tingling increased, but this time without the warm bright light that usually came to dazzle him. He gazed up expectantly into the darkness, accepting the change. After all, it had been so long.

Suddenly a cold came upon him, colder than the chill of the winter plain. Icy, unseen hands touched him, as though exploring his shape in the same careful way Gom had just fingered his treasures.

He reached out to push the hands away, and with surprise met with nothing. Still the probing went on.

He sat up, angry now, and afraid. This was not a waking dream, but something else. He seized his staff, as the fingers moved down his face, his neck until they reached the rune.

There they stopped. In the darkness he heard nothing but his own indrawn breath, and yet he knew that someone or something evil had come upon him.

Suddenly, there appeared before him a pinpoint of light, a tiny star not an arm's length away. As he watched, it grew into the shape of a skull: not a fine, mellow skull like Mandrik's, but a stark death's-head, bone-white.

In a panic, Gom raised the staff to knock it away, but as he did so, the jaw moved, and a voice grated in the darkness with flat, metallic sound.

"Har—ga."

The coldness intensified, creeping through him like death. Another minute and he'd be paralyzed. Quickly, Gom sought the rune, closed his hand over it, and silently called his mother's name.

Harga!

Warmth filled his hand, spread up his arm, chasing out the cold.

"Who are you? What are you?" demanded Gom, his courage returning.

The skull hovered, silent, the dark sockets on him, watching, waiting.

For what? Gom noticed that the cold was creeping in again, despite the rune. In desperation, he struck out with the staff, and the skull vanished at the sparrow's sudden touch.

Gom sagged, exhausted. He drew up his knees and hunched over them, the staff still in one hand, the rune in the other. What evil had chanced upon him, he but one day from home? He peered about uneasily.

Chanced?

He shook his head. He had an uneasy sense of having been sought, and found. But for what? And—*who even knew of him outside Clack?*

He sat up again. It was not Gom that had drawn the death's-head, but the rune! He set the staff across his lap, shivering at the memory of the unseen fingers probing him, lighting at last upon the key to Harga's name—and power.

Harga, the skull had said. *Harga.*

Bright sunlight flaking through his shelter awoke him. He lay for an instant, the bad feeling from his vision still upon him. Then he stiffened, becoming aware of warm breath on his cheek. He opened his eyes to find a sharp-nosed gray fox cub bending over him, sniffing him inquisitively.

Relieved, Gom sat up, but before he could utter a word, the fox leapt back with a bark and raced off.

"Hey!" Gom called after him, in the voice of the brown foxes of Windy Mountain, but it didn't even turn its head. Gom watched it go ruefully. Yet what else could he expect? In the wild, all good mothers trained their offspring to beware of strangers. Up on Windy Mountain, where everyone knew Gom, mothers trusted him, knew he'd do no harm.

Being a stranger wasn't pleasant. He felt hurt that the animal hadn't sensed his friendliness, and it left him feeling small and insignificant. Sighing, Gom stood up. Maybe the fox had sensed his lingering fear from the dream, and had run from that. The idea comforted him, somehow.

He stretched resolutely, and, turning his face to the light, prepared to meet the new day. He'd slept late. The sun was high and climbing. Down in Clack, the townsfolk would already be thinking of elevenses.

Gom pulled out his bread and cheese, took a half-hearted bite of each and stowed them away again. Then he drank from the stream, and gave his face a dutiful splash of icy water.

That done, Gom filled his bottle and returned it to his pocket. Which way should he go? He shaded his eyes, his back to the sun. Why that way, of course, the way Wind was steering him.

He trudged on over the late winter plateau, his eyes on the ground, seeking plantain or fool's-button, any of the wild roots that Harga had taught Stig to use to eke out meager rations. But he found nothing: no dead leaf clumps to tell where roots lay buried, waiting for the sun to touch them back to life. From time to time he glanced back toward the far horizon. Every step he took brought him nearer to his goal—and also farther from home. When he'd said good-bye to his eldest brother and sister, Stok and Hilsa, folk had crowded out to watch, scandalized. Was he still the butt of gossip? Probably, for who else had ever quit that place?

Why, his mother, of course! Gom brightened at the thought, and strode forward with new resolution. He was going to find Harga. He'd fix his mind on that, even though he had as yet no idea where to find her, or how long it would take.

For hours he moved on, but the only thing that seemed to change was the angle of the sun. Slowly, it climbed, hung overhead, then began its downward arc. Gom stopped for a spell, gazing around the plateau at the ring of ever-distant peaks around him. "It's all the same," he cried. "Is this all there is?"

Of course not. Wind breathed on him briskly. *As I've told you often enough. This is but a puny pack of petty peaks. Now move on before you starve and catch your death, for there's neither food nor shelter here at winter's end.*

Gom heeded Wind's warning and stepped up his pace. Time to look for another resting place, make another shelter; to find some dry wood for a fire, and water to drink. The sun's warmth wouldn't last much longer. Then Wind would grow cold again, and the thin air would chill him to the bone.

For four more lonely days Gom trudged on, calling out to the occasional fox and evening rabbit, but to his disappointment, not one came up to exchange news with him. Once or twice migrating birds flew overhead: black-birds, for the most part, and a few wild geese, returning a little early to spring nesting grounds, as Gom would judge, and far too intent on their destination to heed him. Still, it cheered him, going along, to think of warmer weather.

Under the sun he didn't fear the death's-head. But under the night sky when Wind whistled across the dark-ened plain and around his makeshift shelters, he'd re-member his awful vision and he'd wait apprehensively for it to come again. The nights passed, however, without further visitation.

Creeks he found a-plenty to keep his water bottle filled, but by the fifth morning, the bread and cheese were almost gone and hunger shrank his belly. All he had for breakfast that day were a few shriveled berries that even hungry birds had disdained. He must find food soon or perish. It was too far to turn back now.

On, on, Wind shrilled. *Things will get better, you'll see. Beyond those mountains ahead the land drops far. It's warmer there. Things are sprouting tender and green already, and you'll be sure to find something to eat.*

"If I ever get there," Gom answered, eyeing the knobbly spine of low rounded peaks that he must pass to reach it.

By noon, the plateau had come to an end, and the ground was rising. Gom was soon climbing up steep rock face scored with deep clefts—massive cracks big enough for him to shelter in—and pocked with small black holes that promised caves.

All his life, he'd lived among the mountains. Even Clack, at the foot of Windy Mountain, was still high up. The idea of going down into lowland, real lowland, rallied his spirits.

It couldn't quite give him the energy to travel faster, though. Only food would do that. Nevertheless, he struggled along, pulling on his staff until late afternoon, when his strength finally gave out.

Not to worry, he told himself. Perhaps if he stopped now, he'd have enough energy by morning to make that last push over the range—or through it, if he were lucky enough to find a pass.

Looking about for shelter, he spotted a small dark hole

about twelve feet above where he stood. A cave. He stared upward. The staff was a problem, for he'd need both hands to climb.

On a sudden idea, Gom felt around in his pockets and pulled out a spare bootlace of long and sturdy leather. He tied it firmly about the staff at hand height, then knotted the loose ends together, making a loop. Was it big enough? He put his head through the loop, slipped one arm through it, then slid the staff around until it hung squarely at his back. Pleased with his ingenuity, Gom began to climb the sheer rock face.

Have a care, Wind warned him. *That cave may be occupied.*

Wind was right: it was.

Reaching level with the cave, Gom peered in. A huge dark shape lay curled up in the back corner: a great brown bear, creature of fierce, uncertain temper that Gom wouldn't presume to tangle with, not even up on Windy Mountain, where he knew every one. It appeared to be still locked in winter sleep.

Yet even as he stood watching, it stirred, and turned over. Gom left, fast.

It was almost dark before he found another shelter, a second cave, which he entered against Wind's most urgent warnings.

Remember what you found the last time! Agh, you may be sorry.

The cave was small, and sheltered—and empty.

With a triumphant wave to Wind, Gom went in. It was indeed a good find, with solid walls, no holes for chilly draughts. Or sudden bear.

Gom stood the staff by the back wall, and sat down,

leaning against the rough stone, and gazing out at the twilit sky. He took a good swallow of water, then lay down to sleep, rubbing his middle to comfort it. If only he weren't so hungry, he thought, for with hunger came such cold. He pictured a small fire burning in the middle of the floor, throwing welcome golden light onto the walls, filling the tiny shelter with snug warmth. But there wasn't the smallest twig of a tree on this bare rock face.

He sought the rune for comfort, slid his nail along the grooves etched in its smooth, shiny surface. Why had Harga left it with him? And why, if Mandrik spoke true, was he supposed to take it to her? If Harga really were the most powerful wizard in the world, couldn't she get it back herself in a finger-snap? Gom frowned. Did even wizards have their limits?

The sun was suddenly gone. The shadows in the cave deepened, smudging the sharp rock walls, filling the corners with menace. Gom glanced around, thinking of bears—and skulls. Stop it, he told himself firmly. Another few hours and you'll be on your way.

Shadows flowed together into one dark mass, enveloping him. The moon rose, faintly outlining the cave entrance in silver.

He lay on his side, and drew his knees up. "Mother," he murmured, huddling into the warmth of his jacket. "Where are you? When shall we meet?" With his hands clasped about the rune for comfort, he lay facing the dim moonlight and drifted.

When he came to, the moon's radiance filled the cave. Atop the staff, the sparrow's tiny black seed-eyes gleamed mysteriously.

All at once the light cut as a huge shambling shape blocked the cave entrance.

A bear!

Gom went stiff with panic.

A bear, and there was he, lying in the middle of its floor!

Chapter Two

FOOL, FOOL, and fool again, to have ignored Wind's good advice! He thought of running, but where? There was only one thing left to do and that was as his wild friends did on Windy Mountain when faced by danger as sudden and as close: he kept still.

It wasn't easy. The bear entered the cave and shuffled toward him, until it was so close that Gom could see clearly the hairs on its body glistening in the moon's rays.

He stared up at the giant figure, waiting for the bear's growl, for the huge paws to come down and claw him up from the floor. To his surprise, the beast stayed upright, looking down at him, motionless.

Gom tried his throat again, and this time, found his voice.

"Hello, and good evening," Gom stammered in bear, trying to sound calm and normal. The bear didn't answer, but only stood over him, just as though, Gom thought, it were waiting for something to happen.

Something did.

With a sudden flirt of wings, the wooden sparrow darted from her perch atop the staff to light on the bear's right shoulder. There, quickly, deftly, she settled her wings back in place and rubbed her beak against the bear's great hairy neck. Then to Gom's further amazement, she looked at him and spoke.

"You called upon your mother, Gom Gobblechuck? Then Harga answers you. Hear this:

> From Air and Earth comes seed;
> By Fire and Water is tempered:
> In Wood is kernel's secret essence known,
> And purpose comes to light.

"You know what that is?"

"It sounds like a riddle," Gom answered, his eyes fixed on her.

"Quite so. A little box of simple treasures: plain words with deep and secret meaning. If you would meet Harga, find its key. Dear boy," she said, spreading her wings, "your mother watches for you, and hopes for you on your path of experience." With that, she fluttered down from the bear's shoulder, brushed Gom's cheek lightly with her passing, then flew back to her perch on top of Stig's walking stick.

The moment she was settled, the bear lay down beside Gom and curled its great body around him, enveloping him in comfort and warmth. Funny, Gom thought drowsily. He didn't feel at all afraid in the bear's embrace: but rather secure and content as he had the nights he and Stig had gone to bed happy with their hard day's work, while the mellow fire threw its brightness about the hut walls. He sighed deeply, and, the bear's earthy breath upon him, closed his eyes.

"Mother, Father . . ."

Gom awoke with both names upon his lips. He stretched, surprised to find himself warm, and not stiff at all. Remembering, he sat up. There was no trace of the bear:

no sign that it had ever been. He ran to the cave mouth and looked out. Empty landscape stretched away down.

He went back inside the cave, brushing his cheek lightly with his fingertips. Had the sparrow really come alive last night? Or had it been but a dream? For answer, the words of the riddle sprang to mind, clear and in their entirety.

"From Air and Earth comes seed," Gom murmured. "By Fire and Water is tempered: in Wood is kernel's secret essence known, and purpose comes to light." He took the staff and stroked the sparrow's head, the tiny wooden feathers that Stig had carved there. Wood. She was made of wood. But what had that to do with kernels and essences? He looked her squarely in the eye. "It makes no sense," he said. She stared back at him, unblinking.

"From Air and Earth comes seed." Didn't seeds come from plants? Setting down the staff, he took out his pouch and, removing his larger treasures first, he shook out his precious Windy Mountain seeds into his palm. Fine and light, they lay on his hand like grains of golden sand. Who'd ever guess that from such tiny things would come loder trees with strong curving branches high as any oak, and golden leaves as delicate as birch or mulberry?

Wind caught the seeds, scattered them mischievously onto the cave floor. Muttering, Gom got down onto his knees, scrabbling to retrieve them.

Air only dispersed seeds: earth but gave them root. Everyone knew that, even Maister Craw, who didn't know much of anything save how to raise cabbages.

Having found what seeds he could, Gom was just about to restore them to his pouch when he set it aside and instead pulled out the little wooden box.

A little box of simple treasures . . .

He opened the lid and carefully dropped the seeds inside. Reclosing the lid, he shook the box once or twice, listening to the whisper of small dry seeds within, then put it away. Now it was a treasure box indeed.

What a strange experience the vision had been. A gift and a touch from his mother—and a challenge, too: solve the riddle and be reunited with Harga at last.

If all that separated him from Harga was that old riddle, then—a smile spread slowly over his face—his troubles were surely over. Hadn't Stig always said what a quick and clever mind his son had?

Gom collected his other treasures and restored them to the pouch, whistling in great self-satisfaction. Why kill himself running all over the place when all he had to do was stay right there and simply set his brain to work? With luck, he'd have the answer by elevenses!

He put the pouch away and stood up. To think: that very day he could well be handing Harga her rune. He slipped the stone from under his shirt and held it to his cheek, his mother's magic talisman that had saved him from the death's-head's cold.

The death's-head! He glanced to the sparrow in consternation. Harga couldn't know about it, or the sparrow surely would have said. Maybe things weren't so simple as he'd hoped. Dare he stay in that place and wait for his mother to come? He looked toward the entrance uneasily. What if the death's-head came instead?

Better move out of there, he decided. And think as he went along.

He grabbed the staff, and moved out quickly into the open.

* * *

All morning Gom climbed the stone slopes, expecting at any moment to reach their crest. After all, the peaks weren't so high, not high enough for a snow cap, at any rate. But every time he topped one slope, another lay beyond it, going ever up. His knees began to tremble, and his belly hurt. Then he got a stone in his boot. Glad of the excuse to stop, he sat, took off the boot, and shook out a sharp granite chip. The sole was almost worn through, he noticed, pressing on it with his thumb. He slipped the boot back on, and retied the lace. Another day's hard going, two at the most, and he might as well be walking barefoot.

He climbed on.

Elevenses time came and went uncelebrated. He was so hungry by now that he could scarce think on the riddle at all, though he did try. Earth, water, fire, and wood. All to do in some way with seed. But how? He shrugged, looking to the sky for answer.

A single black speck circled above him, too high to identify. Gom shaded his eyes. It could be a buzzard. Or a hawk. He knew both well enough. Buzzards mostly lived on carrion, picking the bones of dead things found lying under the sky. Hawks swooped with deadly aim on living creatures whose only mistake was to stray in the open at the wrong time.

He studied it for a minute or two, until he had the uneasy feeling that it, in turn, was watching him. Gom narrowed his eyes, the better to see. Buzzard, or hawk? Scavenger, or bird of living prey? He still couldn't be sure, though the neck looked long for a hawk's. In any case, a hawk wouldn't go for him. Small as he was, he was no rabbit or squirrel.

Some comfort, that! If not hawk after live prey, then it must be buzzard after worse. The way those birds could sniff out the dead and the dying was remarkable. Gom remembered how those birds would hover over certain spots on the mountain, proclaiming by their very presence some poor creature stranded below.

Gom stopped still. Could it be a buzzard?

Was he even worse off than he felt? Panic rose inside Gom then, pumping his heart, quickening his breath. He saw himself succumbing to hunger, falling headlong to lie out there, unmarked—save by that deathly sentinel. He pictured it slowly spiraling lower and lower, then swooping down at last to pick his flesh.

He tried to go faster, but, oh, what a struggle it was! Where, he thought urgently, was that mountain crest?

Gom stumbled along, one eye seeking out the best way to climb, the other on the circling bird, until his breath began to labor. He was climbing more steeply now, and the staff was becoming an encumbrance, but holding it made him feel secure.

Out of breath, he paused momentarily to take quick stock of the way ahead. To Gom's dismay, about a hundred yards farther up the slope reared sudden rock face; a cliff, too steep and too high to climb in a hurry. But in it, to his right, he glimpsed a dark cleft, little more than a crack in the cliff but surely space enough to shelter him from the bird.

He was just making for it when he heard the beat of powerful wings. The bird had come much lower. It was big: bigger than any hawk or buzzard that he'd ever seen, with a wingspan wide as four arms' lengths, and pinion feathers spread like giant fingers.

Neck outstretched, it banked and dove straight at him.

Gom threw himself down and rolled, shielding his head with his arms, felt a shock of air from the giant wing beats.

Looking up, Gom glimpsed sharp-hooked talons, and a vicious beak. Not buzzard, not hawk, not any bird he'd ever seen. His stomach tight with fear, he picked himself up and ran for the nearest shelter, a round boulder poised on the slope, as though snagged in midfall.

Peering out, Gom saw that the bird had turned about and was preparing for another sweep.

Crouching, Gom shrank under the boulder's overhang. The bird swooped down, and, quick as a snake, thrust out its long neck to strike. Its beak clicked sharply on the stone face, missing Gom by a breath. Screaming in defeat, the evil thing retreated.

Gom closed his eyes and let out a shuddering breath. Much good his shelter was: the bird had but to keep him there until he could no longer resist.

He waited a moment, two, listening, then risked a peek. The massive shape arced high above him, gray wings darkly translucent against the bright blue sky.

Gom's hand trembled about the staff. His whole body was shaking. Why, if he were to stand at that moment, his knees would buckle under him. Was this how rabbits felt, he wondered, when cornered by hawks? Squatting in the cramped shelter of the overhang, Gom pictured the creature waiting above, high enough to draw him out, low enough to catch him when he came.

That thought made Gom angry. His chin went up. He was no rabbit. He was Gom, a human boy, with wits to match any bird's, however big and cunning.

Come on! Wind shrieked urgently. *That is no ordinary crack, as you can tell by my voice, but a pass leading through to the other side of the range. Reach it, and you'll not only be safe from the bird but you'll save yourself a climb!*

Wind's whine vibrating across his ears, Gom eyed the distance to the cleft with even greater interest. Not a blind shelter, but a shortcut, a safe escape route! Could he reach it?

One hundred yards had never looked so far!

Gripping the staff tightly, taking comfort from its solid weight, Gom crawled from under the boulder and scrabbled up the slope on all fours.

He'd gone but a few yards when the bird's shadow covered him and once more the sound of beating wings grew loud.

Shouting in desperation, Gom struck out.

In that instant, pain seared his shoulder, but the bird's screech rang harshly in his ears. The staff had hit its mark.

Gom had no time to rejoice. He stumbled, and went headlong, the staff flying from his hand. Blood oozed from his shoulder, soaking his jacket. Picking himself up, he seized the staff with his good hand and scrambled for the pass. His boots slipped, sent him staggering back a few paces, but with an effort he checked himself, then pressed on.

As he squeezed into the rock cleft, the bird rushed him, but mercifully, it was too late. There came another screech, this time of rage.

Gom slid weakly down the rock face, and sat, doubled over.

Presently, he stirred himself, and peering upward, saw a crooked sliver of sky. Gom breathed out in relief. He was safe for a while at least, for the bird couldn't possibly dive down there.

Leaning heavily on the staff, he pulled himself to his feet and moved on. It wasn't easy. The floor of the pass rose sharply, and shrank in places to a crevice scarce wide enough for Gom to set his feet. Several times along the way its walls, too, grew so narrow that Gom had to slip off his pack and squirm through sideways, pulling the pack after him. But, as he reminded himself, at least he was safe from predatory birds!

At last the pass floor turned downward again, then leveled out and widened, and Gom saw with relief open space ahead. At last he'd reached the mountain's other side. From there, if Wind had told right, the range fell away down into lowland.

Gom paused uncertainly, thinking of the bird.

Was it still waiting for him back on the plateau, or had it guessed that he'd found a way through and out this other side? Whichever, he couldn't stay there for long.

He stumbled on, step by painful step. Then suddenly he was teetering on the brink of a precipice high above open rolling land: little squares of fresh spring greens and yellows all pieced together neat as the patchwork covers worked by the wives of Clack. Tiny white dots speckled the land, farmhouses, probably, and among them lay a sprinkling of bright green pompoms: trees, in leaf already! It looked wonderful: wide, and friendly, and inviting. Gom stared down, quite forgetting the bird. Maybe— his belly rumbled at the thought—he wouldn't have to scratch around for wild roots after all.

He looked up. The bird, gliding in on silent wings, was almost on him!

With a quick drawn breath, he dodged sideways, twisted, and with a cry, rolled off the brink. He fell through the air a short way, bounced, knocking his breath from his ribs. Then he rolled again, slid, and was once more off through empty space.

He thudded onto his back, and lay dazed, staring up into the sun.

There came a scream, and the sun was gone.

The great gray bird was hovering over him, stretching out a neck as long and thick as Gom's arm. As the naked head came close, Gom saw quite clearly that its head was a bone-white skull, half-bird, half-human!

Gom squeezed his eyes shut, waiting for the slash of beak or talon, but felt instead a tug on the thong around his neck.

Of course! Like the death's-head of his vision, it wasn't after him, but Harga's rune!

With a mighty effort, Gom brought up the staff and lashed out. The bird shot up with an angry cry, beat its wings as though to amass its strength, then plunged back down in fury.

Gom tried to stand, but he was finished. Helpless, he watched the bird's descent, closing his eyes at the last minute. There came a rush of wings, then, oh glory, another, more familiar sound:

"Hey! What's all this, then?"

The bird's enraged cries whirled up and away.

Gom opened his eyes.

Standing over him was the figure of a man dressed in bulky layers of warm, thick cloth, so much so that only his face showed. His eyebrows were gray, but his eyes were brown and sharp above his leathered cheeks.

"Hello, young fellermelad." The accents were broad and flat; the voice, hearty and still quite loud. "Whatever's going on around here?"

Gom began to shiver violently, and his teeth to click together.

The man bent down. "Feller? Young feller?"

The man's voice sounded near, then far away. The face leaned closer, and closer, then melted into the dazzle of the sun.

Chapter Three

THE SNAP of settling logs woke him.

Gom opened his eyes. He was lying on a pallet by a hearth. But not his hearth, he remembered with a rush. Where was he, then? Whose hearth was it? He rolled over and tried to sit up. Oh, how his shoulder hurt!

"Hey, hey, hey. Careful does it." A large, ample woman in a black dress and brown apron appeared beside him. Her sleeves were pushed up above her dimpled elbows and her plump, red hands were all over flour. She slipped an arm around his good shoulder and helped him to sit up, deftly placing pillows with her spare hand to support his back. Gom sucked in his breath against the pain, trying not to let it show.

"There now. How do you feel?" Stray strands of wispy hair curled down from her thick, gray topknot to hang about her round, red cheeks.

Gom stared up at her, scarce taking in her words. "Who are you? Where am I?" His voice came out shaky, making him sound afraid, but he wasn't, not at all.

The woman squatted beside him. "I'm Mudge. And you're in my house. My man, Hort, brought you in three days ago. Half dead, you were, from starvation, and"— she waved her plump hand at his shoulder—"that."

Gom peeked under his shirt, saw that his shoulder was heavily bound with clean white strips of linen. He remembered falling, falling away and down, and the great gray bird reaching over him.

"The blood!" Mudge was saying. "I thought it'd never stop. Covered in it, you were, not to mention all your other scrapes and scratches. And bruises: you're black and blue all over!" She threw up her hands, tutting with kindly concern. "On top of it all, you took a fever fit to seethe you, and the ague into the bargain. We had to fetch the herb wife, Mistress Gumby, to physic you. Even then, Hort said you'd not make it, but I said, said I, that one's tougher than he looks. Like a young cub new-slipped from its earth, of a mind to try the world. And here you are. You'll be hungry, I daresay," she added, grinning, as Gom's belly gurgled like an old cistern.

She got up, grunting, and ladled out a cup of amber gruel from an earthen pot standing on the hearth. "Here: careful not to burn your mouth."

She set it on the coverlet and put his hand to it. "Can you hold it steady on your own? I've apples to bake and crust to make, for my man'll soon be in for his tea." She moved to a table in the middle of the room.

The gruel was too hot to drink. Gom shifted his hands on the bowl in frustration. It looked and smelled so delicious, and he was starving. He blew on it a couple of times, then tried a sip. Still too hot. He gave up and looked about him curiously.

The room was raftered in rough oak beams and from the rafters hung strings of onions and herbs and lines of sweet drying clothes. Thick, rippled glass panes beside the door let in small squares of dull gray light that reflected off whitewashed walls, off waxed oak boards, vying with the glow of flames from the hearth.

Gom let out a deep, slow breath. The place felt good

and homely and comfortable, like his sister Hilsa's cottage.

One wall was lined with stout shelves and on the shelves stood rows and rows of tall glass jars labeled cherries, applesauce, cranberries, pickled onions, and buckwheat honey.

Buckwheat honey. He remembered Hilsa, her floury hands holding out a baking tray: *Here, Gom, love. Hotcakes, your favorite. Pick one and don't spare the honey.* Hilsa's own honey, from the hives she'd had built at his urging.

Gom turned his attention back to his gruel. The bowl still felt a mite hot, but he couldn't wait any longer. He took a sip, found it just as tasty as it smelled. He was just about to drink the rest of it down when there came a scraping and scratting of boots on the step outside, a click of the iron latch.

A moment later Hort stepped in, took off his coat, and hung it on a peg behind the door.

"Well, well, well. Look who's back in the land of the living. How do you feel, young fellermelad?" He pulled off his boots, padded over in his socks to sit by the fire.

"Fine, thank you," Gom said. Well, better, anyway. The gruel had burned a track right down his gullet to his middle. He looked down at himself, noticed now that the shirt he had on was not his own but brown and many sizes too big. The man's, obviously. His own faded blue tunic lay washed and folded with the rest of his clothes on the floor beside him, and—joy of joys—his boots were by them, cleaned and polished, and mended good as new with stout patches of leather.

His staff? There it was, propped against the wall beside him.

And the rune? Gom's hand went inside the shirt, closed about it.

He glanced up, caught the woman's eye. She nodded, though she didn't speak, but only got on with her baking.

Hort leaned forward, studying Gom's face. "How's that shoulder?" Without waiting for answer, he went on, "Halfway up the Bluff, I found you. Or down, depending on which way a body was going, like." He cocked an eye at Gom. "Me, I was looking for a ewe. Cranky things they are, close to lambing time. Get themselves into the most surprising places. But lucky for you, or you'd be—"

Gom closed his eyes, saw the great gray bird swooping, neck outstretched, the death's-head looming closer, closer . . .

"Hort!" Mudge warned.

Hort covered his mouth, grinning sheepishly. "Oops. Trust me to put my foot in it. Sorry, lad."

Gom nodded, tried to smile.

"I must say," Hort went on, "that bird gave me a terrible big shock, too. But nothing like what you must have had, seeing it go for you like that. The moment I clapped eyes on it, I says to myself, I says, that's where yon ewe went. And that little feller'll follow if I don't do something fast. One yell from me and that there bird took off, and I've not seen it since. I can't help but wonder where it came from."

"Same place it went back to, we hope," Mudge cut in. "Hort, the lad's as white as a sheet. Leave him be to take his gruel in peace."

Grunting, Hort sat up and folded his arms.

Gom drained his bowl and leaned back against his

plumped up pillows, his fear gradually subsiding. Outside, Wind rattled the windowpanes in impatience, then tore off to whoop and whirl across the far hillside.

He sighed contentedly, feeling the heat of the broth spreading from his middle, and outward through his whole body. It was good to lie there by that friendly hearth, safe from evil birds, with nothing better to do for the present than to listen to Wind's mad capers.

He did wonder drowsily where that bird might be. He stirred slightly. It was linked with the death's-head, he was sure. And like the death's-head, it was after the rune.

He looked over at Hort's solid figure now sprawled by the hearth, slid down beneath the covers, and fell into a deep, deep sleep.

"Looking for your mother? Where is she?"

Gom, fully dressed, stood at the window watching the sun set over a burgeoning countryside. Wind was right: spring did come earlier down here. He turned away, went to take his place at the supper table with Hort and Mudge, before plates of vegetable pie. "I don't know. She left home when I was born." Already he was beginning to regret telling them that much.

"Oh, you poor boy," Mudge cried. "How could any mother go off like that? If I had you for a son, I certainly wouldn't do such a thing."

Gom was stung. "She had to go. She's a w——" He bit the word back just in time. "Wizard" he'd been about to say. "Wanderer," he said, quick to hide his falter.

"A *wanderer*?" Mudge's homely face crinkled in distaste.

Gom stared back at her, disconcerted. The word sounded

so cold in Mudge's mouth. It made his mother sound feckless, and uncaring. And it made him feel bad, as though he'd done Harga a great disservice. But how to tell those folk the truth? How his mother had stayed thirteen long years with Stig, raising nine beautiful children, caring for them all, cooking them the most delicious meals out of practically nothing. How his mother had taught her growing family mountain ways, and had kept them well with her herbal lore. How she'd taught them to look out for themselves and one another, ready for the time when she knew that she must leave them—and that for good reason, Stig had told Gom, even though he'd never known exactly what it was.

"Wanderer?" Mudge repeated. "What kind of no-good occupation is that to make a woman leave her boy with neither mother nor father now to tend him?"

Gom looked to her in surprise. He hadn't said anything about Stig.

Mudge reached over the table and laid her hand on his. "You shouted terrible in your sleep you did, didn't he, Hort?"

Hort sighed in agreement, and gathered up a forkful of pie. "Aye. Cried and sobbed, an' all. For your dad, and your sister, Hilsa, and Stok. He's your brother, right?"

Gom nodded. Of his nine brothers and sisters, Hilsa and Stok were the eldest, and his favorites. In fact, the only ones who'd ever had time for him. Of course, Gom thought, excusing the rest, they'd known their mother the longest, had learned her lessons the best, loving him and looking out for him just the way Harga had taught them.

"Fair wrung my heart out to listen to you, it did," Mudge said. "There shouldn't be that much sadness in such a young 'un. Where are you off to, anyways, leaving a brother and sister that you love so much?"

Gom looked from one to the other, touched by their sympathy, yet also irritated that they'd found out all that about him and he unaware. He wondered anxiously if he'd mentioned the riddle, and sincerely hoped not. Mandrik had warned him to beware of strangers and to keep his secrets close. Like the fox, he'd do well to maintain his distance, he told himself, then felt ashamed. Hadn't they saved his life twice over? And there he was, thinking mean, suspicious thoughts.

"To find my mother," he repeated, patiently.

"But how will you know her?" Mudge asked him. " 'Specially when you've never seen her."

"And where?" Hort chimed in. "Where would you look for her, lad? 'Tis a fair big place out there."

Gom considered his answer. "They say I look just like her," he said at last. It sounded feeble, he knew. But how could he begin to explain to them that the rune—and the riddle—would bring him to his mother in the end.

"As for where to look," he went on, "I thought of trying Far Away."

Hort glanced up, grinning, his fork halfway to his mouth. "I'll say."

"I mean the land of Far Away," Gom told him. "It's somewhere in this direction, so a man once said. It has a castle, and soldiers, and a queen, and lots of people. I thought I'd try there."

Hort and Mudge exchanged glances.

"Well, now." Hort put down his fork. "There may be such a place, and such a queen, but I've never heard of them. Come." He went to the door, and opening it, stepped outside, letting in a gust of crisp, spring air.

Gom went to follow him, but halted on the stoop, looking upward anxiously.

"It's all right," Hort said, catching on. He drew Gom over the step and into the front yard. "That pesky bird's gone. Anyways, nothing'll touch you whilst you're by me, I swear it."

Hesitantly, Gom moved with Hort out into the center of the yard, along a single line of square paving stones that stretched unevenly from the doorstep to the small front gate. Gom's knees felt weak, and the air cold after the cozy warmth of the kitchen. He crossed his arms, hugging himself.

"Hey, hey," Mudge called from the door. "Look at the lad a-shivering. Don't you make him ill again, just as he's getting his strength up."

Hort waved a hand at her. "Do be quiet, Mudge, and let me answer the lad. See here." Hort took Gom's arm and pointed all around them. "Keep on long enough in any direction, *any direction*, and you'll be far away. It's no one partiklar place. Somebody's been fooling you." He looked at Gom closely.

Gom kicked at an edge of paving stone with the toe of his boot. He'd thought as much. Hadn't he said at the time that the thieving peddler Skeller had spun the Clack townsfolk a yarn to trick them out of their home-made treasures? Royal Purveyor, indeed!

"Of course," Hort went on, "I might be wrong, not being a traveling man. But I do know who can tell you better. In three days time there's to be our annual spring fair. Village'll be crammed with all kinds of folks passing through: tinkers, peddlers, basketmakers, balladeers, jugglers, and the like. They're the ones to ask."

A spring fair.

By the neat white fence, delicate light green leaves stippled the stark tree branches, and the hill that rolled away to the low horizon showed fine new grass spikes richer than any he'd seen in Clack. Away to Gom's left, behind a low, red barn, an orchard of white and pink and crimson blossom glowed in the evening light.

A spring fair. It sounded like Clack's annual sale. Once a year, toward the end of summer, the Clack merchants set out stalls along the main street to clear out all their old scuffed up stock. This spring fair sounded grander, and much more exciting.

Gom turned to Hort. "Which way does the village lie?"

"Green Vale?" Hort pointed forward, over the hill. "About two mile that way, lad. 'Tis not far."

A spring fair, with tinkers, and peddlers, and basketmakers, and the like. Gom swallowed, thinking of Skeller. Skeller, who'd nearly sent Stig and Gom to their deaths.

"These peddlers, and such: are they—safe?"

Hort wrinkled up his brows. "Safe?" His face cleared. "Ah, I see what you mean. You've obviously had a bad experience, as they say." He pondered for a minute or two. "Put it this way," he said at last. "You keep your hand on your pouch and your back to the wall and you'll fare fine. Not that they're all bad, as you'll see for yourself."

"That he won't," Mudge yelled from the door. "Not if you don't bring him in from the cold. Come on, or he'll be back in bed and we'll be fetching Mistress Gumby again and then there'll be no spring fair for any of us, for we'll not go and leave him alone."

Hort laughed. "Stop your fussing, Mudge. Lad's tougher than you think, I already told you that."

Gom looked to Hort in surprise. If he remembered right, it had been quite the other way around.

Hort leaned down toward Gom's ear. "We'd better do as she says, Gom, or we'll not hear the last of it." Smiling, he started back to the house.

But Gom lingered, still looking about him curiously. To his right, and directly opposite the barn, chicken coops clustered, already silent for the night. Behind them was a milking shed, and a low stone dairy.

Over all wheeled the deepening sky, blue-green edged with violet. Ahead, toward the horizon, two large stars were already out, twin bright points drawing his eye. These he knew well from back up on the mountain, remembered exactly which peaks they marked. Strange, to see them over this gentle setting.

His head tilted back, Gom turned full circle, gazing all about him. When he left here, he asked himself, which way would he go? He couldn't rely on Wind forever.

Just then, from above his head, came a weird moaning, as of some forlorn creature crying out in mortal pain.

Catching his breath, Gom glanced sharply to the barn roof, minded of the great gray bird. He relaxed. Above the roof, stark against the luminous heavens, reared the most curious device: a horizontal wheel wrought in heavy black iron, with teeth running around its outer edge. Quartering it were four strange signs that could be letters. One of them, bigger than the other three, was made of brass, and it looked like this:

Gom studied the signs intently, wishing that he could read. Set above the wheel, and piercing the spindle on which it was mounted was a rusty arrow that Wind slapped fitfully to and fro.

"What"—Gom pointed—"is that?"

" 'Tis called a weathervane," Hort said, obviously pleased that Gom had noticed it. "Got it a few years back from Carrick, master tinker, in exchange for a couple of cow hides. Not a good swap, but I wanted it so bad that I gave in too hasty, as I'll readily admit. Maister Carrick's no cheat, though he drives a right sharp bargain. See that arrow? Tells you which way the wind's blowing. Though to tell you the truth, I can do that fine well without the help of yon tarrymediddle but it do look rather grand up there, don't it?"

"How does it tell you?"

"See which way that there brass squiggle lies?" Hort pointed straight ahead, out past the neat white fence and up over the hill. "That's called north, and that's what that squiggle stands for, according to Carrick."

Gom looked skyward. "That's in the same direction as those two stars."

"Aren't you the quick one!" Hort clapped him on the back. "Oops, sorry lad," he went on, as Gom grunted with pain. "I clean forgot your bruises. The tinker told me that when he's on the road, miles away from anywhere and anybody, or any weathervane set up on top of a body's barn roof, all he has to do is look for them two stars and he knows exactly where north is."

"And the other three directions?"

"Turn your back directly on north, like so . . ." Hort turned Gom to face about, and pointed up over the cottage's thatched roof. ". . . and you're facing what's called south. That way . . ." He pointed past the dairy. ". . . lies east. You can't miss it, for east is where the sun comes up. And where it goes down . . ." He turned Gom full about again to where the sun had set behind the barn. ". . . is called west. All this Carrick told me when I bought the weathervane. It's all I know and all I want to know. Now let's get inside out of this wind."

Gom called after him. "Where's the Bluff?" The high cliff face where Hort had found him.

"The Bluff?" Turning, Hort pointed. "Thataway."

Gom stared in the direction of Hort's arm. Over the dairy roof, the chicken coops, and the milking shed. Beyond them lay the Bluff. Beyond that, the plateau. And farther still, lost among the higher peaks, Windy Mountain. "East," he murmured. "I came from East."

"Aye, lad." Hort eyed Gom up and down. "You must be of real tough stock living that high—though you don't look it."

"He certainly don't, poor lad," Mudge called again. "Just you get him back in here, Fer Hort, afore he takes the fever again! And let's shut out this awful wind!"

Shut me out, indeed! Wind shrieked after them as Hort pushed the door to. *When are you coming, Gom Gobblechuck?*

Too preoccupied to heed Wind's angry cries, Gom followed Hort indoors. "North, South, East, and West," he said aloud. "My mother must be in one of those directions. But which one, Hort, do you think?"

"Eh, lad, that's for you to find out at the fair. As for me, I'd rather be here than there any day."

"You don't have to take any direction at all," Mudge said suddenly. "There's more than enough room for you to stay on here, and we're needing an extra hand this spring, aren't we, Hort?"

"I thank you for your great, good kindness," Gom said firmly. "But I must move on as soon as I can."

"Oh," Mudge said, and, jumping up, began to clear the table busily.

Gom went to the window where the weathervane stood stark in the day's last luminescence, its brass symbol softly gleaming. Above the weathervane shone the bright twin stars.

A sign, he'd asked for. An omen. He'd gotten two, both pointing north. Was that the way he should go?

A faint excitement riffled through him. When he spoke with the peddlers he'd know for sure.

At the spring fair.

Chapter Four

S PRING FAIR day dawned bright and clear.
Gom awoke well before first light to good strong
smells of wax and grain and burlap and pickling
spice. He slept now in a lean-to off the kitchen; a pantry,
really, into which Hort had pushed his cot. A small stone
cell lit by a tiny skylight through which Gom could see
the stars. Along one wall were pickling crocks, sacks of
meal and flour, bags of barley and wheat, while over all
hung coils of rope, and bunched candles made of beeswax.

He crept out in his nightshirt, crossed the kitchen to
the front door, and peeked out just as the sun topped the
dairy roof. He took a hearty breath, savoring the fresh,
damp earthy smell of the new morning.

"My, we're feeling better today." Mudge stood behind
him, beaming, a big blue washbowl in her hands. "But
don't get too ambitious. You've a long day ahead. Sit by
the fire whilst I heat some water for your wash. After
breakfast, you can help Hort hitch up the pony cart."

A couple of hours later, they were moving up the hill
toward the village. Gom sat happily on the cart seat,
squashed between Hort and Mudge, bouncing and swaying as the iron-rimmed wheels bumped over the narrow,
stony track. To be sure, Gom felt an occasional bump,
and a certain tenderness in his yellowing bruises, but he
wasn't going to let matters like that spoil the day.

He glanced from side to side at his companions resplendent in their feast-day clothes, aware of how plain he looked beside them. Hort's suit was deep blue, with a red checkered shirt and a bright blue neckerchief. Mudge's yellow dress was trimmed in green frills, and her wide straw hat was topped with tiny purple flowers. She wore a shawl against the morning chill, and carried a basket filled with sweet pastries. For Mistress Gumby, she said, in extra thanks for tending Gom.

As they crested the rise, Hort drew rein. "See, lad? Green Vale. What do you make of it?"

Gom leaned forward eagerly.

The track wound down before them toward a mass of whitewashed cottages haphazard as a child's scattered building blocks.

" 'Course," Hort said. "Coming from a town, you'll find Green Vale small, it being only a village."

"Oh, no," Gom said. "It's much bigger than Clack." And much more inviting, he thought, gazing around at the green rolling hills and remembering the tall peaks that towered over Clack, shutting it in.

In the midst of the thatched roofs was an open space crowded with bright pennants flapping in the breeze: the fair. Faint sounds wafted up toward them: the murmur of a jostling crowd, the shouts of peddlers, scattered applause, a snatch of song.

Hort moved the pony along.

" 'Tis started early today," he said. "The juggler's already juggling, by the sound of it. And the balladeer's a-singing his songs." He sniffed appreciatively. "And, my, can I smell hot peas already?"

"For shame, Hort," Mudge said. "You've only just had your breakfast."

"Hot peas?"

"A specialty of the village," Mudge told Gom. "You take a kettle of yellow peas and boil them up for two days until stuff's so thick you can stand a spoon up in it. Makes a fine hearty pottage to warm the belly, and tastes grand with a dash of malt vinegar."

"Ah, the lad won't want that," Hort said. "He'll more likely pick a caramel stick, or sugar floss, or a roll of brandysnap."

They reached the first of the houses.

Gom looked from side to side at neat front gardens, where crocus and grape hyacinth were already blooming. Sprays of golden forsythia arched over white picket fences, and buds of dogwood swelled to palest green. Gom felt a pang of homesickness. Another two, three weeks, and Hilsa's garden would look the same.

They turned into the crowded main street.

" 'Morning, Hort, Mudge. How's the invalid?" folk called on every hand.

Invalid? Gom stirred uneasily. The whole village knew about him, it seemed. He felt all at once exposed and conspicuous. Hadn't Mandrik told him to go about quietly? He shrank himself up as small as he could between Hort and Mudge, avoiding the eyes of the curious villagers as Hort steered the cart into a cobbled inn yard and summoned a stableboy.

With a smile and a wave, Mudge took herself off to Mistress Gumby's while Hort led Gom out into the throng.

Gom stayed close by Hort, trying not to feel uneasy. He might have guessed from his experiences with the townsfolk back home that he had no hope of visiting the village unnoticed. For a start, he was a stranger. But there was more to it than that. He was an odd-looking stranger. Uncut now since last fall, his unruly brown hair bushed out around a thin face pale from a long winter and fever. His quick dark eyes were sharper than the regular child's and altogether too sharp to encourage well-meaning adults. Some folk thought him ugly, he knew. One of his brothers, Horvin, had even scorned him publicly. But Stig had only reminded Gom of how he resembled Harga, and that those who mocked him weren't worth a pinch of salt.

Hort took him on leisurely tour, in and out among the crowd, stopping at this stall to buy Gom a caramel stick and at that for Hort's pea pottage. The fumes from hot malt vinegar were very strong, and stung Gom's eyes. One taste of the pottage and he declined Hort's offer of a second, preferring, as Hort had predicted, the sweetness of the caramel.

From Gom's right came the twang of strings as the balladeer tuned up. By common consent, Gom and Hort pushed through the crowd to where the man sat under a tree.

Gom studied him with great interest.

His hair was gold, his cap and hose were bright orange, his tunic and breeches were motley green and purple. On cap, and cuff, and collar, he wore tiny silver bells that jingled at his slightest movement, and from a braided lanyard about his neck hung a finely crafted mandolin. The fingers, playing up and down the strings, were white and soft, and very long.

So this, Gom thought, was a balladeer. How different from Stig, in his rough shirt and worn breeches, swinging the axe in his great brown hands, his rich voice ringing out through the high thin air.

The man struck up a chord, his white teeth gleaming.

Winter's dead, and spring is here,
The sun grows warm ab-o-o-o-o-ove;
And ev'ry head now fills with cheer,
And ev'ry heart with lo-o-o-o-ove.

The man paused. A coin landed at his feet, and near the front, a knot of young girls tittered. The balladeer smiled up at them and winked. Then, his eye upon them, he struck into a second verse:

Now ev'ry mother's lusty boy
Would seek himself a girl;
Of rosy cheek, and glances coy,
And shining, tossing, curl.

The girls giggled, lads hooted from the back of the crowd, and more pennies arced to the singer's feet.

Gom turned abruptly away.

"You don't like it?" Hort asked.

His throat too tight to let him speak, Gom could only shake his head.

"Well, now." Hort looked around. "Mudge'll be along soon." He reached out to Gom's shoulder, let fall his arm. "I know," he said brightly, "let's find the juggler."

Juggler? Gom pushed his way behind Hort, looking from side to side at the stalls piled with wares of every kind: laces, linens, clay pots, and dishes and cups and mugs and wallets and purses and pouches and fancy belts; cheap trinkets, shells, ribbons; and curtains and carpets and rugs, and—

Gom stopped before a stall piled with little wooden carvings of wild animals: squirrels, rabbits, foxes, frogs;

and birds of every kind. The very sort of things that Stig had loved to make of a winter's evening. He picked one up, turned it over in his hand. A wild goose, neck outstretched, wings spread, just about to take flight, by the looks of it.

"What's that? You like it?" Hort asked, his hand to his pouch.

Gom set it down hastily. The carving was crude, the finish, shoddy. He didn't want Hort to waste precious money on such an ill-turned thing. "Oh, no, thank you," he said. "I was just looking."

Hort picked up the goose. "Nice, isn't it?" he said. "Why, I'll buy it anyway, as a memento of this day. Make a nice ornament for the mantelshelf. And cheap: only half a silver piece."

Hort opened his pouch.

Half a silver piece sounded like a lot of money to Gom.

"Don't!" he cried. "I'll make you one, if you like." The moment he said it, he regretted it. How was he going to carve Hort a goose, when he wasn't going to be around for long enough?

Hort smiled delightedly. "Well!" he cried. "I do believe you could!"

Just beyond the stall full of carvings, the crowd was so thick that Gom and Hort had to fight their way through.

"Ha!" Hort cried. "The juggler!"

Gom stood on tiptoe, craning his neck, but could see nothing.

"Here," Hort said. "Follow me." He pushed a way through for them until they stood by the corner of a gaudy red tent.

Before it, on a low wooden platform, a man was just

in the act of tossing a handful of wooden skittles into the air. He was fairly tall, though not as tall as Hort, but he was broader and more muscular. His face, fleshy and red, was topped with slick black hair shiny as paint. Shirtless, he wore tight green breeches and a wide silver bracelet that flashed with the movement of his bare arm.

Gom watched the skittles fly into the air and waited for them to come crashing down again, but instead, to his amazement, the man kept them going around and around without dropping one.

The people began to clap delightedly. Still the man kept them going until there came the chink of a coin, and another, and another, into a cap by the juggler's feet.

When the coins stopped at last, the juggler stopped the skittles, catching them one after the other in his left hand without dropping one, until he held them all up like a bunch of wooden flowers.

Amid fresh applause, the man bowed again, then, reaching into his tent, he set down the skittles and brought out a long black robe splashed with brilliant suns and moons and stars.

"Oh my!" exclaimed Hort, against an excited murmur from the crowd.

Gom went very still. He well knew those signs from Harga's little blanket. Wizard's signs, he was sure. Was this man a wizard?

The man raised his fists, and opening them, displayed two large, white eggs. The crowd fell silent. Closing his fists again, the man turned a full slow circle. Then, stretching his arms to the sky, he spread his palms.

There was an "ooooh!" as two snow-white pigeons rose up and fluttered away over the heads of the crowd.

The man bowed low with a smile that reminded Gom of Skeller.

Gom tugged uneasily at Hort's sleeve. "Is he a wizard?"

Hort looked down, his eyes alight with pleasure. "A what? Why, no, lad," he said. "You'll not find one of those at a public fair. The man's a conjuror, as well as juggler, which is lucky indeed, for we rarely see such!"

The man bowed again, then straightening up, he put his hand to his ear and pulled out a silver chain with a locket dangling from it.

"Hey!" A woman on the front row clutched her bare neck. "That's mine!"

Amid loud laughter, the man handed back the chain with a solemn nod. Coins chinked into the cap at his feet until they began to spill over onto the platform.

Gom's hand went to his chest, feeling the rune secure under the cloth of his tunic.

The man caught Gom's movement, glanced toward him. For a moment, their gaze held, then, smiling, the conjuror turned back to the crowd.

Gom froze. That man knew him. But how could he, when they'd never met?

"Well, I never!" Mudge edged up, panting, behind them. "How clever! What did you think, Gom?"

As Gom watched, the man bent down and picked up the bulging cap. It was velvet, black, with a jaunty red feather waving in the wind.

Gom shuddered, remembering another hat, another feather, belonging to Dismas Skeller, peddler, swindler of simple folk. And would-be murderer.

"A trick, it was a trick," he muttered.

"Of course it was," Hort laughed. "That's the difference between real magic and conjuring. And the fun is trying to guess how it's done!"

Fun! Why, Gom hadn't felt so afraid since the time of Skeller.

"Gom, are you getting tired?" Mudge peered down into his face.

"No!" Gom said, a trifle loudly, turning heads. "I'm— hungry, I think."

"Oh, you poor boy," Mudge cried. "Hort, let's go and find something to put in his belly." She put her arm around Gom's shoulder, gave him a quick hug. "I'm that glad you're working up your appetite, lad."

They found a booth laden with hot pies and baked potatoes, and soon Gom was doing some juggling of his own. They stood, watching and listening, Hort and Mudge exchanging nods and smiles with passing folk.

"Hey up!" Hort cried suddenly, setting down his empty plate. "There's Carrick!" He pointed through a gap in the crowd to a green-and-white striped awning under which, surrounded by pans and kettles of all shapes and sizes, a man sat on a stool, tapping away at a round, black pot.

Hort led the way toward the master tinker.

The man jumped up when he saw them, his face creasing into a deep smile, his tight black curls bouncing about his dark tanned face. His blue eyes were kind, yet sharp enough to put Gom on his mettle. He stood a good head shorter than Hort, yet he had a stocky strength about him, and the patient air of one who lived life on the open road. His clothes, if threadbare, were plain and neat, and his boots, laced to his knee, were of serviceable brown leather, well oiled.

Gom liked him at once.

Before Hort could introduce Gom, Carrick nodded solemnly. "So this is the invalid. Pleased to meet you, young man. I hear you've had a bad time."

"Well!" Mudge put her hands on her hips in mock indignation.

Carrick laughed. "*Before* he met you, Mistress Mudge, not after, I'm sure. I hope he's left some of your good onion broth for a hungry traveler."

Mudge blushed with pleasure. "There'll always be a bowl for you, Carrick, even if I had to feed a whole town."

"Then you shall prove your word tomorrow, ma'am," Carrick said. "That is, if you have work for me, I hope."

Mudge nodded vigorously. "Indeed. My best preserving pan, and the pot I boil the linen in, and my good iron skillet, all want patching. And I need a new stock pot."

"Carrick, Gom would like a word with you," Hort said.

"Oh?" Carrick looked down at Gom seriously. "What about?"

That was the difficult question. Gom could hardly say, do you know the wizard, Harga? Have you any idea where she lives?

"Do you know of a place called Far Away?" he asked.

"Far Away?" Carrick appeared to give the question serious thought. "Far Away. Now let me see . . ."

"Man as told Gom about it said as it had a queen, and royal soldiers, and all," Hort said.

"Soldiers? Queen?" Carrick shook back his black curls. "Not that I've heard of. There's King Galt, of Sundor, but no queen, and I'd not recommend that vile swamp to any traveler. There's Queen Balivere, of Quend, but that's nearby. And there's King Furly and Queen Rialan of Ringing Valley over in the west. Everywhere else is mostly lords and ladies, and no Far Away."

"I want to go where most people are," Gom said.

"Then you must travel south, to the lakelands," Carrick said promptly.

"South?" Gom made a wry face. So much for his omens, the twin stars and the weathervane. They had been pointing him in quite the opposite direction. "Not north, then?"

"Oh, no," Carrick said. "North of here there's no people, no trails. Nothing but mountains all the way to the Great Northern Sea. No, south's where you must go. There's lots of places down there. Cities, swarming with folk. Like Dune, and Hornholm. And most of all Pen'langoth, on Lake Langoth in Long Valley. Huge place, that is. Do you know their market's open every single day of the year? You'll find twenty tinkers at a time there, all with more work than they can handle. It's the biggest market in all Ulm."

"Ulm? What is that?"

Carrick's eyes widened briefly. "Why, Ulm is—" He waved his arms about. "Ulm is Sundor, and Quend, and Ringing Valley, and Dune, and Hornholm, and Pen'langoth, and this village, and wherever you come from and any other place you can think of. It's the world, the whole world."

"I never!" Mudge cried. "How do you know that, Carrick?"

Carrick shrugged. "One learns much in the big cities, if one keeps one's ears open in the right places."

Gom felt the excitement rising within him. That was

it. All he had to do was go to one of those cities, Pen'langoth, maybe, it being the biggest, and keep his eyes and ears open. Then sooner or later he'd surely hear of Harga. Except that—he'd still have the riddle to solve even then.

"Look at the lad," Mudge said. "He's going home. Come and see us tomorrow, Carrick. Gom can talk to you then."

Mudge pulled Gom away, back toward the inn.

"But you'll miss the fair," Gom protested, though he did feel dizzy, and a little weak and glad to be going.

"Don't you worry yourself about that," Mudge said. "We've seen all we need to see, haven't we, Hort?" She hustled Gom along. Hort had gone ahead, was just passing the conjuror's corner.

"A volunteer!" the man was shouting. "To climb inside this box!"

Hort stopped in his tracks, so suddenly that Gom bumped into him. "What for?" Hort cried.

"I seen it earlier," a nearby man explained. "He shuts someone up in that black box there, and chops it in two with that big knife he's holding. Then he pulls the two halves apart, and do you know, the person's gone!

"Next, he fits the two halves together again, and do you know—he opens the lid and the person steps out, lively as can be!"

"Why," cried Hort, "I'd surely like to see that before we go. Gom, would you mind?"

Gom bit his lip. The juggler-conjuror terrified him and yet he could hardly refuse.

"N-no," he said.

"A volunteer, I want a volunteer. A body small and nimble."

Heads were turning, folk were looking around, and Gom saw to his dismay that those looks were converging upon him.

Leaping from his platform, the man moved quickly through the crowd until he reached Gom, where he shot out an arm and seized Gom's wrist in a grip tight as a trap. The man smiled down at him, his mouth curling. "You, little man. You'll do."

Little man! Skeller had called him that, and in that same sneering way.

"Here, here," Mudge said. "You just mind your words."

With that encouragement, Gom tried to draw back his arm.

"Let me go!" he cried, but the man only tightened his hold.

"Don't be shy," the conjuror said, his smile belying the cruelty of his fingers. He raised the curved blade and waved it over his head, the wide sleeve of his conjuror's gown slipping back, exposing his arm. For one split second, the man's eyes dropped to Gom's chest.

"You surely don't want to disappoint—the folks."

In a flare of panic, Gom began to struggle, twisting in the man's grasp, and as he did so the sun caught the silver bracelet on the man's upraised arm: a plain wide band, for the most part, except that on its center was embossed the unmistakable shape of the death's-head.

Chapter Five

"**H**ERE, HERE." Hort spoke up. "The lad's not well. You'd better be letting him go."

For one minute, Gom wasn't at all sure that the conjuror would do as Hort said, but then he released Gom's arm and slowly lowered the blade.

"Well, now," the man said to Gom, loudly for everyone to hear. "You've done folk out of a rare treat. Too bad." With that, he strode into his tent and dropped the flap behind him.

The crowd broke up, muttering in disappointment.

Conscious of unfriendly glances, Gom slunk away between Hort and Mudge, into the inn yard.

"Don't fret, lad." Hort took his arm to help him up into the cart. "You weren't to blame. There were plenty of other young folk there. He could easy have picked one of them."

Gom climbed up and sat, slumped in total exhaustion. He scarcely noticed driving back through the village, past the fluttering pennants, the bright tents and awnings. The candy booths smelled sickly now, and the odor from the hot pies turned his stomach.

It was a miserable ride. Once or twice, Hort and Mudge started up a conversation over Gom's bowed head, and faltered. The day had turned out more like a wake than a festival, thought Gom. Oh, the shock of seeing the death's-head on that bracelet! He glanced up, fearing to see the skull-bird wheeling above him, but the mild spring sky was clear.

The moment they reached home, Mudge bustled Gom off to bed, and Gom let her. He undressed, and lay with his back to the door.

He shuddered in the darkness. The way that conjuror had seized his arm, in broad daylight, in front of everyone. And the way he'd looked to Gom's chest, as though he'd known the rune was lying there. First the vision of the skull, then the great gray bird, and now this man. They were all connected, Gom didn't doubt it, and they all sought the same thing.

All his life, his mother's rune had brought him comfort, had warned him of dangers. Now it seemed to be bringing him nothing but danger.

If it hadn't been for Hort and Mudge today, something terrible would have happened, Gom was sure. Somehow, between blade and big black box there'd have been an "accident." The crowd would have been shocked, and Hort and Mudge would undoubtedly have made a great fuss. But it wouldn't have done Gom any good, and the rune would have disappeared—and the conjuror certainly wouldn't have plucked *that* trinket from his ear afterward.

Lucky indeed that Hort had found him, Gom thought vehemently. What had he said? "Nobody'll touch you whilst you're by me, I swear it." Gom went over the events of the day in his mind, taking comfort from the way Hort and Mudge had stood by him, the way they'd answered the conjuror. The way Hort had supported him against the general mood of the crowd, the way Mudge had hustled him off to bed.

Like father and mother to him, they were.

And what of his own, real mother?

Gom turned the rune over in his hand, his resentment growing.

"Dear boy," Gom mimicked softly, "your mother watches for you, and hopes for you on your path of experience . . ."

Some path! Some experience! He tossed about to face the door.

When that bird had first attacked him on the plateau, had almost killed him during the second attack up on the Bluff, what had his mother done for him then? This very day when the conjuror would have put him in that awful black box, what had her "watching" and "hoping" done for him? Did Harga even know what was going on? If she didn't, she surely was not as great as Mandrik had said. And if she did, then she'd stood by and let him be almost killed!

Was Mudge right after all?

He took off the rune and drew back his arm to hurl it from him, but resentful as he was, he couldn't bring himself to do it. Leaning over the side of the bed, he slipped the stone under the mattress, then once again lay down, face to the wall, and went to sleep.

The moment Gom awoke, he felt his bare throat, remembering. His anger had faded, yet his resentment against his mother and his sense of betrayal remained strong. It felt strange to be without the rune around his neck, yet he felt so out of sorts that he would like to leave it where it was. But a lifetime's habit was too strong to break. He pulled the rune from under the mattress, and, grudging, put it back on.

Mudge was at the kitchen table, busy baking.

"My, you're up late," she said. "I says to Hort, I

says, the lad's tired out from yesterday. Let him sleep. Looks like rain," she added, as Gom crossed to the window. "Lucky the fair were yesterday. How're you feeling anyways?"

"Quite better," he said, without much conviction. "It's time I was off."

"Nonsense. You don't look better," Mudge said. "Besides, Carrick's coming today to talk to you special."

No, he wasn't, Gom thought. The tinker was coming to mend Mudge's pots, but Gom didn't argue the point. It really was late. By the time Gom was washed and dressed, Hort came in for elevenses.

"Eh, you look right chalky, young feller," Hort said.

"You tell him," Mudge cried. "He won't listen to me!" She handed Gom a mug of hot broth and a fresh cheese scone.

"You're not thinking of leaving, lad?" Hort said. "Two, three more days, a week or two, that's what you need afore you go off into the blue."

Gom glanced toward the window uncertainly. His head hurt, and his knees were shaky. Perhaps they were right. He sat down at the table and took up his mug, looking from Mudge to Hort, the only folk who'd ever been really friendly to him, save for Stig, and Hilsa and Stok. Homesickness welled up inside him like a pain. He set down his mug, threw Hort's old raincape over his head, and went outside.

He stood on the stoop, leaning against the door, fighting self-pity.

Across the yard, the hills lay soaking under steady drizzle. Wind was elsewhere, leaving the weathervane still and silent. He crossed the yard dodging puddles to stand by the gate, gazing gloomily over the dairy roof.

Gom's fingers stole toward Harga's rune. He forced his hand down, into his pocket. Fool, to be always seeking comfort from that.

"With you she left it . . ." Gom could hear his father's voice now. ". . . special, to keep care of, like. Not with any of the others. Not with me, even. Just between you and me, boy, you understand?—you're the child she was really after, much as she loved the rest."

Gom had believed Stig, for his father would never tell a lie. But what if Stig were mistaken? Because when all was said and done, one question always remained in Gom's mind: if Harga loved him as much as Stig had said, then *why had she gone off and left him the moment he was born?*

All those stories about what a wonderful mother Harga had been to the rest of her children only made him feel unwanted and abandoned.

What had his mother ever done for him? When the Clack folk had been mean to him, had she been there to defend him? When he'd had the fever, had she been there to nurse him? No. Stig had been both father and mother to him, and when Gom was older they'd both cared for each other, washing, mending, sweeping, cooking, and keeping each other company. All his life he'd managed without Harga. Why need her now?

Why, he thought, growing angry again, why should I go risking life and limb to take her the stone? For all she either knows or cares, I could be dead by now. She wants her rune? His chin went up. Let her fetch it!

A distant shout startled him. Without stopping to look, he turned about and dashed for the front door, only to collide with Hort on the stoop.

Hort peered out through the rain. "Hey, it's Carrick

coming down the hill. Fill up a mug, Mudge, for a wet body in need of nourishment!"

Sheepishly, Gom watched Carrick striding down toward the house. The tinker's wiry body was hung with bulges that clanked and chinked with every step: pots and pans and kettles and skillets, and a knapsack full of gear.

"Good heavens!" exclaimed Mudge, helping the tinker off with his load, "Just look at you, Carrick! Walking through all this rain. Where's that horse of yours?"

Carrick smiled down at her. "Finnikin's not as young as he was, Mudge. This kind of wet doesn't agree with his feet. I spare him when I can."

Gom took off his wet boots and at Mudge's bidding sat opposite Carrick by the hearth while the tinker drank hot broth helped down with chunks of fresh brown bread.

At last, Carrick stood up, his clothes steaming in the fire's warmth. "Here, lad. I've something for you." Fishing in a deep side pocket, Carrick took out a wad of yellowed parchment, and set it down on the kitchen table.

Something for him? A *gift?* Gom felt a little prick of excitement, which he quickly suppressed. Carrick didn't even know him. Was it some kind of jest? Eyeing the wad warily, Gom got up and went to stand by the tinker's chair.

Mudge exclaimed as Carrick spread the parchment, holding it flat between his capable, square hands.

"Whatever is that, Carrick?"

" 'Tis called a map." Carrick looked around at all three of them. "A tinker's map for our young traveler here."

Gom's heart swelled. No joke, but a real gift. He could scarcely believe such generosity.

"I'll be!" cried Hort. "If that doesn't look like the weathervane you traded me a while back." He pointed to a small device in the bottom left-hand corner of the parchment. Gom saw that it did indeed look like the weathervane atop the barn roof: the wheel, the squiggles, and the arrow, pointing north.

"That's to tell Gom in which direction everything lies," Carrick said. He smiled at Gom, his blue eyes crinkling at the corners. "Where you're going and where you've been, and to help you remember where places are." His smile widened as Gom hesitated. "It's all right, lad. I don't need it anymore."

Gom flushed with pleasure. "That's very good of you," he said, and at once thought how lame that sounded, but he didn't know how else to answer such kindness. He eyed the map again, then looked up.

"I can't read," he admitted in a low voice.

Carrick laughed merrily. "No more can I. But I do know places and how to find them. So will you when I've finished with you, without having to know them letters. Let's get to work."

For the next hour, Carrick patiently went over the map with Gom, teaching him the names of towns and cities in all the different lands, making Gom repeat them over and over until he knew them for sure. Then just as patiently, he taught Gom how to distinguish roads from trails, which to take, and which to avoid if he could. Being a tinker's map, he said, it was measured not in miles, but days. Each mark on a road or trail told one day's travel: for a tinker.

"Now let's see," said Carrick at last. "I think we're ready to plot you out a route to someplace. We decided on the lakes yesterday, didn't we?"

Gom nodded slowly, his eyes still on the map. That was yesterday. Today, he wasn't so sure that he was going anywhere.

"Well, that is where most people are," Carrick reassured him, misreading Gom's hesitancy. He traced a path on the map with his finger. Gom was to go from this dot, which was Green Vale, up north aways, he said, then east through Deeping Dale until he reached Bragget-on-the-Edge at the northern end of Twisting Valley. Then all he had to do was to travel due south, through Twisting Valley, then through Middle Vale, passing at last into Long Valley.

Gom watched Carrick's finger, tried to keep count of the days, and, getting hopelessly lost after the first dozen or so, let out a big sigh.

Carrick looked up. "If you told me exactly what you sought," he said, folding the parchment and holding it out, "I could maybe help you better. As it is, I might well be sending you in quite the wrong direction."

Gom avoided the invitation, taking the folded map with a polite thank you, and setting it by his place.

"I don't like the idea," Mudge said, "of such a young 'un going out there all by hisself. Couldn't he travel with you, Carrick?"

Carrick looked to Gom. "That would be nice," he said. "But Master Gom may not want a tour of these hills. I'm not due back south just yet."

Carrick mended Mudge's pots then got down to hard bargaining over a new one. Mudge won. Gom, sure that the victory had to do with hot broth and scones, watched as Carrick packed up his gear and prepared to take his leave.

Mudge pushed a package into the tinker's hands, a hard, square package wrapped in butter muslin.

Carrick smiled with evident pleasure. "Why, thank you, Mudge. I'd hoped you hadn't forgotten me." He waved the package at Gom. "Mudge's good waybread," he said. "Enough to last a four-month. And a wondrous weapon swung around in one's pack—enough to hold the worst of robbers at bay!"

Mudge laughed, patted the tinker's shoulder. "Be off with you, Carrick, afore I take it back. Good speed until we meet again."

The rain had stopped temporarily, and a watery sun shone down through dark, bulging clouds. Over Mudge's objections, Gom put on his own jacket and walked Carrick to the top of the hill.

As they passed through the gate, Gom turned up his collar. He smiled at himself. He was growing soft, down in the lowlands.

"You all right, Gom?" Carrick asked, seeing the collar go up.

Gom nodded. "I grew up in this kind of weather. It's just that I've been ill, I suppose. You don't mind the rain either."

Carrick grinned. "Tinkers get used to it. It's their way of life."

Tinkers, and peddlers . . . and conjurors, thought Gom.

"Tell me—" he asked. "That conjuror at the fair— do you know him?"

"Zamul?" Carrick was not smiling now. "Aye, I know him well enough. I'd as soon as not bad tongue any man, but—" He frowned. "I was most surprised to find him here. I've never known him stray from the lakelands, where fools are thick on the ground and a new one is born every minute. He's a trickster, and a rogue, who gives conjury a bad name. Seeing him here made me wonder. There has to be a purpose, which won't bode well for some poor body. Why do you ask?"

Gom, much disturbed by Carrick's words, thought quickly what to say. "I wondered how one learned those tricks."

Carrick stopped, his frown deepening. "Lad, if you would learn that craft, then find another master. You wouldn't seek an adder's company, would you, knowing of its poisonous fangs? Neither would any wise man get too close to Zamul." He laughed, as though to soften his words. "My imagination runs away with me. What could Zamul possibly want of you? You've neither treasure for him to trick you out of, nor promise of any. Truly, one small question has loosed a torrent of words about your head! Forgive me."

"Is Zamul still in the village?" Gom asked him.

"Not to my knowledge. He left the inn this morning. The noise he made arguing his account with mine host would have awakened the dead. The last I saw him, he was walking down the main street toward the north road. And good riddance, say I, on behalf of Green Vale."

They reached the rise. There, Carrick stopped and held out his hand. "Master Gom, I wish you good journeying, and should we meet again, then shall we have a merry time."

Gom took Carrick's hand and shook it. "Good-bye."

Wistfully, he watched the tinker stride away. He'd have so enjoyed going with Carrick.

As it was . . .

Gom picked up a pebble and aimed for a nearby puddle. The pebble hit its mark with a small splash, and disappeared.

. . . there was the rune.

He turned back down the hill, thinking of Zamul. Had the conjuror really gone, as Carrick thought, or was he lying in wait somewhere?

A sudden cloudburst sent Gom scurrying back to the house. When he got inside, Mudge made him change his clothes and sit by the fire.

Gom stared into the flames, brooding. Carrick had been surprised to find Zamul there. Something was up, the tinker had said, to bring such a one so far out of the way. Not that it concerned Gom, as Carrick thought. *You've neither treasure for him to trick you out of, nor promise of any.* But Carrick didn't know about the rune, did he?

Zamul did, Gom was sure. Yet Zamul was only a conjuror, not a true magical man. He couldn't have known about the rune by himself.

Gom put his hands to his brow, thinking of the death's-head and the bird. If Harga's riddle weren't enough, now there was this puzzle to tax him too.

While Gom moped around the house, debating with himself whether or not to go, he grew stronger. He began to enjoy the rest, to eat more and more of the good food that Mudge set before him, and to relish the comfortable company of her hearth. The fear of Zamul faded, and life began to feel like the good old days when Stig had been alive.

Mudge made him over a set of Hort's old clothes, and in these he went with Hort about the farmholding: a large area extending over four hills, on which grazed plump gray sheep and half a dozen sleek brown cows.

After elevenses one day, Mudge gave Gom a deep wicker basket, and sent him to collect the hen's eggs from the yard. Gom was glad of the chance to speak with the fowl in their own tongue.

As he stepped into the first coop, the hens crowded close, their sharp beaks threatening. "What do you want?"

Gom shocked them by answering in kind.

"Mudge's sent me for eggs," he said. He raised the basket to show them.

"Eggs!" they squawked indignantly, getting over their surprise. "Night and day we work hard laying, and all for nothing. That woman takes them all!"

Sympathizing, Gom set down the basket and squatted down among them.

"Tell you what," he said. "For every five I take, I'll leave one in the straw. Deal?"

There was a squawking, and a clucking, and a scratching, and a shaking of bright red combs, then they shouted all at once: "Deal!"

With that, Gom gathered up white and brown and speckled eggs, some still warm and sticky with tiny feathers clinging to them, wispy scraps of down. Every sixth one he carefully laid back in the straw.

"Funny," Mudge said, as Gom stepped back into the house. "They made such a noise that I nearly came to rescue you. Then they all went quiet. Whatever happened?"

"Oh, we just passed the time of day," Gom replied, handing over the basket. Mudge laughed, not remotely guessing that he spoke the truth. "I really enjoyed that," he added. "May I do it again?"

"You're a funny lad," she said. " 'Tis a thankless job that makes a body sneeze. As far as I'm concerned, you may do it every day from now on."

Hort was out, gone up the hillside, Mudge said, to inspect dry walls.

Left to himself, Gom investigated the barn. Just inside were scattered wood bits, remnants of the winter logpile.

Gom picked them over until he found the piece he wanted. A silvered, weathered piece, well seasoned. He ran his hands over it, feeling the grain. Here, it would be just right for a gray goose's outstretched neck, here, the knotty bit was perfect for the head. And here, where it widened, would be the wings as the bird poised to fly.

Yes, it would do well. He reached automatically for his knife. Not on him, of course. Muttering, he went into the house.

Mudge let him have a couple of old kitchen blades, which he sharpened until they were bright and keen as new. A little more scavenging and he'd collected an old whetstone, a rasp, and some sand, to rub the wood clean and fetch up the grain. He worked away in the warm afternoon sun, doing his best just as though Stig were watching over him.

By the end of the afternoon, the bird was already taking shape. He traced the flare of the wings with his fingertips. Stig would surely have been proud.

"My," Hort said, crossing the yard. "That's a goose you're making, just like you said. What a clever lad you are."

Gom put the carving things away, went with Hort to watch him clear a ditch, then, the shadows lengthening, he helped Hort bring in the cows. It would have been much easier to do it alone, for he'd simply have asked them to follow him, but he couldn't, not in Hort's hearing, so he did as the man did, switching a stick about, and whistling, and hupping, just as the farmers in Clack. A clumsy and awkward process, he thought, this working with animals without using their tongue.

To Gom's great delight, Hort even let him try his hand at milking, though by the time he'd half-filled a pail his fingers were too sore to pull more. He looked down at his hands. Strange. He'd been carving wood all afternoon without their once feeling tired. Evidently strength from one skill didn't always help a body in another!

Midway through that night, Gom awoke to rain driving hard against the skylight. Hort was bending over him, his finger to his lips.

"Come on, lad," he whispered. "I need your help."

Gom got dressed, threw on Hort's spare raincape, and followed him out into the storm. They crossed the yard, went out the gate and up the hill, each carrying a lantern.

"There," Hort cried, pointing.

Halfway up the dark hillside huddled the darker mass of a ewe.

Gom squatted with Hort and watched the birth of a spring lamb.

"Here, Gom," Hort said, as the lamb emerged under the driving rain, "hold up your cape until we've got it on its feet."

Hort no sooner had the newborn upright, when the ewe got up and began to wander away.

"Quick," Hort said, pulling the ewe down again. "Put the lamb to her while her scent is on it."

Gom picked up the little wet thing and moved it around to the ewe's belly, where it began to suck noisily.

They moved on.

Gom almost fell over the next ewe.

"Dead," Hort shouted over the noise of the storm. Beside her, a little lamb bleated piteously. "We must find it another dam to suckle or it will foller!" Hort handed Gom his lantern, picked up the lamb, and strode off through the dark.

Gom hurried after him, swinging the lanterns to light the way, the rain streaming off his face and down inside his clothes.

"Over here, lad! Put them lanterns down!"

Hort handed Gom the motherless lamb and stooped over another ewe who had just given birth. Hort stood up her newborn, set it to suckle.

"Now, Gom."

Reaching for the orphan, Hort rubbed it in the ewe's strong birth scent, then stood it to her belly also. A moment's anxious wait while the ewe sniffed the newcomer, then she licked it, and let it in.

Hort straightened up in relief.

"Whew. That were a close 'un, Gom. Another hour and it'd have been too late to bond them. There's three more around here, as I guess. Are you willing?"

Gom nodded, regardless of the rain streaming over them. He worked away beside Hort, driven by the urgency of their task.

It was almost dawn when they finished. They birthed not three, but seven more lambs that night. And thanks to Gom, Hort said gratefully, every one with a dam to suckle it. Gom fell onto his cot exhausted and slept until late morning.

His first thought on waking was of Harga. Harga, who'd left the day he was born. Too soon for a bonding.

There was only Mandrik's word for it that Harga ever wanted to see her youngest son again.

And the riddle? The vision of the bear and the sparrow was fading fast. Maybe that had been but a dream, a kind of wish-fulfillment, after all.

After that, he went about the farm every day, helping Hort, watching the lambs grow stronger, nurtured by their mothers' milk and warmth.

Every morning, he collected Mudge's eggs, and soon he was carrying three baskets.

Mudge was delighted—but puzzled.

"Eh, lad," she said. "Them hens's taken to laying themselves silly. How do you do it?"

"Secret," he said. "Something I learned in Clack. Tell you one day."

Each night, he'd sit by the hearth, just as he used to do with Stig, carving away at the goose. After he had finished the carving, he polished its beak smooth with the sand, then oiled it all over until the wood fairly glowed. It was perfect, down to the last quill and feather.

Gom found a small slate slab in the yard to mount it on.

As he walked back to the house, Wind screeched, *Haven't you been here long enough? You look recovered to me. When are you moving on?* It whipped the last fading blossoms off the trees and scattered them in Gom's face, reminding Gom how late in spring it was.

"Soon," Gom said. "Soon."

How soon? Wind demanded.

Without answering, Gom walked on, all the way to the farmhouse door.

Coward! Wind shouted, slamming the door shut almost on Gom's heels.

What does Wind know? Gom asked himself, and set about fixing the carving firmly to its base.

After supper, he stood it on the mantelshelf for Hort and Mudge.

"Eh, lad, you've caught it exceeding well," Hort said. "I wouldn't be surprised to wake up one fine morning to find it flown away!"

Mudge tapped the stone base. "Don't worry, Hort. Gom has it bedded down real safe." Abruptly, she turned away. "I don't know why," she said, "but I find that terrible sad."

That night Gom came suddenly awake. He'd been dreaming, about what he couldn't remember, but he must have been weeping, for his face was wet. He lay staring up into the dark.

Coward! Wind had called him. Not fair, not fair, he thought. And not true. Restlessly, he turned onto his side and as he turned, his hand caught in the rune's leather thong. For nigh on two weeks now he'd ignored that stone, neither touching it, nor even thinking of it. It was almost as though it had melted from around his neck and disappeared. How honored and excited Gom had been to learn that Harga was the greatest wizard in Ulm. But now he felt only bitterness. What use was he to her, or she to him?

Here in this house for the first time he was enjoying true motherly care, the sort of care his nine brothers and sisters had taken for granted every day of their childhood down in Clack. And it was good to have Mudge fuss over him, cook his meals and wash his clothes. So why, he thought, as he had a hundred times since the fair, should he now go running out to goodness knows where after a stranger who'd abandoned him on the day of his birth?

On an impulse he took off the rune and flung it into the darkness. It landed with a clatter and slid across the floor.

For a moment he lay rigid, feeling guilty, and not a little afraid, half-expecting something bad to happen.

But nothing did.

With a defiant shrug, he turned over and went to sleep.

Chapter Six

RILLIANT sunshine shafted down through the little skylight, dappling the pantry's whitewashed walls, bouncing on Gom's eyelids, waking him up. He rose with a will, ate a huge breakfast, and went out onto the pasture with Hort to mend dry rock wall. Wind was cold and choppy, gusting in his face, at his back, butting him impatiently as the cows at milking time.

After elevenses, Hort led Gom around to the back of the barn where he'd stacked a pile of fallen tree limbs, victims of the past winter's gales. From the barn he brought out a large axe with a handle tall as Gom.

"You're the son of a woodcutter," Hort said grinning. "Let's see you swing this."

Gom took the axe handle, felt its smoothness. He lifted it, hefted it. Not so well balanced as Stig's. And the blade was blunt and rusted. Frowning, he handed it back.

"This axe needs sharpening," he said. "Mudge couldn't slice butter with it."

Hort laughed delightedly. "You're right. Let's see . . . there was a grindstone around here somewheres . . ."

A short while later, Gom swung the new-shining blade and cleft a stout oak branch in two, releasing a strong and fragrant scent that brought back sharp memories of times gone by. A glade back up on Windy Mountain. A tidy stack of logs ready for loading into the cart. Stig leaning on his axe as Gom picked up stray branches for kindling.

"What's wrong, lad? That thing too much for you?" Hort's brown eyes twinkled.

Gom stared down at the brightness of the new-exposed wood grain.

In Wood is kernel's secret essence known,
And purpose comes to light.

He ran a finger down the oak grain as if searching out its secret.

"Lad? Lad, are you feeling all right?"

Gom looked up to find Hort's hand on his arm. "Yes, yes. I was only thinking." He swung back the axe again and brought it down full force on the wood a second time, splitting off another log.

Hort whistled in admiration.

Gom swung again. And again. And as he swung, his muscles stirred to life, his body took up the old familiar movement patterns. It felt good, to be chopping wood once more. Faster and faster neat logs replaced untidy branches. Hort stacked them in the barn, marveling.

"My, that was no idle claim of yourn," Hort said, as Gom cleaned and oiled the axe. "I wouldn't have looked for such strength in a boy. How do you do it? With magic?"

Gom smiled a little. "It's neither magic, nor just strength."

"Well, I couldn't have done thus," Hort said. "And I'm a great big man."

"You're also a sheep farmer," Gom told him. "And not a woodcutter. You have your tricks, and we have ours. See."

Gom took the axe again and swung it back behind him and up over his head. "You swing the axe up, so. Then when you bring it down, you must pull in the handle toward you, tucking your elbows into your ribs, real sharp, like so." Gom brought the axe over and down with a thwack that made Hort jump. "This way, the axe-head's own weight works for you, as well as your arms, saving your strength quite well. Here, you try, Hort."

Gom handed Hort the axe.

Hort tried once, twice, several times to do as Gom had done but it was a while before he began to get the knack.

"My," he said, "it makes it easier all right. But," he added, putting the axe away, "it's fair tricky pulling that blade in close like that. One slip and a man could lose his toes!"

Gom walked back to the house in silence, his hands in his pockets, too minded of his father to trust himself to speak.

"You should a' seen him," Hort said at supper. "I nearly came to get you, Mudge, but then you might've made the lad stop. My, he were that strong, with his arms going up and down, reg'lar as the pump in the yard. How do you do it, lad, I said. It must be magic. Not so, he said. 'Tis more an art, like sheep farming. And he shows me how. All these years I've been chopping that wood stack all wrong. No wonder I've allus pulled my back."

"Art or no, it still takes muscle. You didn't let him strain hisself, Hort?"

"No, my gal, I did not. Now, lad, tell us something

about them other folk where you come from," Hort said, trying as usual to avert Mudge's fussing. "Tell us what they're like and how they live."

Gom told them. Of Bok, the butcher, of Maister Craw, the greengrocer, of Pinkle, the blacksmith, and of Winker, the host of The Wild Green Man. Of the rows of small, neat houses with their small, neat gardens. Of daily life and festivals when Maister Sproggins played his bagpipes to make the townsfolk dance.

"Sounds such fun," Mudge said dreamily, her elbows squarely on the table propping up her chin. "All that music and dancing and singing. We don't have nothing quite like that, not even at the spring fair. Give us one of them songs, Gom."

Gom shifted awkwardly. "I can't."

"Can't? Why, there's nothing you *can't*, lad, I'd swear," Hort said, glancing proudly to the carving on the mantelshelf.

"Leave him be, Hort," Mudge said, her eyes on Gom's face. "He don't want to sing, that's his affair. I'll sing one for him."

Hort raised his eyebrows. "You? You don't sing, girl. What song can you know?"

"Wouldn't you be surprised," she retorted, and began to sing.

> If I had a boy,
> Here upon this farm,
> I would tend him
> And defend him,
> Keeping him away from ev'ry harm.
>
> If I had a boy,
> One and only one,

I would know him,
I would show him
How to be a gentle, loving son.

If I had a boy,
For a little span,
I would love him,
Watch above him,
Grow him up to be a fine, strong man.

"Well," Hort said, looking at Mudge in surprise. "I'd
never have thought it. That were as good as what that
there balladeer were singing at the fair."

"Better," Gom said. He got up and, putting his arms
about Mudge, he buried his face in her shoulder.

Mudge squeezed him tight, enfolding him in her
warmth, and rocking back and forth. " 'Twere nothing,
really," she said, releasing him at last. "It's surprising
what a body can do from the heart."

"Sure you wouldn't like to match it, lad?" Hort asked,
with a twinkle.

Gom only shook his head.

"Never mind." Mudge touched Gom's arm. "He'll
maybe change his mind someday."

"How d'you mean, *someday*, Mudge? The lad's moving
on soon."

Gom looked from one to the other, clearing his throat.
"As a matter of fact, I've changed my mind."

Mudge beamed. "You mean you want to stay along of
us after all?"

Gom nodded. He did, and he'd been meaning to say
so for some time.

Mudge blushed with pleasure. "You're a dear, good
lad," she said. "And sensible, too. You're far better off

with us than out there looking for her as don't even want you."

"Mudge." Hort looked shocked.

"It's true, or she surely wouldn't have left Gom all this time."

"Mudge!"

Gom looked down at his plate. "It's all right, Hort. Mudge is only being honest." *But she's wrong,* he found himself thinking, much to his surprise. *For she doesn't know about Harga.* He rubbed his chest absently, feeling for the rune. It wasn't there. He looked up, startled. Of course it wasn't. He jumped up, and ran into the lean-to. The floor was tidy and bare. He got down onto his hands and knees, scrabbling about in the sacks of grain. It wasn't there, either.

He looked to the darkening skylight, his heart racing. Zamul!

Mudge and Hort watched from the doorway. "Try your pillow," Mudge said quietly.

Gom scuttled across to his cot on his knees, threw down the covers and ripped the pillow aside. There, on the sheet beneath, was the rune, stark black against the whiteness of the linen, its thong coiled loose around it. Shaking with relief, Gom picked it up and slipped it back around his neck, and under his tunic.

Something was wrong.

He looked down. The rune lay cold on his chest, not warming to the heat of his flesh. He took it out, held it in the palm of his hand. Nothing. Not even the slightest vibration.

"What is it?" Mudge sounded anxious.

Gom peered at it closely. It really was the rune, but it was dead. Like an ordinary stone.

"Eh, well," Hort said. "Supper's getting cold." He went back into the kitchen.

But Gom lingered, replacing his bedding, taking a moment to recover. When he straightened up, Mudge still stood in the doorway, watching. " 'Tis hers, isn't it?" She barred his way.

He nodded.

Mudge sighed. "I thought so. Well, come on," she said, with none of her usual whys and wherefores, and moved aside to let him pass. And not one word did she say for the rest of the evening, about the rune or anything else.

Gom lay awake long into the night, holding the rune, listening to voices churning within him.

Dear boy, your mother awaits . . .

Coward . . .

Oh, Mother, he whispered into the dark. Mother, I'm so sorry.

What had he been thinking of, to turn aside at the first sign of trouble? What sort of son was he? He held the rune to his ear. It might have been a pebble from the farmyard. For the first time in his life, he and the rune were no longer attuned. Oh, how could he ever have thrown it away! What if it never "spoke" again! What a fool he was, and no match for his task!

As Stig himself had said: *. . . for all your smartness you're still but a simple mountain boy and ignorant of the great wide world out there . . .*

Stig had told Gom to stay at home. But Mandrik had told Gom that Harga wanted her rune back. What would Stig have said to that? Why hadn't he confided in his father? Now Stig was dead, and life went on, and Gom must answer these voices alone.

For hours he stared up at the stars shining through the skylight, and never remembered falling asleep at last.

The next morning when he awoke, he felt different: scoured, empty, light, as though a terrible force had passed from him. The rune still felt dead, but just then he had more pressing business on his mind. He walked out into the kitchen trying to think what to say.

Mudge forestalled him.

"Sit you down, lad." She pushed a plateful of pancakes in front of him. "Stoke yourself up for the day ahead."

"But—" Gom said.

"Eat first," Mudge said firmly. "Talk after."

He ate in silence while Hort announced their next chores: putting new shingles on the dairy roof, and cleaning out the ditches in the far pasture. Gom listened, growing more and more uncomfortable. He'd come out all set to tell his news: that his grief, his madness had finally left him, that he was going to seek his mother after all.

But Mudge had told him to eat. So he ate the pancakes, all of them, and a second plateful, too. At last, however, he pushed away his empty plate and stood up.

So did Mudge. "Here," she said briskly. "You'll be needing this." To Gom's surprise, she produced a large leather satchel with stout back straps and set it before him on the table.

Into it she put a loaf of bread, and cheese, and honey cake, apples, a pack of waybread wrapped in butter muslin, a bag of sunflower seed, and Stig's green bottle filled from the well. And Gom's old clothes, rolled up tight.

To all this she added a small wool blanket, also tightly

rolled, which she tied to the satchel. "Your traveler's pack," she said.

Gom stared at her in surprise. "But—"

"No speeches, lad. You'll be off now."

"I—yes." Gom hung his head.

Hort laughed awkwardly. "I told her, I says, he's only just said that he's staying. But she would put up this pack. My missus, she's allus right."

Mudge stood by the hearth, her back to them, looking up at the mantelshelf.

"Eh, lad," Hort clapped him on the back. "We be that right sorry to see thee go, but it's no bit of good trying to keep a body against his inclination." He nodded to the goose. "At least we have summat to remember you by."

Mudge ran from the room.

Gom went into his lean-to, where the neglected staff lay amid the grain and the candles. He dusted it off, softened up the thong between his finger and thumb, and polished up the sparrow's feathers on his sleeve.

"We're on our way at last," he whispered. "I'm sorry I've taken so long." He took up Carrick's map from beside his cot, and folded it into his jacket pocket for quick reference. He looked around the little room, up through the skylight to small white clouds scudding by.

Maybe, he thought, going to the door, maybe I'll come back one day, when I've found Harga. What a good time we'll all have of it, and Mudge will see how wonderful my mother really is.

He walked with Hort and Mudge to their northern boundary, by-passing the village. The pack felt heavy, but comfortable, and it was good to have the staff in hand again.

As they went along, Gom kept a wary eye out for large birds and conjurors, but the hills—and the sky—seemed clear. At last they came to the parting of the ways: a little trail north of the village that would in due course turn east.

"Take care of yourself, do." Mudge, her eyes getting red-rimmed suddenly, hugged him tight. But even then, she tried to rally. "Them eggs, Gom," she said. "What shall I do about them?"

"It's like this: for every five you take, leave one." Gom's voice caught. "That's all."

"It is? Well, I never!" She wiped her eyes on her shawl.

Hort shook Gom's hand. "I'll not say good-bye, lad. In fact, I'll be keeping an eye out for you." He looked slyly back to Mudge and lowered his voice. "There'll be a fine new set of ewes to lamb come next spring. Bear that in mind."

"I will," Gom said. "Thank you, Hort. For—for everything."

He turned abruptly and walked away. Every time he turned around, they were still there, waving, getting smaller all the while. At the crest of the next hill, Gom halted for one last wave, then stepped over and down the other side.

Part

2

Chapter Seven

THE SUN rose higher and hotter. Gom strode along, uphill, and down. As he went, he found himself thinking wistfully of the two friends he'd left behind. By now, Hort would be up on the barn roof, fixing shingles, and Mudge would be baking bread in time for Hort's elevenses.

With a deep sigh, he stopped beside the trail, sat with his back against an elm tree, and ate a crust of the new-baked bread. Then, out of curiosity, he opened the pack of waybread. There were four cakes in the pack. Gom took one, tried to break a piece off, but it was too hard. He banged it on a boulder, but still it wouldn't break. So he nibbled at a corner, the way a mouse gnaws hard cheese rind. At first, the waybread seemed tasteless. But then Gom became aware of a pleasant aftertaste, of malt and bran. And of a comfortable feeling of fullness in his middle.

Carrick was right, he thought, contented. A little did go a long way. Good old Mudge. Lonely he might be, but he wouldn't go hungry, at least. Rewrapping the waybread pack, he stowed it back in his satchel and stood. He was just brushing crumbs from his clothes when he sensed movement above him.

He looked up.

A squirrel perched on an overhead branch, watching him.

"Good day," Gom called, fully expecting the animal

to run away as all the other wild creatures had done. To his surprise, the squirrel answered.

"Good day yourself. That's tasty-looking bread you have down there."

Gom smiled, delighted. "You know, you're the first wild creature to speak with me since I left home," he said. "Folk must be friendlier around here."

"It's not surprising," the squirrel answered him. "Considering the number of strangers that pass through these parts. *Generous* strangers," the creature added, eyes on the satchel.

"Oh, here." Gom knelt down and took out a piece of Mudge's fresh bread, and offered it.

The squirrel ran down the tree, took the bread with practiced ease, and began to nibble greedily. Gom noticed now the squirrel's sleek coat and plump belly. Too sleek and too plump for a wild creature's, he reasoned, a little disappointed. The animal must be almost tame, and well used to human company.

The squirrel looked up. "This is good. My name's Acorn. What's yours?"

"Gom," Gom answered. "Gom Gobblechuck, of Windy Mountain."

" 'Mountain?' That sounds rather grand." Acorn waved his arm about. "I live here, in Elm Coombe, as they call it. Look around: what do you see?"

Gazing about, Gom saw hills smoothly shaved and patterned with neat fields: green patches dotted with gray sheep, and rich brown squares of newly tilled soil fresh-sown with grain. But being the son of a woodcutter, his eyes went to the tall stands of elm trees here and there from which came the raucous cries of rooks about their clustered nests in the elms' high branches.

Gom frowned. The tree clumps looked like nothing he'd ever seen up on Windy Mountain. Their edges were too neat, not having the ragged spread of a regular wood. And the trees were not only of a height, they were all elms.

"Well? What do you see?" Acorn chittered impatiently.

"Those trees," Gom pointed. "They're all of one height, and of one kind, and they're planted in neat circles. They didn't seed naturally."

"Exactly!" Acorn jumped up and down. "They're not woods, but *coppices*, planted on purpose by the farmers to shade their stupid sheep and provide timber. And what did they pick to plant? *Elms!*" The squirrel sounded disgusted. "No oaks anywhere. Do you know how hard it is to find a decent acorn? Oh, one doesn't starve. There're beech groves on the farms, and hickory hedges, and hazel bushes, and sycamores. But oaks? I tell you, one of these days I'm off to find a place where a body can eat what he likes."

While the squirrel nibbled and grumbled, Gom took Carrick's map from his jacket pocket and looked at it. On the parchment the way seemed clear: a simple dotted line rolling over open space. In reality, as Gom had already found, the trail wound in and out and around those hills, meandered beside streams to fords of stepping stones, and once or twice dipped into dark and narrow gullies overhung with trees. He set aside the map and leaned back. A few more minutes and he'd have to move on. He was nowhere near the sign on the map that marked the end of his first day's journey.

Beside that sign, a small dot denoted Bragget-on-the-Edge, the next village. Much like Green Vale, only with a better inn, so the tinker had said—for all the good that information was to Gom, he having no money. No matter. He'd likely find a friendly meadow or even a haystack to unroll his blanket in—if he reached there by nightfall.

He stretched out on the grass. He shouldn't, but his legs had grown unused to all the walking. It would take them a day or two to toughen up again. He closed his eyes and felt the warm sun on his lids, thinking how wise it was to take a rest now and then.

When Gom awoke, it was midafternoon.

He jumped up, shouldered his pack and began to hurry along the open trail.

"Hey!" Acorn bounded after him.

Gom stopped, waited for the squirrel to catch up.

"Well?"

Acorn reared up on his hind legs, his tail waving behind.

"I've decided," he said. "You're my omen, my sign. Today's the day. May I tag along?"

The prospect of Acorn's company cheered Gom. "By all means." He patted his shoulder. "Hop up."

"I was hoping you'd say that," Acorn answered promptly. Leaping onto his perch, he turned around and about to make himself comfortable.

"Ow!" Gom cried, as Acorn dug in. "Paws, not claws, if you please."

Gom trudged on with his new companion over the gentle, rolling slopes, some quite wild, most just like Elm Coombe: very pleasant country to walk through on a clear, sunny day. Acorn kept up an incessant chatter, about his old noisy quarters under the rookery, and the quiet roomy hollow oak that he hoped to find farther on.

Birds circled overhead.

Gom looked up, apprehensive, but saw only more rooks flapping over a nearby coppice—yet another shady stand of high elms. He watched the loud birds with unease, not so happy suddenly with the bare countryside. There was little shelter anywhere but for the scattered coppices and distant farmhouses. Even the clear blue sky took on a menacing aspect now, for sharp eyes up there would spot him from miles away. He began to wish for cloud or mist or drizzle, anything to cut down visibility.

Gom also now felt uncomfortable about Acorn innocently riding his shoulder. He should never have brought this new friend along. What if they met trouble?

As the shadows lengthened, he began to have the feeling of being watched. Even Acorn fell quiet.

"We must find somewhere soon," the squirrel remarked. "This is a treacherous time of day for small animals."

"We'll find a place, don't worry," Gom said, trying to sound confident in the fast fading light. It was all right for tinkers, he thought. They knew their roads, and distances. Wherever Bragget-on-the-Edge might be, it was too far to reach that night.

"Look!" Acorn cried, sitting up in great excitement. "At last!"

Over the next rise loomed another coppice, neat and round like the others, but with one great difference: it was a stand of sturdy oaks.

Acorn chattering in his ear, Gom passed warily under broad branches, alert for sign of bird or Zamul, until he reached the center of the coppice.

There he stopped, and stood, listening. The place seemed empty enough.

Acorn leapt eagerly into the nearest tree: an old gnarled grandfather, festooned with leafy creeper and boasting a small, dark hole way up high out of ground reach.

With a wave of his tail, the squirrel disappeared into it. Gom sighed and turned away. At least one of them had good shelter for the night. He thought regretfully of his own little cot back in Mudge's pantry, could almost smell the pickle and beeswax.

Outside the coppice, the late sun shone red-gold on the gentle hill slopes. Inside all was dark. Gom was safe enough in that place from any old skull-bird or human conjuror, he was sure.

Out in the field, a lapwing late to bed sang evensong.

Gom leaned the staff against the grandfather oak, un-slung his pack, spread Mudge's blanket on a patch of straggly grass—all that covered the ground under the gloom of the trees—and sat down to eat his supper.

With a slight scratching sound, Acorn darted down the tree to sit at his feet. The hole in the oak was snug, and small, and unoccupied. Maybe, Acorn said pointedly, they could have a last supper together, a sort of house-warming.

"With pleasure," Gom said. He set down a chunk of bread before the squirrel who ate quickly, and waited for more.

"You're very kind," Acorn said. "And wise, too, for it never hurts to make a friend."

Gom smiled at his companion's patent flattery. But he took Acorn's hint that he might need help one day quite seriously. Many times on Windy Mountain small crea-tures had helped Gom—even helped to save his life on occasion, just as he'd helped them in return whenever he could. It was hardly likely that this squirrel would be of any service to him, though, for at dawn Gom would be on his way again. Still, he gave Acorn more of his precious bread. Then, thinking to give the squirrel a special treat, he opened the bag of sunflower seeds. Inside the bag was a little bundle wrapped in cotton. Curious, Gom unfolded it, and into his palm rolled four silver pieces.

He spread them out, tears pricking somewhere back of his nose.

Hort and Mudge had known he'd not accept money, and so they'd hidden it there—and he knew why. That couple were even now sitting at their supper table, thinking him securely settled in the Bragget inn for the night.

He rewrapped the coins, feeling uncomfortable. Those two kind folk had little enough money to go wasting on him. He slipped the bundle in his pocket, then on second thought, put it back in the satchel, on its own.

He looked up to find Acorn staring fixedly at the sunflower seeds. Gom shook out a handful, only too glad to share his food as he and Stig had always done.

As they ate, darkness fell. Overhead, branch and creeper wafted gently in the wind, and through them twinkled a tiny star or two. Acorn, swallowing his last seed, bade Gom good night, and ran up the tree.

Gom sat for a while longer, looking up into the waving creepers, enjoying the dark, the sounds around him: some last sleepy bird calls, the chirp of crickets. A family of raccoons went by, on their way out to take supper. Reassured, Gom leaned back and closed his eyes contentedly. Even though he was without bed or shelter, it was good to be among trees again.

He reached for the rune, and, on touching it, thought he felt a faint vibration. He sat up eagerly, put the rune to his ear. Nothing. Not to worry, he told himself, encouraged. He really had felt something, he was sure: a tiny, promising sign of reawakening.

Run, run, Acorn cried. You're sitting in a trap! The squirrel flagged him with a quivering tail, and fled down inside the oak. As Acorn disappeared, the tangled creepers overhead came alive and began to writhe like a skein of adders. Before Gom could move, they slithered over his arms, his chest, pinning him down among the tree roots. Then, still curling in and out, they meshed into a living net, enclosing him.

A large hand grasped the mouth of the net, hoisted it into the air, and hung him from an overhead branch.

"Help!" Gom shouted. "Let me down!"

The death's-head stared in on him, two dark eye sockets set in a bone-white skull. As Gom stared back at it, the skull grew brighter, and brighter, exploding into silver light, filling him with terror.

Gom squeezed his eyes shut against sunlight flashing on his face down through the branches overhead. He stayed quite still for a moment, caught up in the horror of his nightmare. He tried to sit up, but found with a shock that he couldn't. He pushed out with his hands to feel rough mesh all about him, hemming him in.

He opened his eyes in alarm. He was doubled up, knees to chin, suspended high above the ground, in a net of the sort that the Clack farmers sometimes used to capture live quail. He went still as a wild thing caught in a snare. Had he somehow fallen asleep by one of these traps and gotten caught up in it? If so, then he must call the farmer out.

Gom took a deep breath to shout, but before he could let it go, he caught sight of a figure sitting against the trunk of the tree below him.

His breath held. He knew those bright green breeches, and the black velvet hat with the bright red plume waving above it.

He reached for his mother's rune, and cried out then.

For his neck was bare.

Chapter Eight

"**O**HO! You're just in time to say good-bye." Zamul sprang up, popping a last morsel of food into his mouth and batting crumbs off his hands with obvious satisfaction. "I'm so glad we had a chance to make magic together after all." The conjuror put a hand to his ear, drew out the rune with a great flourish, and held it up by the thong.

The small black stone dangled, swinging like a pendulum, marking the next few stricken moments, while Zamul waited, watching Gom expectantly.

At last Gom found his voice. "Magic? Cheap, swindling, thieving trickery, you mean." He tried to sound scornful, but fear cracked his voice. Horvin, Gom's brother, had once snatched the rune from him and had come to grief within moments of taking it. Nothing bad seemed to be happening to Zamul. *Why?* Was the rune's strange deadness the reason? If so, thought Gom soberly, he had only himself to blame.

"Trickery, you call it?" Zamul sounded amused. "Perhaps it is, but soon, little man, I'll make magic of quite a different kind, after I've delivered this." He twirled the rune around by its thong, so fast that it looked like a dark gray circle.

"Delivered it where?" Gom stared down at the dark circle, transfixed.

"Now wouldn't that be telling?" Zamul caught up the

stone in his fist, then bending down, he retrieved a large pack lying alongside Gom's and shouldered it. "Good day, Master Gom. Oh, and thanks for the extra supplies." Zamul took up Gom's satchel and shouldered it, too. Then, swinging the rune jauntily, he began to walk off.

"Wait!" Gom eyed the rune in anguish.

Zamul paused, half-turning.

"You might at least let me down!"

"So that you can trot after me, little man? Not likely."

"But I'll starve to death."

Zamul grinned up at him. "You think I'd let you do that? I, who could have slit your throat while you slept? No. There's a croft a mile over the hill. The farmer's sure to be along this way, some time before fall, anyway. He'll fetch you down—if there's anything left of you by then." Chuckling, Zamul strode off through the trees.

"Wait!" Gom shouted again at Zamul's retreating back. "Who sent you?"

There was no reply.

Gom took a deep breath and shouted, really loudly this time. "Help! Help me, somebody!"

With a flurry of wings and loud protest, a lone pheasant started from the coppice. That was all. If farmer lived about as Zamul had said, he was too far off to hear.

Remembering Acorn, Gom began to chatter urgently, then stopped. That was the worst he could do. Distress calls only warned squirrels to lie low and stay away until danger was past.

He pressed his lips tightly together. He thought of the creek back home on Windy Mountain, and became as old Leadbelly squatting on a lily pad, unmoving save for his fat green sides going in and out with his breath, his eyes swiveling as a damsel fly came closer, closer in the still quiet. He saw himself sitting there, the fly darting to and fro, zigzagging nearer, tempting him to move, and he resisting, waiting for the right moment . . .

Around him leaves rustled softly, and out in the field the lapwings flapped over rising wheat.

Gom tried to think who else might help him, a creature with friendly teeth who could climb. One of the raccoons? They'd be asleep by now. Which left Acorn.

Oh, what a situation he was in! But it only served him right, Gom thought, twisting his fingers in growing anxiety. He remembered the rune's faint stirring. The little stone had tried to warn him, even though he didn't deserve it, and what had he done? Carelessly allowed himself to fall asleep!

Gom recalled his bad dream of the night before. No, not all dream, and not all the night before. Some of it had in fact happened, and only minutes since. He really was caught in a net and hanging from an oak.

And the adders?

You wouldn't seek an adder's company . . . Carrick had said about Zamul.

Gom's own mind had been trying to warn him of danger, turning creeper into adder, even as Zamul was hoisting him up.

What of the skull?

That had been on Zamul's bracelet, as Gom would guess, remembering its silvery shine. The bracelet connecting the conjuror with the death's-head of Gom's vision and the skull-bird back on the plain. Zamul's master. Hadn't Zamul boasted that he'd be practicing "magic of a different sort" after delivering the rune? The skull had sent the conjuror after him, as it had sent that great gray bird.

Where was the skull—or whatever power had manifested it—now? And what did it want with the rune? Power? To harm Harga in some way?

Or both?

Oh how could he have let himself get so taken! Forgetting his resolve, he began to struggle desperately, setting the net bouncing, and the leafy branches creaking above him.

Acorn appeared outside his hole, tail bushed out, and twitching.

"If you don't watch out, you'll bring this whole house down! Whatever's going on?" The squirrel turned about, peering warily above and below.

"Will you please get me out of here?" Gom called.

Acorn ran down the tree trunk, and, clinging by his hind legs, he hung upside down, nose to the net, whiskers quivering. "Will I get breakfast?"

"Breakfast?" Gom's outraged cry sent Acorn scurrying back out of range. "Zamul took everything I have! Hey—didn't you say that we were friends? Come back here!" he shouted, but the squirrel had vanished.

Gom cursed himself for his quick, sharp tongue. He wriggled about, trying to squeeze his hands through the meshing, to reach the rope that bound the net to the tree branch.

"That won't get you far!"

Acorn was back, hanging upside down once more, his tail curled around the neck of the net like a furry collar.

"Go away," Gom snapped. "If you won't help, don't hinder. Some friend you've turned out to be!"

"I only went to see if it was safe," Acorn said. "You shouldn't blame folk for being—careful." The squirrel, sounding hurt, nevertheless began to gnaw at the meshing.

Gom watched, his anger, his resentment, giving place to shame at having judged Acorn so rashly.

Six, seven, eight strands of the netting broke and Gom could push his head through the hole. A few more, and Gom's shoulders followed. A few more still and Gom was able to squirm out and up onto the branch, leaving the remains of the net dangling like an empty cocoon.

"Thanks, Acorn," he said.

"Pray don't mention it," the squirrel replied. "Now, if you'll excuse me, I'm off to breakfast. Do you know—there are acorns everywhere! They're not exactly fresh, of course, but they're still good eating." With a twist of his gray furry body, Acorn ran down the tree trunk and looped away through the undergrowth.

Gom followed him to the ground, and searching anxiously for his staff, found it lying behind the grandfather oak.

Dusting it down, Gom wondered how to find Zamul. How long had the man been gone? It seemed like hours. He went to the edge of the coppice and looked out.

Wind blew upon him, ruffling his hair. *Where to now, young one?*

"Maybe you could tell me that," Gom said. "There was a man in that coppice a little while back—"

The one who raised you to a higher station in life? Wind sniggered. *Don't get so huffy,* Wind went on, as Gom scowled. *He's going directly northward, I know, for I've had such fun trying to blow him back my way. I'm off south, you see, to visit cousin Zephyr for a while.*

Northward. That certainly made sense. Wind was always icy when he blew from there. He thought of the vision of the death's-head back on the plain. Of its paralyzing cold. Yes. Zamul might very well have gone that way. Remembering Hort, Gom took his bearings. The sun rose in the east, so Hort said. Gom turned to face it, picturing himself back in the farmyard, looking out over the dairy roof. If that was east . . . Gom took a quarter turn to his left to face Hort's front gate . . . then there was north, just as Wind had said.

North, he thought, with a tiny prick of excitement. So his two omens hadn't been so wrong after all! His excitement died. Wasn't he getting ahead of himself? Solve the riddle, the sparrow had told him, and Harga will come. It had sounded simple enough. But now with the rune gone, the last thing he wanted was to solve it, and the last person he wanted to see was his mother. Whatever would she say if she knew? If this were his "path of experience," he was treading it backward!

He gazed at the northern horizon, a low, wavy rim of hills. The rune had gone that way. And not only the rune, he thought grimly. So had the pack Mudge had given him, full of good things, including his father's old green water bottle. And precious silver pieces. It hurt to think of Hort and Mudge's hard-earned money in that rogue's pocket. Thank goodness, Gom patted his own jacket pocket, that he still had Carrick's map.

He gripped the staff and moved off, but after a few steps he pulled up short. There he went, rushing off again without thinking. Hadn't Stig always cautioned him not to go anywhere without preparation, no matter how much haste he was in? "Your very life may depend on it one day," his father had insisted, how many times?

Gom turned back to the coppice thoughtfully. When he caught up with Zamul, how would he get back the rune? Wait his chance and knock Zamul senseless with the staff? Gom tested it against his palm. It was certainly heavy enough, and Gom did have the knack of adding weight to it.

No, he thought, setting the staff upright again. Striking down a man in cold blood would be wrong. Stig had always taught him to shun violence. Only once had Gom seen Stig raise his hand to any man, and that had been in the heat of saving their lives. Furthermore, bad as Zamul was, he'd not killed Gom when he'd had the chance, but only caught him in a net.

Gom ran back into the coppice.

A few minutes later he reemerged, rolling the damaged net into a tight bundle, and tying it with the rope that Zamul had used to suspend it from the oak branch. Zamul, fancying himself the hunter, had gloated over his catch. A mistake, which the man might yet regret. For now the hunter was the hunted, and with luck—maybe the catcher would be hoist in his own trap!

The net tucked securely under his arm, Gom called farewell to Acorn, and leaning once more into Wind, hurried north.

After an hour's travel over the ever-rolling hills, Gom made out a ragged, misty band along the horizon: mountains, high ones, higher than any he'd ever seen in his life.

Another hour, and the ground was rising sharply and becoming rocky and uneven. Not easy territory for Zamul, it seemed, for Gom caught up to the man so soon that he almost fell over him.

The lakelander was sitting on the ground, opening Gom's pack.

Gom dodged behind a pile of rocks to take a better look. Only just in time as Zamul's head came up. Had the man heard him? Seen him, perhaps?

Several minutes went by before Gom dared peek out again.

The conjuror was eating an apple. One of Mudge's apples, by the look of it. Gom's belly rumbled.

Stig's green glass bottle and two small bundles lay untouched beside Gom's pack: the bag of sunflower seeds, and another, wrapped in butter muslin. Gom's mouth twisted wryly. Zamul had no taste for Mudge's waybread, it seemed. The regular bread, the cheese, and the honey cake, however, were gone.

As Gom eyed the remains of his rations, the conjuror set down the apple and, taking the rune from his pocket, examined it closely. Surely—it wasn't vibrating for Zamul? He watched his mother's stone dangling idly from the conjuror's fingers, wanting to rush out and snatch it back. But he didn't. Coward, he thought in disgust.

To Gom's surprise, Zamul suddenly leapt up onto a nearby boulder, his hands raised.

"Ladies and gentlemen."

Gom blinked and looked around. The conjuror appeared to be addressing empty space.

Zamul bowed low to his imaginary audience, then raised his hand high above his head, the little stone flashing in the bright sunlight. Enclosing it in his fist, he turned around three times, then opened out his hand.

Gom caught his breath. The rune was gone, and in its place was Mudge's apple!

Zamul bowed right and left, displaying the apple above the heads of his unseen audience. Gom still didn't breathe.

With a laugh, Zamul clapped his hands together over

the apple. When they parted again, the fruit was gone, and there was Harga's rune!

Gom let out his breath. Conjury! So vain the man was, he thought angrily, watching Zamul preen himself and turn about to acknowledge his imaginary crowd. If only Gom had a few of those tricks, he'd soon whisk the stone out of Zamul's hand.

But he hadn't.

Zamul spoke up.

"You see before you a stone of priceless worth. Ah, you may well laugh, but I speak true. This stone, un-prepossessing as it looks, contains magic of the highest quality. How do I know, you say?" Zamul puffed out his chest. "My master told me so, and he"—the conjuror leaned forward and dramatically lowered his voice—"will be the most powerful being in all Ulm, once he has this." Zamul held the rune up by its thong, then twirled the thong around his fingers, winding it up until the stone rested on his palm.

Watching him, Gom was minded again of his brother Horvin, who'd snatched the rune from him so long ago. Horvin had been arrogant like that, and overweening. A blustering bully. And a coward, when pressed. Gom frowned. Zamul was also a coward, come to think. The way the big man had backed down from Hort and gone off to sulk. And squeamish. Why, Zamul had taken Gom asleep, and without hurting a hair on his head. He wouldn't anymore likely offer Gom physical harm now, would he? Gom felt a touch of hope. Perhaps there was a chance after all of face-to-face victory. He sighed. Not really. Zamul might be a coward, but so was he, and much the smaller of the two!

Zamul's head came up so suddenly that Gom drew

back, thinking that Zamul had spotted him. But the man only pointed to some invisible person in his audience. "Fool, did I hear you say, madam? To be doing all this work for somebody else?" He dismissed the unseen woman with a contemptuous wave. "Not so. For my master has promised me power that you wouldn't dream of when I deliver this stone. Perhaps the power of invisibility— think how much that will help my conjury! Or, with luck, a touch of his own special power, which I own I do most highly covet. And what is that, you ask?"

Zamul struck a pose, pointing skyward.

"Picture yourself a bird, way up there, looking down on all this from a great height! Picture yourself swimming deep with the fishes of the sea! Or racing across the face of Ulm as the swiftest of horses! All this my master can do at will, for he is a *shapechanger!*"

He leaned forward, scooping his audience up into his confidence.

"This is the power that I would have my master give me. But if not—he will give me other magic that will make my great feats of conjuring seem like cheap trickery!"

Apparently tiring of his audience, Zamul put away the rune and sat down to finish his apple.

Gom watched him, while the sun climbed overhead.

Zamul claimed that his master was a shapechanger. Gom would bet that it was the death's-head—and that the death's-head and the gray skull-bird were *one and the same!* Gom shivered under the bright sun. Zamul sounded so pleased with himself. But did he really know what evil he served?

The conjuror tossed the apple core aside and lay down, gazing skyward.

Gom scanned the space above him anxiously. Was the

man expecting the skull-bird? Gom shrank into the shelter of his rocks.

Zamul's master was clearly going to use the rune's power. Did that make him a *wizard?* Surely not. Stig had always insisted that wizards were only good, whatever the Clack folk said.

Stig would say that, in defense of Harga. But wizards were only human, after all, and no human was all good or all bad, as Stig had also always insisted. Even Harga must have her faults, Gom reasoned thoughtfully.

And the death's-head? By comparison, Zamul was a paragon. He was greedy, and vain, and unscrupulous, but when the man could have killed in cold blood, he'd not harmed Gom one bit.

No. Zamul wasn't all bad. But then, he was human.

The death's-head was not. Gom had suffered its touch, and met the pitiless eyes. It was evil, totally.

And it was after Harga's rune, her wizard's magic locked within, and after it to what purpose Gom could not begin to guess. Gom shook his head. Through pride and anger and carelessness he'd put his mother's very power in jeopardy!

He looked up. The skies still seemed clear. He ventured to peep out. Zamul appeared to have fallen aleep.

How deeply? Soundly enough for Gom to steal out and reach into the man's pocket for the rune? He cast about on the ground, took up a small pebble, and threw it by Zamul's ear.

The conjuror was up in an instant, looking about suspiciously. He was no heavy sleeper, that much was clear. And Gom was no light-fingers, either.

Stealing was too risky. For now, anyway.

He'd have to wait for dark.

About an hour later, Zamul jumped up, shouldered his pack, and went on his way, looking this way and that, even stopping sometimes to listen. But near as Gom could judge, this was only the conjuror's natural caution, the result of a life spent on the road, and not the result of any particular suspicion.

Gom waited until the man was well and truly out of sight. Only then did he venture out to retrieve his satchel. To his great relief, he found Stig's old bottle still almost full. He stowed the waybread for suppertimes, and sprinkled sunflower seeds onto his palm. These he chewed slowly, thoroughly, to get every last bit of goodness from them, then washed them down with a swallow of water. After that, he closed the pack, then reached for the old gray blanket that Zamul had also disdained. Into this he rolled Zamul's rope and broken net. The first chance he got, he'd mend the net and hope to use it, somehow.

He caught up with Zamul easily, and tracked the conjuror all afternoon, the mountains drawing ever closer until the slopes towered over them both.

As they went, the air grew colder and thinner. Gom didn't mind. He was adapting to the familiar mountain heights very quickly.

Zamul was not. Gom was amused to see him take from his pack a fancy brown jacket with shiny braiding, wide padded shoulders, and a thick fur collar, and put it on. Gom eyed the conjuror's back with interest. Was this how folk dressed in the big cities? He'd not seen anything so fine, though it did look bizarre up in these mountains, and totally unsuitable for such rugged wear.

Zamul's progress slowed markedly, until Gom could even hear the man's labored breathing.

Gom's spirits lifted. The balance between them was shifting. How lucky that I was born a mountain boy, he thought. I'm in my element. The longer the lakelander goes on, the worse off he'll be. If I keep my wits about me, I might well have my chance against him at last.

Zamul stumbled, rolled down a short incline. They'd not go much farther that day, Gom bet, as the man struggled up again.

He was right. Well before the shadows lengthened into evening, Zamul stopped and sought shelter in a rock cleft.

Gom stopped likewise, finding himself another cleft not far away. He sat down, wrapped himself up in Mudge's good warm blanket and, taking out the tinker's map, studied it in the clear evening light. Up north, Carrick had shown him, were only mountains, all the way to the Great Northern Sea. No trails. No people.

He ran his finger along the band of broad blue wavy lines running off the top edge of the map. The sea. Wind had told him that it was like a giant creek, ever flowing toward the sky.

He traced the sea's edge from east to west, a ragged line, like Zamul's fancy braiding, a series of tiny inlets, fetching up against a really big one, a crooked, pointing finger, dividing the high ranges from north to south. A wide fjord, or sound, as Carrick had called it. Gom tried to imagine what it would look like, with those steep mountainsides on either side plunging sheer into its depths. Small, neat letters told the sound's name. Two short words, of five letters each. Carrick didn't know it. How Gom wished he could read it for himself!

Sighing, Gom put away the map again. He unrolled Zamul's net, and, taking the rope, threaded it in and out of the torn webbing. A rough repair, but—he tested it with his hands—effective enough. With that net, in a little while, perhaps Gom would give Zamul a taste of his own medicine. Once Zamul was asleep, Gom would slip the rune from the man's pocket, then throw the net over him and run. By the time Zamul had freed himself, Gom would be well away, and the lakelander wouldn't have a chance of finding him, not up among those mountains.

Gom leaned against the cleft wall. Ahead glimmered the bright twin stars that he and Hort had gazed at in the farmyard. It comforted Gom that night to think that they were shining on both him and those two kind folk alike.

After a while, the moon rose: time to move. Gom took up the net, slipped from his crevice and into Zamul's.

The conjuror was lying on his side, his pack under his head for pillow. Gom stood gazing down upon him. It had all seemed so simple earlier. But now he could see clearly how heavy and big the man was. What if the rune were not within reach? Or what if the man woke up now? He remembered how fast Zamul had come alert that afternoon at the sound of a pebble.

Holding his breath, Gom bent and reached for Zamul's nearest pocket.

Zamul stirred, and turned over to face him.

Gom held quite still. If Zamul opened his eyes now, it was all over. Maybe he should use the net first, tangle Zamul up in it, then feel for the stone. He waited a moment, then cautiously, he began to unroll the net.

Zamul must have sensed something, some faint stirring of air. The man stretching, rolled over and began to sit up.

Gom ran out around the corner, and waited, pressed against the rock wall, listening. Had Zamul seen him? In the deep night silence, the conjuror coughed and opened his pack. Then Gom heard him take a loud swallow of water, and smack his lips.

Gom slipped back into his own shelter and sat, turning the net over in his hands, ashamed. He had failed. His courage reached no farther than his mouth, apparently. He was nothing but a coward, too squeamish to wield the staff, and too timid to cast the net. How was he ever going to get back his mother's rune?

He sat miserably, his arms wrapped about his knees. But though he stayed awake almost until dawn, not one answer did he find.

The next morning, Gom awoke to new resolve. Today, he thought, today I shall try once more for the rune, and this time I shall succeed.

It was late when Zamul emerged. Gom's hopes rose to see how tired the man looked. But in spite of his apparent tiredness, the conjuror pressed on with dogged resolve, not stopping to sleep once, giving Gom no chance. Going to his reward, Gom thought. Maybe he'd get more than he bargained for!

A river crossed Zamul's path. Gom watched the man wobble across smooth, slippery stepping stones, aged boulders lying like stranded sheep on the stream bed. At the far side, the conjuror stooped and plucked a purple flower from the clusters about his feet, and stuck it in his hat to bounce jauntily beside his feather.

Crossing the stream in his turn, Gom regarded the tufts of dark green leaves and patches of tiny purple pompoms nodding in the clearing. Fool's-button, growing in abundance. A plant aptly named, for who but a fool would pick those flowers? Those who knew better left flower to seed itself, taking only from plants bearing empty pods.

Finding several of these, Gom uprooted them, washed them in the river, and tied them to his pack by their stringy stems. He and Stig had eked out their meager food supplies with fool's-button many a time, root and leaf, eating them raw, or boiled, or toasted over the fire, just as Harga had taught Stig many years before. A most sustaining root, if somewhat bitter: a potent herb to liven one's steps and quicken one's blood. Pity Zamul didn't know that. Gom, smiling wickedly, watched the man pick his way ahead, up and down the stony slopes, the purple pompom nodding at his brim.

The whole day passed, and in spite of Gom's resolve, Zamul still had the stone.

For most of that night, Gom sat brooding, plucking up the courage to try Zamul again. But he stayed where he was, not for the first time regretting his small size. With heavy heart he watched the sun come up, and soon afterward, they moved on again.

For eight days more, Zamul continued north, then, on the ninth day, turned directly eastward, through narrow, twisted glacial valleys dark green with pine. By now, the conjuror was weary, and less inclined to look about.

Gom, pleased at first, eventually found the slow pace

trying—yet not without its compensations. All along the way, he came across discarded scraps of bread, and apple—already turning brown, but still sweet inside—and even cake. In fact, Zamul left so much food behind that Gom's waybread was still almost intact. No self-respecting traveler would be so extravagant, Gom thought, picking up a sizable chunk of stale bread and nibbling on it for elevenses on the third morning of going east—unless—he broke off in midthought. *Unless he knew he hadn't much farther to go!*

Gom reached for the map anxiously. They'd almost reached the sound. Was that their journey's end? If so, Zamul would hand over the rune and then Gom would never get it back!

Later that day, Gom was following Zamul through a steep, narrow valley that sloped downward, when he saw sunlight flashing off distant water. The sea!

Wind had been right. It was like the biggest creek one could ever imagine. But how restlessly it glittered! Way beyond, in the misty distance, Gom could just pick out the farther shore: more mountains, tier after tier of them rearing back.

It was late evening when Zamul, reaching the end of the valley, halted on a cliff high over the sound. Gom watched the man settle into a rock cleft by the cliff edge, then found himself another not far away. The death's-head was close, Gom was sure. Tomorrow, Zamul would hand the rune over. If Gom were ever going to get that stone back, it would have to be now.

Gom took out the net, gripped it tight, and set himself to watch.

* * *

How long had passed? Not too long, he was sure. But enough for Zamul to fall asleep.

Still. A fine rain, mist, really, at that height, hung in the air, drifting across his face, as Gom crept the short way along the cliff top to Zamul's shelter.

Two steps inside the cleft Gom almost tripped. All but crying out, he caught at the rock wall to steady himself. Then crouching, he groped about for what had tripped him, and encountered Zamul's open pack.

Strange. Gom frowned. The last time he'd found Zamul sleeping, the conjuror had been using it for a pillow.

Gom shrugged. Zamul was exhausted. He could have dropped off to sleep before he got himself properly prepared. Gom inched the pack toward him. Since it was there, he might as well look for the rune. Aware that Zamul might be but a foot or two from him, Gom raised the pack's flap carefully and felt around within. No rune, and not much of anything else, either.

Dare he try the man's pockets?

He dropped the flap and edged along the cleft wall, not wanting to kick Zamul by chance. It was very dark in there. And quiet.

It also felt empty.

Gom blinked to accustom himself to the darkness, and looked about. With a cry, he ran the length of that short space and back again.

The cleft *was* empty.

Zamul was gone!

Chapter Nine

GOM ran to the cleft mouth. Only steps in front of him was the edge of the high cliff. Where could he go? He had no idea which direction Zamul had taken, and it was perilous to move about that cliff edge in the dark. He decided to watch by Zamul's pack and hope for the man's return. And if the conjuror didn't come back? Don't even think it, Gom told himself.

He squatted, his back to wet rock wall, pulled his collar up about his ears, and waited.

Dawn came late and slow. The rain was gone, yet a layer of higher cloud still blocked out the sun. Brushing the surface damp from his clothes, Gom got to his feet in the cold light, stretched stiffly, went to the cliff edge, and peered over.

Directly below him was a small island, a miniature mountain poking up out of the dull gray water like a Clack wife's Sunday hat, with pointed peak and round, white-laced brim. Had Zamul gone down there? If so, how? The cliff overhang looked impossible to climb even for him, let alone the conjuror.

A large bird circled overhead.

Gom looked up apprehensively, but it appeared to be a raven: blue-black, not gray, and with no sign of a skull.

"What a *fool* of a creature, standing out here in the

middle of nowhere, gawping at a chunk of rock!" it screeched. "Whatever will Tak see next?"

Gom breathed in relief. It was a raven, and as cantankerous as any he'd ever bandied words with.

"Tak will see," he cawed back harshly, cupping his hands about his mouth. "Tak will see a *fool* of a big black bird tumble into grief if he doesn't mind his manners!"

Tak was so surprised he tumbled down anyway. "Well, I *nev*er! How extra*ord*inary! A human: *talk*ing!" He tucked in his glossy wings and cocked his head. "You *are* human, aren't you? It's difficult to tell, such a *scraw*ny thing that you are. What are you *do*ing here, and how came you to speak the Tongue?"

"I learned raven up on the mountain where I was born," Gom replied. "As for what I'm doing, I'm looking for a man: a big man, in bright green breeches, a black velvet hat with a red feather, and a thick brown coat. Have you seen him?"

"Man? There's no man here." Tak glanced nervously toward the island.

Gom caught the glance. Ah! Tak *had* seen Zamul, and Zamul had gone down there. But not by climbing. How, then? Tak knew, Gom would bet. But would the raven tell him? Ravens were stubborn, and willful. And for all their sober plumage, inveterate tricksters. Even if Tak did speak, it might not be the truth . . . unless Gom could con it out of him!

Gom cleared his throat.

"That island down there . . ." He pointed. "I want to explore it."

Tak squawked in disgust. "What an *odd* creature is this human: clever and stupid both at once. Caws and claws, listen!"

As he spoke, the island began to shake with a great rumbling noise that sent huge waves thundering against the cliffs.

Gom's hand went to his chest. "What was that?"

"A monster!" Tak squawked. "A *monster* lies under there, that would tear you limb from limb!"

A *monster?* Did Tak mean the skull-bird? No. It wasn't heavy enough to set a whole island shaking in this way. Gom's eyes widened. But it might in its true form. The death's-head: was it the *monster?*

Monster.

Mother Chubb, the herb wife back in Clack had a brass knocker on her front door, in the shape of a snarling face. To keep bad spirits away, so she said, but the townsfolk called it a "hideous monstrosity" in itself. During his run-ins with old Gaffer Gudgeon, the old man would complain of Gom's forward tongue, or "monstrous lip," as the gaffer called it. The Clack merchants called their annual clear-out a "monster sale," a term that Gom linked not so much with the goods as with their prices.

Monstrosity, monstrous, monster: a hideous thing, or offensive, or of extraordinary size. If the death's-head were this monster, then it was all of these things and also evil into the bargain.

Come on, he urged himself. You lost your mother's stone. You must get it back, and fast! He chose his next words with care.

"Sounds interesting," he said casually. "How do you get over there?"

"I don't!" Tak snapped back. "Nor does anyone else with sense, these days. But if I went, I'd *fly.*"

"I don't mean you," Gom said. "I mean you—that is, me."

"You?" Tak sounded scandalized. "Are you com*pletely* daft? Didn't you hear that racket? Do you *want* to get yourself killed?" He surveyed Gom critically. "If I did know a way for humans, I certainly wouldn't tell you."

The old bird prepared to fly off.

"Wait!" Gom urged. "There is one, isn't there? And you do know it." He stared at Tak until the old raven fluffed out his feathers nervously.

"I've just remembered an urgent appointment," Tak said. "Got to go. Good-bye."

Good-bye! Tak mustn't go, not until he'd told all Gom needed to know. Gom thought fast: bluff was the only way.

"Good-bye," Gom said. Bending down, he picked up a pebble and weighed it as though he meant to throw it the moment the raven left the ground. Of course, he'd never actually have thrown it, but the bird didn't know that.

"*Well!*" Tak thrust his head out indignantly. "To be held to *ran*som in one's own back*yard!* Whatever next?"

"Tell me the way onto that island and I'll let you go," Gom said.

"Certainly not," the old bird snapped back. "And folk *stu*pid enough to ignore good ad*vice* deserve all they *get!*"

Tak turned his back on Gom and began to peck angrily in the dirt.

Gom sighed. Stubborn old creature! He gazed down at the water, then at the island so close to the shore. There must be a tunnel, or more probably a shaft, running down to the base of the cliff, then bending under the sound to come up under the island peak like the handle of an upside-down walking stick.

Tunnels and shafts were nothing to him. He'd learned

about them under Windy Mountain. But the surrounding area atop the cliff was all folds and clefts like the ones in which he and Zamul had sheltered. Finding the tunnel entrance could waste precious time. Therefore, Gom concluded, the bird must show it to him. Gom studied Tak thoughtfully. As well as being stubborn and willful and inveterate tricksters, ravens were also vain, especially about their wit and wisdom. Maybe he could outsmart this old creature after all.

"There is a way, I'm sure of it," Gom muttered, as if to himself, yet loudly enough for Tak to hear. "But this poor thing, for all his airs, clearly doesn't know it."

Tak hopped around. "Don't know? Don't *know?* Of course I know!"

"You do?" His eyes gleaming, Gom pretended to think. "Is it by boat?"

"Silly!" Tak screeched. "How would you reach a boat from up here?"

"If not *over*, is it *through* the water, swimming, maybe?"

"No, indeed! You'd still not get down there. One more try."

Gom could scarcely hide his excitement. "What a pretty riddle this is," he said, ruffling up his hair. "The way onto that island lies not *over* the water, not *through* the water, but . . ."

"Go on, go *on!*" urged Tak.

"I'm trying. Not over, not through, but . . ."

"*Under* lies the way!"

"Under? How?" Gom held his breath. One wrong word and all would be lost.

Tak croaked derisively. "A tunnel, a *tunnel!* What a ninny you are!"

"Tunnel! Of course!" Gom smacked a hand to his brow,

trying to hide his glee. Now to find out where its entrance was! He was just about to pitch his next question, when Tak shot loudly into the air.

"Why, you've tricked me, shameful creature! You want the tunnel entrance? Find it your*self!*" he cried, and flew away.

"Come back!" Gom called after him, but in vain. The sun was climbing, lightening the haze. Had Zamul handed over the rune now? Gom bit his lip. He must get on, without the raven's help.

Quickly, Gom stowed staff and pack in the cleft where he'd spent the night and was just leaving when the cliff began to tremble and shake. Gom braced himself against the cleft wall, while the ground moved under him.

A monster . . . that would tear you limb from limb . . .

The trembling grew more violent until Gom was thrown to the floor. There he stayed, his arms over his head, until all was quiet again.

As he got up faint hope stirred within him. The death's-head monster seemed angry. Maybe Zamul hadn't delivered the rune yet after all!

With renewed will, Gom set to work to find the secret tunnel, exploring each crevice in turn along the cliff top.

The sun was almost overhead when he found it, a fissure so narrow and crooked that he might have missed it had it not been for the tiny bright green thread snagged on a sharp rock spur at knee height.

He picked it off with care and held it up. It was a vivid green, the green of Zamul's breeches exactly.

So, Gom thought, eyeing the crack in excitement. This was the tunnel's entrance. Zamul had squeezed his great size through there to take a dark and surely dangerous way? He must have had help of some sort. Gom pictured the death's-head and, shuddering, resolved to watch his step.

He held up the bright green thread for Wind to take out over the cliff edge, then, with a deep breath, he turned and squeezed through the crack.

He'd taken no more than a few steps into the tunnel beyond when daylight suddenly vanished, leaving him in darkness thick as fog. He stood quite still, listening, feeling the drafts on his face.

"Sessery!"

Mmmnnn. Who comes into my halls this time, disturbing the peace?

Gom smiled.

"Good-bye, Sessery," he'd bade the breeze under Windy Mountain—Sessery, who'd taught him how to find his way about tunnels and shafts in the dark by judging her subtle drafts on his face. "I shan't forget you."

I know you won't, her mocking voice had answered. *Wherever you go there'll be a relative of mine and that will be me . . .*

Now Sessery laughed delightedly, caressing his face.

You know me, then. Or a cousin of mine, which is the same thing. What are you doing here?

"I'm trying to get down to the island. Is there a shaft leading under the sound?"

That there is, and a treacherous one too. You are the second body to come down here in a short space. But the other was not like you. He was clumsy, and noisy. I thought he'd not survive the first step down but . . . Her voice trailed away.

The second body to come down? Zamul? Gom's heart began to beat faster.

"But what, Sessery?" Gom asked, trying not to sound impatient.

. . . the Other aided him . . .

Gom's skin pricked with fear. "Other? What do you mean?"

Sessery didn't answer. She never answered once Gom betrayed interest in what she said, but she did blow gently along the way ahead, and Gom could tell at once that a few steps farther along, the tunnel floor ended abruptly.

Step by careful step he advanced, guided by Sessery, until suddenly, just as he'd judged, level tunnel fell away sharply into vertical shaft that should lead down inside the cliff, fetching up beneath the sound. From there, a tunnel running under the sound should connect cliff to island and then bend up again under the little peak itself.

He took off his boots, tied their laces together, and slung them around his neck. Then, turning about, he lowered himself over the edge of the shaft, and slid first one foot, then the other down the rock, searching for toeholds. Secure at last, he let go of the floor above his head, and climbed, slowly, steadily, going lower and feeling the air growing colder, until suddenly, he heard a sort of growling, and a slow, rhythmic beat, as of a great heart pounding.

He paused, the sweat starting all over in spite of the cold. "Sessery? Is that the Other?"

Sessery's light laugh answered him. *Oh, no, little one. What you hear is the Deep Sound, the pulse of Great Krugk itself.*

Great Krugk: the name of the sound, that he'd not been able to read on the map. Thanking Sessery, Gom climbed on.

Still he descended, until once more he felt the solid

floor of a passage under his feet. He went on slowly, aware now of the ground curving gently down. Aha, he thought. He'd climbed down the shaft, and he was now treading the underwater tunnel from cliff to island. If he judged right, when he came to the end of that, he'd be at last under the island peak.

On he went, downward over wet, slimy rock. And on. He began to grow anxious. Surely the tunnel should have bottomed out by now?

"Sessery, aren't I almost there?"

Oh, yes, you are, you little quick thing. And now I'm going to leave you . . . for I've other things to-o-o . . . do-o-o-o-o-o . . .

Sessery was gone, but sure enough, the ground began to turn upward again, until he was climbing well above sea level, under the tiny island peak.

At last the tunnel merged with a deep and noisy stream. Gom stopped, listening intently to the rushing water. If the echoes told right, the way ahead opened into a high, wide cavern.

The monster's lair?

He pictured the bone-white skull hovering in the darkness, above whatever hideousness it possessed for a physical body, its dark eye sockets staring toward the tunnel, waiting for Gom to emerge.

Coward, he told himself sternly, and made himself walk on.

Chapter Ten

A LITTLE farther along the tunnel, Gom noticed a dim glow coming from around a wide bend in the rock wall. He stopped a moment, until, his curiosity getting the better of him, he moved on again beside the stream toward the tunnel bend. As he went, the stream got wider, and the glow, brighter.

At that bend, Gom paused once more to consider. Did the glow come from the death's-head monster? The thing was likely around there, with Zamul. He clenched his empty hands. Fool that he was to have left his staff behind. Too late to regret it now! Gom squared his shoulders, and moved forward.

He emerged into a vast lighted cavern. The stream, too wide now to leap over, rushed straight across the cavern floor into the tunnel's continuance at the far side. Along to his right, a little cave, or grotto, led off the main cavern. That grotto entrance was crammed with a bulging mass covered in glowing scales: the light source. From the base of this mass something long and thick, like a tail, curled out onto the cavern floor.

Gom stared.

It *was* a tail, attached to a great, broad, fat back: a back of *extraordinary size.*

The monster. It had to be.

And yet—Gom didn't sense evil from that back. In

fact it put him more in mind of Mudge. And those scales, come to think, of the warm glow from Mandrik's skull.

Gom looked around cautiously. Zamul had come down here, the green thread had told him that and Sessery had confirmed it. Yet if he had, then the skull was here somewhere. But save for that back crammed into the tiny grotto mouth, the place seemed quite empty. So where was Zamul? And where was the skull?

Perhaps through the tunnel at the far side?

Gom started toward it, and was just even with the grotto and the monster when a sparkle caught his eye. There, just beside the little entrance, the glowing back, and the long, thick tail, shone a large pile of gemstones. Intrigued, he turned aside and moved quietly toward them, a wary eye on the tail. One blow from that and he'd be clear across the cavern floor—or worse! Closer, closer, and still the monster didn't move.

He reached the pile, and, still mindful of the awesome bulk glowing before him, looked down. Some of the stones were set in rich ornaments and diadems of silver and gold. Some, lying like pebbles on their own, shone all colors: red and yellow and blue and green and white and—

Gom reached for the small black stone lying on top. A smooth black stone carved with many magical fine lines, hanging from an old leather thong.

Slowly he took it up. Dead as ever, but—he rubbed it between finger and thumb—it was the rune. He closed his hand over it, and squeezed.

"Amsatla-lassoom?" The question boomed out from the small grotto, muffled by the bulk of the monster's body.

Gom leapt back, all but dropping the rune.

"Amsatla-lassoom!" The question came again, more insistently, but just as muffled: a curious sound, a blend of boom and hiss. Snake, with a measure of some other tongue Gom didn't even recognize.

"Pardon?" Gom said, in snake, measuring the distance to the far tunnel.

The voice came again, less boom, more hiss, a strong overlay of snake, primitive snake, but at least Gom made some sense of it.

"Who be is?"

Gom stood frozen, wondering what to say.

The glowing tail tip, round and flat as a butter paddle, began to wave ominously to and fro.

"Make voice sound," the monster demanded. "Say who be is."

With practiced speed, Gom slipped the rune around his neck and under his shirt, and made for the far tunnel.

"To I speak, soft belly!" The words continued, boom overcoming hiss, deteriorating into an incomprehensible tirade.

Gom paused, curious. The monster was clearly very agitated and growing more so by the minute, and yet apart from its lashing tail, it hadn't moved, not even to turn about to take a look at him.

As Gom watched, the round back heaved against the grotto's entrance arch. The strange rumbling began again, more violently than ever. The floor tilted, sending Gom teetering toward the stream's edge. Quickly, he righted himself and called out.

"Peace!"

This was no evil creature, for all its size, Gom was even surer, now. It was clearly in some sort of trouble, and was surely going to damage itself if it didn't stop.

"My name is Gobblechuck," Gom said, "Gom Gobble-chuck."

The rumbling subsided. The long tail withdrew, stacked itself into neat, tight coils, like a glowing rope. "Gom?" There followed quiet while the monster apparently considered this. "Is Gom of Katak? You be not feel is."

"Katak?" Gom said. "What's that?"

"If not of Katak, say who be is, and how is in this place."

Katak again. Gom didn't like the sound of that word. What was this Katak, that such a huge beast feared it? Even as he wondered, another question began to form at the back of his mind.

Could Katak be the skull?

"What does this Katak look like?" he started to ask, but the monster cut him off.

"Shush!"

In the stillness that followed, Gom heard only the noise of the stream rushing along behind them.

The monster cried out again.

"Is wish stay is, must step inside tail!"

Step inside tail? Gom stared, puzzled. The coils moved, the tip waved like a flag over the hole that they formed. Oh. Step down into those great coils? Gom retreated uncertainly. That back suddenly didn't seem quite so harmless. Was this a cunning trap? Maybe the monster was an enemy after all.

He began to run across the wide cavern floor.

"Stop!" the monster cried. "Is Katak here!"

Gom halted. "Where?"

"Haste!" the monster urged him. "Is last chance hide!"

Gom hesitated. He could be wrong, but the monster really did seem to be sincere. He ran back and climbed over the warm bright coils, and squatted down inside them. Immediately, the tail tightened about him, and the flat tip flapped shut over his head with a soft leathery thud.

Gom flinched at the muffled impact, then looked around uneasily at the glowing pile of tail that enclosed him like the inside of a lamplit well.

Was it refuge? Or trap?

How strange it was in there. He put his hands to the tail wall, saw them looking golden in the warm light. He bit his lip. Had he been too hasty? He was shut in so tight that surely no air could get through. In a little while he'd be unable to breathe! In a panic, he raised his hands, pushed against the tail tip. It held firm. He opened his mouth to cry out, but at that moment a tiny speck gleamed before him, brighter by far than the tail's soft glow.

The speck grew before his eyes into the ghastly death's-head, hovering like pale smoke before the grotto entrance. And somehow Gom could see it quite clearly, right through the thickness of the monster's shining coils!

Katak!

This was magic, thought Gom, shrinking. Real magic. He took the useless rune, closed his hand over it protectively. If he could see the skull—could it in turn see him? He tried to twist away, to avoid those hollow eyes. But they were not upon him.

A cry, harsh and angry, grated upon Gom's ears. A wordless wail of rage.

Gom froze. He could well guess its cause. Either Katak or Zamul had left the rune on that pile, and now it was gone. Gom remembered his vision, how Katak had found the rune out. Why did he not do so now?

Of course! Then, the rune had been alive. Now its power was dead. At this moment, Katak no more sensed the rune than he would an ordinary stone.

The harsh, angry voice filled the cavern, speaking in the monster's alien tongue. The monster answered, sounding defiant and sullen.

What were they saying? Perhaps Katak was accusing the monster of taking the rune, and the monster was denying it. Katak was clearly growing angrier by the minute. Whatever trouble the monster was in, worse was coming, and on Gom's account.

What now? The monster surely guessed that Gom had taken the rune. Would it regret hiding him and offer him up to save itself?

A sudden silence fell.

In that silence, the glow of the monster's tail faded. A deathly coldness filled Gom's hiding space. It touched Gom's skin, and his skin went numb. It touched his heart, and for a fraction, his heart stopped beating.

Yet Gom's awareness still remained. He still saw that death's-head hovering before him, stark now in the darkness as it had been in the vision on the plain, looking more substantial. Even as Gom watched, the death's-head, its eyes still upon the monster, flared malevolently.

The monster's voice sounded out in anguished protest, then died away.

"Kataaaak . . ."

The skull faded, but the echoes went on and on through the dark:

Katakataaakataaaakataaaaaaaak . . .

The cold was agony. Whatever Katak had done in his rage to the monster, he, Gom, was caught up in it.

Another minute and he'd not be able to move. Remembering his vision, how the rune had brought warmth and life back into him on the plain, Gom squeezed the stone tight.

Mother! he called. *Help me!*

A faint itch in his palm, gentle as the tickle from a hen's feather, grew into a warm tingling, which spread up his arm and outward. Healing, liberating warmth flowed through him, until at last he could move. His shoulder began to hurt, and some of the old bruises, too, from his fall down the Bluff.

The rune was alive again, had answered his need. He let it go and rubbed his aching body.

Then straightening up as much as he could, he pressed both hands against the monster's tail tip, and with great effort heaved it aside. He leaned against the cold dark coils for a minute until his strength came back, then he climbed up and out of his refuge.

The cavern was also cold—but not quite dark. From above the grotto arch came a dull red light quite unlike the warm glow of the monster's scales. Wonder what that is, Gom thought, not fancying the looks of it. He'd maybe investigate—after he'd seen to the monster.

"Hello," he called softly.

There was no reply.

He put his hand to a coil and patted it.

The monster still didn't respond.

In his spite, had Katak killed the creature? Gom slapped the monster's tail harder. It not only felt cold, but different. Like—he could scarce bear to think of it. The night Stig died, Gom had woken up to find him still sitting in his chair by the hearth. At first he'd thought his father to be sleeping merely, but when he'd touched his father's body, this was how it had felt. Cold. Dead. With nothing inside.

Gom pulled his thoughts back to the present. If the monster were not actually dead, it was as good as, and totally under Katak's power. It might have saved itself by giving Gom away, but instead it had gone down protecting him. Even so, Gom had fallen under Katak's spell and would be still were it not for the rune.

The rune!

It had brought Gom back to life. Could it help the monster, too?

He took off the stone and pressed it to the lifeless tail.

After a minute, Gom thought he felt a faint trembling against his hand, then nothing. The pile of coils was still dark and cold.

Mother, hear me! This poor unfortunate beast tried to save me from Katak. Please, please help me to save it in return! Gom cried silently, and willed with all his might for the rune to respond.

Suddenly, the monster's tail tip flickered with a faint, uncertain light.

Encouraged, Gom intensified his efforts. "There," he murmured, stroking the rune against the rough scales. The light increased steadily, up and around the coils. "Feel the good warmth chasing out the cold. In a minute, you'll be moving that tail of yours—see? Didn't I say so?" he cried, as all at once, the blunt tip began to wave to and fro.

Gom sighed with satisfaction. "Take good breaths," he said. "One, two, three, that's right. Now. How do you feel?"

The monster shuddered, then heaved a deep sigh.

"Is I from deathsleep loosed?" It sounded puzzled.

Deathsleep? Gom slipped the rune back around his neck.

"Say what be is," came the muffled demand. "Say what stronger than Katak be is."

Gom shifted uncomfortably. The monster clearly thought that he'd brought it back to life. Perhaps simple honesty was the best policy.

"I'm human," he said. "A human traveler."

"Human? Human, you say?" The monster's voice came with great force, its tones rich and sonorous as ever. But, to Gom's astonishment, the clumsy hybrid language was gone, replaced by Gom's own tongue.

Gom stood astonished. All those languages he'd had to learn of other creatures. For the first time, one addressed him in his own.

"How do you know the human tongue?" Why didn't the monster turn around? Gom wondered. Was it simply stuck?

"I was taught it long ago by one of your kind." The monster sighed into the grotto's back wall. "I promised not to tell the name, but I'll go so far as to say it was someone great and powerful, like you who overcame Katak's deathspell."

"Who is this Katak?"

The very mention of the name seemed to turn the monster once more into stone. When answer came at last, it was so low that Gom could scarce hear it.

"Katak in my tongue means evil one. He has come like a blight upon this world, and if unchecked, he'll work its destruction. He wants power, I've heard him talk. Power over those who rule the people, to bend them to his will. That I know. But to what purpose, I don't know. Nor what he is, nor where he comes from, either. All I've seen of him is that skull: he's not human, certainly."

"What's he doing down here? And you, too, for that matter?"

"I might ask you that, young human. What is this stone that he accused me of taking, me who can't stir from this grotto and he knows it?"

"The stone belongs to—me. He stole it—or rather had it stolen. I came to get it back. I'm so sorry," he added, "that you got the blame. If there's anything I can do—"

"There certainly is," the monster cried. "You must release me from this place. Quick, for I need water urgently."

"Release you?" If the monster was wedged in that place, Gom was surely not strong enough to pull him free. "Can't you wriggle your way out?"

"I wish it were that simple," the monster replied sadly. "Katak has shut me in here with a sealstone. But your magic could undo its power."

"Magic? I have no magic," Gom said. "I'm just a boy."

"No magic? And you roused me from Katak's death-sleep? Come!"

Gom thought fast. The monster clearly had expectations of him now. He patted the great tail absently, withdrew his hand smartly, rubbing his fingertips. The monster's scales had certainly grown very warm. And brighter than when Gom had first come into the cavern.

"I tell you, I have no magic," he insisted.

The monster cried out in anguish. "Then why did you wake me? You must put me to sleep again at once!"

"Put you to sleep again?" There's gratitude for you! Gom thought. "Whatever for?"

"Can't you see? At any moment, this place will fill with fire!"

Gom looked around. The walls ran wet, and the center of the cavern floor was dotted with puddles from the stream's upheavals.

"I am Ganash of the kundalara," the monster said.

"Kunda-what?"

"Serpents of the sea. If I don't reach water very soon, kundalara becomes *mangatla-aczai*: fire-breather, treasure-hoarder, man-slayer—dragon! Unlock the seal-spell! Hurry!" The monster's voice rose.

"Seal-spell?"

"By its magic none can pass in nor out of this place! See: my tail was outside when Katak set the seal-spell and there it stays while the rest of me—oh!" The monster broke off in terror. "The heat flowers within me! Go!"

Gom could see nothing but the monster's own bulk jamming him in. He reached out to feel the magic barrier but had to draw back from the heat. Ganash's scales, fairly blazing now, gave off a stench of rotten eggs that caught at Gom's throat and stung his eyes.

"Ganash," he called urgently. "Where is this seal-stone?"

Silence, then Ganash's voice came as from far away. "Red be is, and upsssssss . . ." The voice trailed off.

Red? Gom suddenly remembered the faint red light he'd seen above Ganash in the dark after Katak's visit. That must be it!

Gom sprang for the wall and climbed. There, at the top of the arch, tight as a spider in its crack, was lodged what looked like a sliver of red glass, its shine dulled by the brilliance of Ganash's glow. Now what? It seemed a simple matter to reach in and dislodge it. He stuck in a fingernail.

There was a bright flash, and Gom cried out, almost falling at the burst of pain in his hand.

Ganash moaned, a mixture of agony and grief, and a thin wisp of yellow smoke trailed up from the grotto.

Gom eyed the sealstone anxiously. What could he do to break its spell?

Why, nothing—*but the rune might!*

He took it off and slid it into the crack. "Break the sealstone's spell," he muttered urgently. "Break the seal-spell and release Ganash!"

Concentrating all his energy upon the rune, he touched stone to stone.

A second flash, more brilliant this time. Gom squeezed his eyes shut against the flare, expecting more pain, but none came.

He opened his eyes.

The sealstone lay dark in its niche, its light extinguished. The grotto was open. Now Ganash could squeeze his way out!

"Ganash! Quick! Get out of there!" he called, but the kundalara appeared not to hear him.

Gom scrambled down the wall. Oh, the pity of it! The way was clear at last, but too late to save Ganash. Gom reached out to nudge the beast, and pulled back sharply. The scales were now too hot to touch.

"Ganash!"

The beast didn't move.

Gom leaned his forehead against the cavern wall. Ganash would never get away from Katak's evil spells now. Wouldn't even want to change back, once he'd ignited, Gom thought grimly. The gentle kundalara would be gone forever. In deep despair, Gom swung the rune, hitting Ganash. A shudder went through the giant back. Then another, and another.

With a rumbling that shook the cavern floor, Ganash burst backward from the little grotto. Gom had a quick glimpse of big body, long neck and small head, then the kundalara turned about and lumbered forward to the stream.

Blue sparks spat and heat like lightning shimmered over the shining scales as, with a roar, Ganash reached the water's edge. With a loud hissing and clouds of steam, Ganash toppled in. The glare faded from the bright body, wavered, and went out, leaving the cavern in total darkness.

The hissing flared, then died.

A few moments later, Ganash's shape pulsed with faint, uncertain light. Not the hot coppery glow of before, but a green-blue luminescence, as of a glow-worm's tail.

The light grew brighter, steadier, filling the cavern with cool radiance.

Gom stirred. "Ganash?"

The kundalara didn't move.

Gom crept over to see.

The monster's eyes were closed.

Ganash was even more huge than Gom had thought. Almost as big as Stig's hut. His serpentine neck, thick at the shoulders, tapered to a small horselike head, flanked by pointed ears, crowned with a pair of horns that ended in small round knobs.

The belly was large, and round, and covered in smaller, paler scales than the rest of him. The forearms were short and shaped almost like a human's. The hindquarters were immense and looked very, very strong.

Gom sneezed, and wiped his eyes. The smoke and the reeking stench were clearing, carried off by gentle drafts blowing through the cavern.

"Ganash?"

Ganash opened one large green eye and looked up.

With a sudden swoosh of water that knocked Gom off his feet, the kundalara surged from the stream to tower over him, scales glistening, all hint of fire gone.

As Gom lay there on his back, water running from him, the huge beast leaned down his long neck and peered closely into Gom's face.

"Harga?" he said.

Chapter Eleven

HARGA? Gom scrambled to his feet. Ganash knew Harga? And thought himself to be looking at her! Why, thought Gom, I must really be like her, just as Stig had always said.

"Harga!" Ganash cried—this time in a voice none too friendly. His great tail rose from the cavern floor, lashing slowly from side to side.

Gom drew back. "I'm not Harga," he said. "I'm her son."

Ganash's nostrils flared, his green eyes blazed. "None of your old tricks!" he roared angrily. "Oh, how could you be so cruel, pretending that you couldn't help me, and I in terror for my life? I declare, your humor has grown too strong, even for me!"

"Won't you listen?" Gom cried. "Ganash: I—am—Harga's—son!"

"Son?" Ganash leaned closer until Gom could smell the sweet watery smell of his breath, could see the wet spiky lashes rimming the luminous green eyes. "Son, you say?" For a moment, he looked uncertain. Then the anger was back. "No! No mere boy could do what you did today, not even Harga's son."

"Quite right," Gom agreed, his eyes on the sharp claws starting from Ganash's outspread hands. "I didn't break the deathsleep, or the sealstone's spell. This did." He held up the rune by its thong.

"Ah!" Ganash exclaimed, but he made no effort to touch it. Instead, he put his face close to it, waving his head to and fro on the end of his snakelike neck. Then, to Gom's astonishment, he laughed. "I do believe," he cried, "it's the very stone I gave Harga from my treasury, as a parting gift for teaching me to speak the human tongue. For her wizard's stone, she said, she being new to the calling. It was so many years ago, and she a tiny young thing, just like you now. Amphory, they call it. She chose it above my finest diamonds and emeralds and rubies." Ganash turned and waved a hand back to the shining stones piled outside the cave mouth.

Gom stared in surprise. Those stones belonged to Ganash?

"Amphory is so rare that few ordinary folk have even heard of it. Nor would they want it if they had, it being so plain, so Harga said. And yet there are those, she told me, who'd kill for it. 'The quintessential wizard's stone,' she called it. I certainly never thought to see it again. Yet here it is—" He broke off in alarm. "Harga's not come to grief?"

"Oh, no," Gom said. "At least I hope not. I haven't met her yet, you see. She left me and my father the day I was born—and this rune on top of my blanket. For me to mind for her, as Father used to say. Now he's dead, and here I am, taking it to her." Gom eyed the stone. "All the years I've worn this, I've seen scarcely any magic, until this day."

How strange and wonderful, thought Gom. This gift to Harga from Ganash, returning to save its giver.

"Mmmm." Ganash bent closer, his nose practically on the tiny thing. "It's much changed. She has shaped the stone into her own sign, and wrought many wondrous spells within it." He held a hand out.

After a second's hesitation, Gom let the rune settle onto the radiant palm, while still keeping hold of the thong.

Ganash studied it intently, then looked up again.

"So, Gom—Gobblechuck, is it? You're Harga's son. Why would she leave this treasure with you, an untried boy?"

Untried boy, indeed! "One who," Gom retorted, "nevertheless pulled you from the deathsleep *and* the grotto."

"Quite so," Ganash murmured, "but as you yourself have admitted, only with this."

With a swiftness that belied his clumsy bulk, the kundalara swept the thong from Gom's grasp and dangled the rune out of his reach.

Gom's mouth fell open, but Ganash, laughing, only slipped the little stone back around Gom's neck. "Fear not, young one. Harga's son won't come to grief by my hand. I'm doubly glad that I harbored you today. And I admit: your wit is worthy of your dam. You're looking for Harga, you say? You'll not find her here."

Gom told Ganash how Zamul had stolen the rune for Katak. How Gom had followed the man down into that cavern. "And here I came thinking to find conjuror and skull. I never expected to find the likes of you. You say Katak has imprisoned you here. Why?"

The monster glanced back to the pile of gemstones lying beside the little cave mouth.

"He is stealing my—modest—treasure trove, and would have me guard it for him. That is why he was forcing me to ignite."

"Forcing you to ignite?" Gom frowned. "I don't understand."

"Once I became mangatla-aczai again, I would be a perfect watchworm—dragon, you know? Once rumor of me got around, not a body in the whole world would come near looking for the treasure."

"But if he wanted you to ignite, why freeze you with the deathsleep?"

"I don't know," Ganash said. "I only know he was more angry than I've ever seen him. Maybe he thinks I did manage to take the stone somehow."

Gom paused to consider. If, as Ganash said, Katak sought to gain power over those who ruled Ulm, Gom could well understand the efforts to possess Harga's rune. But not the need for Ganash's hoard.

"If Katak is after magic, why does he want your treasure?"

"Because—" Ganash hesitated. "From precious gold and silver and priceless gemstones is much magic made," he said at last, his voice low.

Gom nodded. So that was it. "Where is Katak now? And Zamul?"

"Katak has gone back to my home farther down the sound, to haul out more of my treasure. And the lackey brings it here, armful by armful on a raft that they keep on the island's far shore. I wondered where that one had gone these past weeks, and now I know that he'd gone to steal the rune from you. I heard him return earlier, though I couldn't see him. And I heard him place something on the treasure pile—the rune, of course—then go to find Katak. A mistake, I think, for which he'll dearly pay." Ganash smiled maliciously.

Gom nodded, recalling his thought that Zamul might get more than he bargained for.

The monster was no longer smiling. "Katak will be back soon with his slave to look for the rune. What are we going to do?"

What indeed? Gom considered. There was no point in running.

"We're going put a stop to Katak once and for all," he declared.

Ganash's head came up. "Oh? How?"

"That's the catch," Gom replied. "But I do have the germ of an idea. Tell me: when Katak and Zamul come back, they'll be expecting to find you still in your death-sleep, won't they?"

"That's right," Ganash said.

"Which means no smell, no smoke, and no light."

"Ye-es."

"What if Katak were to find the cavern full of smoke?"

Ganash considered. "He might think I'd somehow warmed up through his deathsleep. He'd certainly be confused."

"Enough to go into the cave to investigate?"

"Perhaps. But the sealstone's spell is broken, too. That would surely seem very strange and suspicious to him. Why?"

"I'm thinking to shut him up in your place."

Ganash first looked surprised, then his brows came together wryly. "And I'm wondering how, you not having your own magic."

Gom huffed at this last remark. But it was true. The rune was the thing. He squeezed it in his palm again. It had done so much for them. It had even broken the power of the sealstone.

On a sudden thought, he walked over to the cave mouth to stand beneath the place where the sealstone lay dark in its crack. If the rune could break the sealstone's power, perhaps it could restore it.

Gom climbed, touched the rune once more to the sealstone. There was a flash and the sealstone shone dull red as before.

"It worked! It worked!" Gom cried. "I think we have a chance!"

"By heavens, you may be right," Ganash said, lumbering over. "You said you wanted dark. That's no problem, for I can glow or not at will. But the smoke and smell are another matter. What are we going to do?"

Gom clung to the rock face in the dark, trying not to cough. Ganash waited across the far side of the cavern: dark, motionless, and alert for the first sign of Katak's return.

Black smoke drifted up from the empty grotto, acrid smoke from slowly smoldering cloth—the hem of Gom's tunic that he'd torn off with reluctance, it being the tunic that Mudge had made him.

Gom shifted his position above the grotto entrance, and sniffed the air anxiously. The smell of burning cloth wasn't exactly right for an igniting kundalara, but it was the best he could do.

He glanced down at the sealstone shining red beneath him. When Katak returned, Gom was hoping that the smoke would lure the evil one into breaking the seal to go into the cave. The moment Katak was inside, Gom must quickly touch the sealstone to life, shutting Katak in his own trap.

The trick was to catch Katak right. For the most part,

so Ganash said, Katak was invisible, showing himself as skull only when he chose. So silent and secret would be that one's coming, Ganash said, that Gom wouldn't even suspect it.

A moment later a small piece of rock hit the floor, Ganash's signal.

Katak had arrived.

Gom could see nothing in the sealstone's dim shine, no white light, no skull, nothing. The only token he had of Katak's presence was that beneath him, the sealstone suddenly went dark.

Katak had broken the seal on the grotto entrance, and was now inside looking to see what the smoke was all about. Quickly, Gom leaned down and put his hand to the crack.

Flash!

The red stone shone once more. The grotto entrance was resealed, and Katak was inside, out of the stone's reach—so Gom hoped!

Would the spell hold? Or could Katak break it somehow from within?

A scream of fury issued from the grotto. It burst against Gom's ears, and roared inside his head. No words were spoken, and yet into Gom's mind came the threat that if he didn't break the seal and release Katak at once, he'd pay an unimaginable penalty.

Gom shut his eyes against the sound, but it went on and on, echoing through the cavern—or was it through his head? He seemed to shrink until he was no more than a small white worm before the might of Katak's power.

He began to wonder how he'd ever dared defy that terrible force. Slowly, he reached down again to break the seal. But before he could touch the sealstone, large hands found him in the dark and hoisted him so high into the air that he felt Sessery's playful currents across the cavern roof.

"Let me go! Put me down!" Gom kicked and struggled against the kundalara's grasp. But Ganash, a radiant green again, only shook him gently, then held him out before his face as a mother her wayward child.

"Stop up your ears, young one. Katak's powers of persuasion are great."

"But the voice is within me also," Gom protested weakly.

"In that case," Ganash nodded toward Gom's chest, "use the rune."

Gom touched his mother's stone, and shut his mind against Katak's urgings. Although he felt nothing still, little by little the voices inside and outside ceased.

Gom whispered, "You may put me down now." And added, with a touch of resentment as Ganash lowered him, "You kept your head clear."

"And so I should, for I've had enough practice. Don't worry, I was just like you at first, before I learned not to listen, and even then I fell into that deathsleep. Come," he warned Gom. "We're not through yet. We must get out of here."

Gom took up his boots, slung them around his neck, and went with the kundalara into the far tunnel, Ganash swimming in the stream, Gom walking along beside it by the cool green light of Ganash's scales, until they reached a fork. There, the tunnel split into two, each way winding downward.

"Choose," Ganash told Gom, pointing. "Go right, and you take the stream down under the island and into the sound. Go left and the other tunnel will bring you out on the shore. You'd best come by water with me, if you want my advice. It's safer."

"Thank you," said Gom, "but I'd rather take the dry tunnel if you don't mind. I travel well underground, and I'm not overly partial to water."

"As you will." Ganash sighed heavily. "Good luck. I'll watch for you topside," he said, and with that he dove beneath the stream and disappeared.

As soon as Ganash was gone, Gom called out. "Sessery? Are you there?" Then stood in the darkness, listening.

A faint shout from the cavern behind him answered. Not Sessery, but a human call!

Zamul?

Gom listened. The voice came again, still as distant, but this time the words were louder, and quite distinct.

"Gom! Gom!"

Gom spun on his heel. He'd never heard that voice in his life, but he knew it. He moved fast, back to the cavern, to find a short, slight figure all in brown: brown shirt, brown skirt, brown shawl, brown boots, and brown hair drawn neatly to a coil at her nape. The figure, lantern in hand, was watching the tunnel entrance.

As he emerged into the lantern's light, she raised her other hand and beckoned.

"Mother!" Gom cried, and ran across the floor.

Chapter Twelve

THE FIGURE didn't come to meet him, but stood her ground, holding out the lantern directly in front of her, almost as if warding him off. Gom faltered, lowered his arms. Not the kind of meeting he'd expected. Oh well, he told himself. His mother no doubt had her reasons. And a little trust this time on his part wouldn't go amiss!

At least she was still smiling.

Stig had described her remarkably well: the quick, dark eyes deep set in the long face; long nose, bent just like his at the bridge; and three moles at the end of her chin. How mysterious and distant she seemed in the lantern light. Was that how she'd looked the night she appeared on Windy Mountain?

He looked down at his chest. Maybe his boots were in the way, he thought, slipping them from around his neck and dropping them to the floor. But she still made no move to embrace him, or even to touch him.

Her smile faded abruptly.

"So," she said, in a low and husky voice, just as Stig had described it. "I had to come after all to pull you out of this mess. Serves me right, I suppose, for having expected too much."

Gom stared at her in disbelief. What was his mother saying! Hadn't he just rescued Ganash and shut up the evil one in his place?

Harga was shaking her head at him reproachfully. "Such a big world, Ulm is. Too big for you, it seems. You think that is Katak in there?" She nodded to the grotto mouth. "Think again. Katak, you freed, and it's Ganash who lies behind that seal. Oh, to think the shapechanger duped my own son!"

Shapechanger? No! Incredulous, Gom thought back to his meeting with Ganash, how the kundalara had first spoken with him. That couldn't possibly have been Katak. "Besides," he said aloud, "we were both under Katak's deathsleep."

Harga shook her head. "A simple trick to make you think he was Ganash. Simple—but effective."

Gom stood stricken, recalling now the beast's fierceness when supposedly warming up. Oh, the cunning of it. The cleverness in winning Gom's sympathy. Why, Gom had actually *liked* the creature! While all the time behind the false form, Katak must have been laughing at him.

He clenched his fists. Fool again! When would he ever learn? He, a woodcutter's son, with a head turned by dreams and the lofty words of an ancient ghost, as Mandrik surely was. And now his mother had had to come to bail him out, before he'd had a proper chance to solve her riddle. He squirmed to think how he'd fancied his own cleverness. Now his worst fears were realized. He'd not only failed his mother, but had been shown right in front of her what a fool he was. He wished fervently that he were back up on Windy Mountain, lying safely under his bedclothes, with no more on his mind than the next trip down into town.

He forced himself to meet her eye. "I'm sorry, Mother. I know no better, being but a simple mountain boy.

Father always said I was no match for the outside world."
He took the stone from about his neck, and held it out.
"Here's your rune."

It was fairly buzzing against his open palm. And why
not, being rid of its bumbling keeper and with its rightful
owner again, Gom thought bitterly.

Harga nodded to the top of the arch. "First," she said,
"you can save your mother's legs and let that poor old
serpent out."

"Yes, Mother. Of course." Gom scrambled for the
cavern wall, eager to make amends, to show her at least
how well he could climb.

He'd no sooner found his first toehold when a deep
voice boomed out.

"No!"

Ganash swept up from the waters of the stream and
lumbered over toward him. No—not Ganash, Gom corrected himself, but Katak, shapechanger, who'd tricked
him into shutting the real kundalara into the cave.

"Gom!" Harga raised the lantern. "The sealstone, quick!"

Obediently, Gom turned back to the wall, but the
beast stamped the ground, making such a rumble that
Gom sat down hard.

Harga's eyes grew small and angry; her mouth, tight.
"Up!" she cried. "Fail me now, and I'll have no more
use for such a son!"

Before Gom could obey, the huge wet shape moved
with surprising speed to block his way.

"Move aside," Harga commanded sternly. "Or it will
go ill with you."

"That I'll not!" The kundalara leaned down its long
neck and murmured in Gom's ear. "You think that's

Harga? Young one, you're deceived. That's but an image of her that Katak took from your mind."

Gom looked up into the luminous green eyes, then to Harga, doubtfully. The beast looked so real. And its words made sense. The sham monster was indeed persuasive.

So was Harga. His mother's eyes gleamed dangerously. "Let my son pass, Katak. Or you'll be sorry, I promise."

Ignoring Harga, the creature leaned down yet closer until Gom caught the strong sweet smell of its breath.

"Young one, think," it urged. "If I'm Katak, *how come you still wear the rune?*"

"Gom!" Harga's voice came sharp. "Beware the shape-changer's power!"

"If you can't trust me," the kundalara went on, "trust the rune. Touch her with it and see what happens."

Harga waved the lantern at the wall. "Up! Quickly!" she cried.

Gom looked from one to the other. They each seemed so real. But one of them was lying. One of them was false. Which one?

What should he do? Touch Harga? Or the sealstone?

He twisted the rune's thong, weighing his options, trying to decide. If that were really his mother, and he touched her, his only risk was more anger. If that figure were not Harga but a sham, and he touched the sealstone, then all was lost.

He swung the rune out by its thong, just enough to tap his mother gently. He felt no impact. Instead, the stone passed clean through hand and body, as through smoke. At once Harga disappeared, lantern and all, and the death's-head glared out from the blackness of the grotto. Words streamed in silent fury through Gom's head:

Release me. Release me, while yet you can. You meddle in matters past your understanding.

Gom looked in horror from Katak to the place where "Harga" had stood but a moment before. So close, so close he'd come to ruin!

"You chose wisely, young one." Ganash laid a hand on Gom's shoulder. "You are truly your mother's son. Come," he went on, "we must go, and fast, before he pulls another trick—and this time together, like it or not."

Gom retrieved his boots, and clutching them tightly, let Ganash scoop him up and carry him to the stream.

Holding Gom above the wet, Ganash swam from the cavern, along the tunnel, passing the tunnel fork, and down until Gom heard the thunder of Great Krugk.

There, Ganash paused. "Don't be afraid. Take a deep breath, and hold it. We're going down under the island, then up again, out into the sound."

Gom obeyed, shivering as the waters closed over his head.

They dove deep. Gom felt the currents grow colder. The water pressed in upon his ears, hurting his head, and lights seemed to explode all about him.

His thoughts grew confused. He opened his mouth to shout, to tell Ganash that he was suffocating. The harsh salt water rushed up his nose to tear at his throat. Mother, he thought. I've failed you. I never solved the riddle. I never brought you the rune. Gasping, choking, he began to struggle. "I wish—" he cried, and his life's breath streamed in tiny bubbles from him . . .

Gom became aware of lapping waters, the soothing hiss of pebbles in the tidal wash. He was lying in something soft and warm, and swinging gently back and forth; a pleasant, lulling motion.

Gom was minded of the cradle Stig had made for Harga to rock their children in. Beautifully carved with small wild animals running all over it, and Hoot Owl presiding from the canopy. Hilsa in turn had rocked three of her own in it already, with promise of more. Such a warm and loving mother she was, and so she should be, having learned her craft of Harga.

Gom alone of all the family had never slept in it, for he'd spent his babyhood lying under trees while Stig went about his work nearby.

That had had its compensations. Gom would swear that was how he'd come to know so much of animals over the years. And yet, he thought, sighing deeply in satisfaction, it would have been nice to be rocked like this by his mother's hand.

He tried to turn over, but in vain.

Stiff with alarm, Gom opened his eyes. All was still dark, but it was the darkness of night, and those twin stars above his head were real. Against those stars glowed Ganash's radiant head, green eyes fixed on him anxiously. Gom peered down. The kundalara was crouched on wet shingle, Gom in his arms.

"Ah! So you decided to live after all." The beast stopped his rocking, and lowered Gom to the shore. "My, but your lungs need building up."

His lungs? The icy waters had sucked all Gom's strength. He sat, his eyes fixed on Ganash, finding the soft green radiance of his mass strangely beautiful.

"Where are we, Ganash? Are we safe?" His numb lips slurred the words.

"We're still on the island. The way you were looking, I thought I'd better let you get your life breath moving again before we go any farther. It's all right: we're safe enough, now."

Gom bent over, folded his arms across his middle, and squeezed, fighting the urge to be sick. Katak was somewhere inside that peak, caught in his own trap. Gom saw again Harga's form, standing beside the grotto, lantern raised, beckoning to him.

"It was just like her," he murmured brokenly.

"No, it wasn't," Ganash answered, his voice low. "Not one bit."

The beast touched Gom's head with great gentleness. "You think your mother would treat you thus? Young one, just you wait. When at last you meet with Harga, you will know the difference."

Gom wasn't comforted.

If I'm Katak, how come you're still wearing the rune?

"I should have guessed," he said, rocking back and forth. "I'm a fool."

"No." Ganash's voice was almost sharp. "Katak's power is strong. He clouded your mind."

Gom straightened up. "He didn't fool you."

"Gom, Gom." Ganash shook his head. "I already told you: how do you suppose I came to be locked up in that grotto? You mustn't blame yourself, or judge yourself a fool on account of this day. Think." He crouched beside Gom. "Who's left behind down there, and who's come out victorious, eh? Who broke the seal on the grotto? Oh, yes, you used your mother's rune. But seriously: can't you see what a great feat it was to bend it to your will? And look what wit and wisdom it took to find the false Harga out at last, against the full force of Katak's power! Oh yes, I gave you the choice, but only you could make it! Young one, you've done great good this day. In fact I do believe you've saved this whole world a packet of trouble."

Gom shifted awkwardly. He had felt the power of Katak's evil. If Katak had gained control over the rune and Ganash's treasures, that power would have grown beyond imagination. Ganash's words were indeed true. But they made Gom feel highly uncomfortable.

"As for me," Ganash went on, "I owe you my life and my freedom. And the return of my treasure. And that Katak shall stay safely shut away in his grotto forever, as long as I'm around, anyway, which amounts to the same thing."

"There's still Zamul."

"I know. When he shows up, I'll get rid of him."

"H—how?"

"Don't worry, I'll not 'tear him limb from limb'," Ganash said, in fair imitation of raven. "You think I don't know what *cer*tain folk say of me in these parts?" He laughed, as Gom stared in surprise. "No. I'll give that Zamul, as you call him, the scare of his life, then tow him on that raft of his to the far side of the sound. He'll not bother us again. Would you sleep here the night, or on the mainland?"

"On the mainland," Gom replied promptly. "But I can't climb those cliffs."

"No matter," Ganash said. "I know a secret little bay where the sand stays soft and warm at nights. You'll have to ride my shoulders, you see, for I'll need my arms to swim the Krugk. Are you fit enough to try?"

"I certainly am," Gom cried, although he wasn't sure he could even make Ganash's back, let alone hold on for the space of a ride across those waters.

Ganash reached down his strong neck, and Gom climbed it up onto the great bony shoulders. Wet as Ganash was, his scales felt surprisingly warm and rough under Gom's hands and knees.

"Lucky for you I burned off all my algae," Ganash explained. "A few days back in the water, and I'll be my old slippery self. Hold on."

Powered by his tail, Ganash swam swiftly under the shadow of the high cliffs. Gom looked all about them curiously in the dark, saw nothing but the gleam of waves gently rippling out from Ganash's luminous body. Wind blew about them, tugging affectionately at Gom's hair, at his clothes, but didn't speak. Gom shivered, wishing that he dared take his hands off Ganash's neck long enough to pull his jacket more closely about him. He remembered Carrick's map suddenly, still folded up in the pocket, and hoped that it wasn't ruined.

"Here we are, Gom Gobblechuck." Ganash slowed at last. "I daresay you're quite chilled from the sea wind, but you'll warm up here fast enough."

With a slight bump or two, the kundalara waded from the water and up onto the shore.

Gom slid off Ganash's shoulders onto sand. He bent down, ran his fingers through it, and found it warm and dry as Ganash promised. To his great relief, Ganash made no move to go, but lingered beside him.

"Tell me, little one," the monster said, working his great body down into a smooth round dip in the sand. "Something you said greatly bothered me back there—about Harga leaving and you just newly born. Tell me more."

Gom gladly complied, telling of Harga right from the beginning: of her coming to Windy Mountain, her marriage with Stig, and of the ten children she had by him. Of the wonderful tales she'd told by the hearth of a winter's evening, of how Stig would set her words to song. How she'd taught Stig the herbal lore. What a good and loving and gentle mother she'd been.

Ganash looked thoughtful. "That sounds like her right enough. The tales—my, could she tell them! And the way she brought her children up and everything—save for one thing: The Harga I know would never have abandoned her family like that, most of all, her newborn. However much of a hurry she was in, she'd have warned your father of her purpose—and she'd have taken you with her. Unless . . ."

"Unless what?" Gom's throat was suddenly dry.

Ganash fixed his eyes on him. "Unless she was hiding you."

"*Hiding* me?"

"By acting as decoy. You've surely seen such in the wild."

Gom's heart beat faster. Yes, yes. Many a spring below Windy Mountain, when Fox got too near Mother Grouse's nest, he'd seen Mother Grouse flutter away from her little ones, limping, or pretending to have a broken wing, drawing Fox after her, back to a safe distance.

He gazed up into Ganash's face earnestly. Was that what Harga had done? He'd dearly like to think so. But—

"Why would she be hiding me?"

"That's for you to find out, young one. But think what happened to you the moment you popped your nose outside your nest."

"To the rune, more like," Gom muttered, but Ganash's words struck home. Odd, he thought. How you can argue whys and wherefores forever, yet know the truth when you hear it. A warmth stole over him, filling him with such joy that it sought to spill out.

Your mother waits for you, and hopes for you on your path of experience . . .

He had to turn away to face the dark waters, barely keeping himself from standing up and shouting out loud. After all those years of doubt! He was certain now and forever that Harga hadn't abandoned him.

He faced Ganash again at last. "The question is," he said, "where to find her. Have you any idea where she would be?"

Ganash wrinkled his brow. "She didn't tell you, you say. Hmmmm. She must have good reason for that, too."

Gom bit his lip. He was inclined to agree. And yet it occurred to him that so far on his travels, he'd always fared better with the help of others. Perhaps that was part of his lesson. Instead of trying to figure the riddle all by himself, perhaps he should ask Ganash to help him solve it.

He told the kundalara about his vision of the bear and the sparrow, and the words of the riddle. "And so as soon as I guess the answer, then we'll meet, the sparrow said. Have you any idea what that answer is?"

Ganash looked at him oddly. "If I did, d'you think your mother would thank me for telling you? I know Harga well enough to give you this advice: whatever help you take from others on this journey of yours—and take it where you may—if you would meet Harga, you must keep that riddle to yourself. A box of treasures, she called it, a secret, private box to which only you must find the key. Never, never mention those words to any other—in fact I've already forgotten I heard them myself. Now, come. Sleep. You've a way to go tomorrow. Don't worry, I'll stay by you. But if you should wake in the morning and find me gone, I'll only be seeing that Zamul to the other side of the Krugk."

Ganash crouched down and closing his eyes, laid his head on the sand. Gom curled up beside him, under the curve of the great body. The sand's really quite comfortable, Gom thought, wriggling around a bit making himself a shallow little hole. Like a nest, he thought. He began to relax. Ganash was right. He was tired. But after all the excitements of that day, he'd never manage to fall asleep. Never, never, never . . .

The next morning, when Gom awoke, the sun was high, and there was no sign of Ganash.

He stood and stretched, aware of stiffness, of pain in his empty belly. How long was it since he'd eaten? He was thirsty, too. He glanced to the cliff top, thought with longing of Stig's water bottle, and Mudge's solid waybread lying in the place where he'd hidden them. He turned to look out over the cold waters, north, south, then west to the faint smudge of mountains at the far side of the sound.

Was Ganash with Zamul, as he'd said? If so, he could be gone for hours.

Gom decided to fetch his satchel.

The ground, snaking back from the beach in an almost leisurely way, looked an easy enough climb. Gom looked around for his boots. They were lying nearby, caked in sand and salt, stiffly drying in the sun. He bent them up a bit to loosen them, shook out grit, and put them on. They felt tight, and damp, but they'd soon soften and warm up, Gom told himself, tying the laces.

Remembering Carrick's map, he pulled it from his jacket pocket. The parchment was half-dry already. He opened it carefully and spread it out. Still intact, and the ink lines not even smudged. But then it was a tinker's map and made for rough weather. Gom laid it flat on the sand to dry, weighed it down with large pebbles. Then he made his way up from the beach to the cliff-top hiding place, leaving signs along the way to mark his path: little circles of stones, with a gap pointing down the way he'd come. As he went, white gulls circled over-head, swooping and diving over the water, watching for fish. Gom paused a moment, eyeing them curiously. There had been no gulls on Windy Mountain, naturally, and so they were strange to him. He hailed them in heron, then in goose, then duck, but they ignored him. They either weren't interested, or couldn't hear him over their own loud calls. He was just about to climb on again when, from a nearby ledge, a late fledgling, with wisps of down still fluttering from its back, took off out into space.

Above, its mother circled, mewing anxiously.

Gom glanced down. Far below, the water boiled about jagged rock.

The fledgling flapped its wings once or twice, then began to plummet toward the rocks at the foot of the cliff, the mother following now with strident calls.

Gom cried out. The little thing was going to dash itself onto those deadly rocks, and no one could stop it!

At the last moment, it suddenly began to beat its wings, pulled out over the water, then fluttered down to land on the glistening waves. A moment later, the mother gull landed beside it, and the pair of them sat, bobbing on the water, turning and turning about in unison.

Gom let out a long slow breath, and turned back to the cliff.

He found the hiding place without too much difficulty; his pack and staff, still stashed safely where he'd left them. He helped himself to a big bite of waybread and a nibble of dried fool's-button root that had grown strong and bitter with age. Quickly, he measured out a generous handful of sunflower seeds to sweeten its aftertaste.

From Air and Earth comes seed, by Fire and Water is tempered . . .

He chewed the seeds thoughtfully, making his way back down to the beach.

Fire and Water . . .

Ganash! The creature of fire and water. The kundalara who nearly became mangatla-aczai! Sea serpent to dragon . . . water to fire . . .

Was Ganash himself part of the riddle? Certainly that one had guessed some, maybe even all, of its answer. Gom opened the water bottle, washed the seeds down with a careful swallow.

He'd come into this region to retrieve the rune. He'd tracked Katak down to his lair, and shut him up in it. He'd lost the rune, and found it again. Somewhere in there was the answer to part of the riddle.

But what?

He was beginning to think that it was no mere exercise of the mind. That his search for Harga itself was both riddle and answer. " 'Your mother hopes for you on your path of experience,' " he repeated, under his breath.

He saw once more the young gull plummeting down from the high ledge, its mother hovering anxiously. For all her love and care, that young one had had to prove its wings alone.

He climbed steadily down, feeling the staff good and solid in his hands again. When he arrived on the secret shore, would Ganash be waiting?

"Hallo there!" Gom heard Ganash hail him long before he reached the sand.

"Well," the kundalara said, as Gom approached. "How are you feeling this morning? Don't you worry about that Zamul fellow anymore," he went on, before Gom could answer. He pointed west to the misty peaks across the sound. "He'll not get out of there in a month of Sundays."

Ganash eyed Gom's staff and satchel. "You're going now? Here."

The beast held out a huge, coiled hunting horn, wrought in gold, and encrusted with pearls and small bright stones that flashed in the sunlight.

Gom stared down at the golden shining thing, minded of the coils of Ganash's tail. He took it, caressed the colored stones.

"Emeralds and rubies, they are," said Ganash. "I found it fairly recently, so it's still nice and clean."

A hunting horn, out in this desolate place? "Where?" Gom asked in wonder. "Where did you find it?"

Ganash nodded to the water behind him. "Same place as I find the rest of my treasure," he said. "Every lost thing ends up in the deep, sooner or later, from pins to opportunities. Listen: if ever you need my help, just come and stand right here, and blow this. Don't worry," he added, "I'll hear it, wherever I am. Try it."

Gom raised the horn to his lips and blew so hard that his cheeks ached.

A blast, deep and hollow as Ganash's own voice, rippled out across the water and curled up through the mountains beyond.

"See? You can blow it well. One note like that, and I'll be here." Ganash backed into the current, the waves swishing about his bulky body. "I hate good-byes," he said. "And anyway, we're going to meet again. Regards to Harga, young one, and good journeying."

A small splash, and Ganash was gone.

Gom watched the swirl dissolve, then, tucking the horn into his belt, he retrieved his map and made his way back up to the cliff top.

There, Gom weighed the horn in his hand. It was heavy, and too big for his satchel. And what would be its use away from here? He decided to hide it where he'd left his staff and pack. Just in case, he thought, he needed Ganash's help one day. Or wanted merely to visit for old-time's sake.

But that could be many years hence. He might forget where he'd put it. To make sure he'd find the horn again, he scratched a sign, a curly line in the horn's own shape, opposite its hiding place.

He settled the rune inside his shirt, closed his jacket over it. It felt alive, tingled almost, against his chest. All this distance he'd come, to get back the stone. And he had succeeded.

Now he must go back and pick up his journey south again from where he left off. Hitching up his satchel, he took up his staff, and went on his way.

He'd not gone far when there came a loud squawk from above.

"Well! And what did you let him out for! A disgrace to the whole *neigh*borhood, that creature is!"

It was Tak, doubtless come to investigate the sound of the horn.

"It was all I could do," Gom answered him. "He was so hungry. And do you know what his favorite dish is? Why, it's raven. So I hope you don't mind my telling him that you live close by. Most grateful, he was, for the—"

Tak shot upward, dwindled to a tiny speck as, laughing, Gom strode on.

Part

3

Chapter Thirteen

SHOULDERING the staff jauntily, Gom moved due east, going by the sun, then south, walking, climbing, retracing his steps to Deeping Dale and Bragget-on-the-Edge. From there he'd pass by Twisting Valley, down Middle Vale, and into Long Valley following the original route into the lakelands that Carrick had given him.

He traveled fast, much faster than he had coming, when he'd had to match Zamul's pace. And he traveled with great zest, for hadn't he gotten back the rune and, with it, defeated Katak, and couldn't he afford to face Harga at last?

It felt so good, going without fear. He looked up at the blue sky lightheartedly. With Katak shut in his deep grotto, there'd be no more skull-bird, and with Zamul stranded somewhere across Great Krugk, the road was clear. He strode along, Wind blowing briskly at his back, glad, it said, to see Gom on the move again.

But though Gom traveled quickly, and with great energy, and without fear of danger from Katak, something was changed.

He was lonely.

Solitary as he'd been for much of his life, Gom's fits of loneliness had never lasted for long. Until now. He missed his father so much: the great warmth, the gentle strength. Hilsa, too, he missed. And Stok. And Hort and Mudge.

Even Ganash.

Such wonderful friends he'd made, good, loving warm-bodies, only to leave them to travel on alone with but Wind for company.

Would it always be thus?

If he had to keep moving, perhaps he should look for a fellow traveler, someone to talk with, to sing with, to share tales with at the end of the day. Like Carrick. Now there was one whose company he'd gladly enjoy.

Keeping up his pace, Gom climbed down from the lofty ranges until he reached their southern end. Things had certainly grown in his absence! He'd lost count of time, but judging from the lushness all about him, he guessed he must have been gone at least twenty days.

The fool's-button grew in greater abundance now beside the ford that he and Zamul had first taken on the way north, so that Gom was able to pick a good thick fresh clump of roots and leaves to tie to his pack, several days' supply.

Farther south, he added wild parsley, lettuce, and asparagus, eking out comfortably the remains of his waybread and sunflower seeds.

Another few days, and he was striding through the gentle hill country where he'd left Acorn, using the map now to pick out the way to Deeping Dale and Bragget-on-the-Edge.

One late afternoon, about ten days after he'd left Ganash, Gom finally hit the Bragget trail. He hurried along, hoping to reach the village by nightfall, and perhaps find a snug haystack to lie in, and maybe hear the sound of a friendly human voice.

Or perhaps, he thought, almost running now, he'd meet another Hort, a kindly farmer ready to trade a cup of milk and a loaf of bread and some cheese for a neat stack of fresh-chopped firewood.

The sun was just going down when, cresting a rise, he saw below him the eastern end of the gentle, green Dale, and Bragget. Smoke drifted up from whitewashed chimneys, along with the mixed and tantalizing smells of a villageful of suppers.

Bragget was bigger than Green Vale. The houses, clustered in that sheltered dip, looked bigger, too: squat, solid shapes smudged by soft haze.

By the time Gom neared the village, the sun was down, and the skies were darkening fast.

He gazed at the twilit houses hungrily, picturing hospitable folk within, gathered around tables loaded with good hot food. But—he hesitated—dare he knock on doors at this hour? Come on, he told himself. You braved Katak, and Zamul, and Ganash, as well, before you found him to be friend. Surely you're not afraid of a homely face or two.

Gom hitched up his pack and moved along.

He paused by the very first dwelling, a croft on the village outskirts. He pictured the farmer's wife, a second Mudge, with amiable face and motherly inclinations, her larder stocked with tasty things for a small, tired wayfarer with a good axe arm.

He pushed open the gate and stepped resolutely into the yard.

A huge black shape bounded up. "Who are you! What do you want!" it snarled, circling him.

Gom started back in alarm. He'd never seen the like, a hound as big as a small calf, of exceedingly thin and hungry body, all set to take his leg off.

"I'm a traveler," he yupped hastily, "looking for a night's lodging."

The hound's mouth dropped open. "Why," it said, "you sound just like a dog—though you don't look like one." It wagged its tail uncertainly. "A traveler, you say?" The dog sniffed around him. "Mmm. You have some good, strange smells about you. You've come far."

Gom relaxed a little. "Aye, I have. Do you think your master would consider a night's bed and lodging for, say, a day's work around the place?"

"My master?" The hound snorted scornfully. "My master beats me every morning to keep me in hand, then at night in case I forgot, and then some more whenever he finds the excuse. And he feeds me scarcely anything at all, so you'll get short shrift from him. Many's the time I've resolved to run away, but where to? Listen, you must go, before he hears you."

Go? Gom was crestfallen. "Is there another house you could recommend, then?" he asked, at the gate.

The hound considered. "Normally, I'd name two or three places right off, but not at present. In fact, right now any stranger showing his face in this place without reason or purse is likely to be whipped out of sight. I tell you: you'd best put as many miles between you and this place while you can."

"But why?" Gom asked. "What has made the folk so angry with strangers?"

The cottage door opened suddenly and a head poked out. "Shadow? Shadow! Cut your racket unless you want a thrashing!"

"Oh, dear," Shadow whimpered softly. "It's my master. Wait here."

The hound ran up to the front door and, wagging his tail, stood on his hind legs and licked the farmer's hands.

"Here, here, back off!" The farmer kicked him off the porch. "I told you afore: them tricks'll not get you indoors. You keep watch, d'you hear, boy? Or I'll come out there and fix ye!"

The farmer went back in and slammed the door.

"See what I mean?" Shadow came back to the gate, his tail between his legs. "Oh, how I hate that man. Tell you what," he said. "If you like, you can sleep in his barn. I'll wake you at dawn before he comes out, and you can be safely on your way."

"That's very good of you," Gom said, and followed the hound around to the back of the house.

The barn was clean and dry, with a pile of empty sacks in one corner.

Gom took off his pack and set the staff aside. Then, too tired to eat, he lay down on the sacks and closed his eyes.

A moment later, Shadow's nose lightly touched his cheek. "Good night. Sleep well," the hound said, and trotted away.

Barely two minutes later, it seemed, Shadow nudged him awake again.

"Quick," the hound urged him. "It's late. I've had the hardest time rousing you! The master'll be out any minute."

Scarcely before Gom could stand up and blink, the dog hustled him out into the early morning sunshine.

"Too late," warned Shadow. "He's coming! Listen: behind the barn is the orchard. Behind the orchard is a wall. Beyond that is a way out of town. Be quick, and be quiet, if you value your skin."

"Thank you for your kindness," Gom said, but the hound was already scurrying back toward the farmyard.

Gom found the orchard wall, and moments later he was standing, breathless, in a narrow lane.

Westward, the lane led away from the village, toward Twisting Valley. Eastward, it led past small neat cottages onto the village green.

Turning westward, Gom hadn't gone far up the lane when he heard a commotion behind him. Folk were flocking onto the green from all directions, to gather under a huge old oak standing in its center.

Intrigued, Gom stopped and pressed himself into the wall to watch and see what brought out all those folk so early in the morning. He couldn't be sure, but he sensed this was no festive occasion. The murmuring that Wind blew his way sounded angry.

Come, Gom Gobblechuck, Wind whipped his hair. *You'd best be moving. There's bad work afoot back there.*

"What bad work?" Gom asked. Heeding Wind's warning, Gom stepped out to hurry up the lane, and dodged back again. He should have curbed his curiosity and gone while he could. Too late now. There was no way he could go up that road without being seen.

Don't say I didn't tell you! Wind cried, and whirled away.

All at once, there came a burst of angry shouting.

Peeping out, Gom saw a tall, foxy youth, with lank pale hair, running toward him as though his life depended on it. A crowd followed at his heels, pelting him with rocks and bottles, making a violent din.

A bottle striking him on the shoulder, the youth fell, picked himself up, and ran on. But he'd lost his lead. Any minute now, the foremost villager, a great hefty man who looked as if he might be the blacksmith, would reach him.

Sure enough, the man drew level with the youth, seized his shoulder, and began to drag him back up the lane.

"Think to get away, do yer?" the man snarled. The folk followed after, shouting and gesticulating angrily.

Gom was so shocked that he stepped from his hiding place and followed them all the way back to the village green.

In the grass lay a long leather whip.

While the blacksmith held the youth, another took up the whip and cracked it. "Flogging we said, and flogging it be, so let's get on with it. We've still a day's work to do after," the whip man said.

Flogging? Gom had never heard that actual word before, but it was easy enough to guess its meaning. He eyed the whip in horror.

The man raised the whip and prepared to bring it down across the youth's shoulders.

"Hey!" Gom shouted, before he could help himself. "Stop that!"

The whip halted in midair, as everyone turned to stare at Gom.

Seizing his chance, the youth pulled away from his captor and dashed through the crowd, brushing past Gom so closely that in his haste he knocked Gom over.

"Here!" Climbing to his feet, Gom started after the youth, but many hands seized him and dragged him back.

"Who are you? What are you doing here?" Voices clamored on every hand.

"I'm G—" Gom struggled wildly. "I'm going west," he said.

There came a shout of laughter.

"I'll say," someone said.

The hubbub broke out again.

"What shall we do? Mat's gone, thanks to him. Who's going to pay?"

"Why, him, of course!"

"We'll flog this nosy busybody instead."

"Yes," the crowd took up a general call. "Flog him instead."

Gom found himself, resisting, being dragged over to the oak tree. He couldn't believe it. If he didn't do something quickly, they'd carry out their threat.

"Wait!" Gom shrugged his captor off. "What has this Mat done to deserve such dreadful treatment?"

"Done?" The blacksmith's face darkened. "What hasn't he done! He's wrecked this whole village, that's what. Fooled us with his bragging and his fine promises, cheated us out of our hard-earned money."

In spite of his predicament, Gom had to ask. "How do you mean?"

A sad-faced man spoke up. "Last harvest, he burned down all our hayfields trying to prevent rain."

"And at sowing time, he flooded our farmhouse," a woman called out, "trying to bring it on."

An old gaffer piped up. "He made me a special walking stick as he claimed would cure my lumbago. I no sooner put my weight on it than it folded and put me abed for this past six-month."

"Don't forget the village hall," said a tall, thin woman, "that Mat promised to clear of riddley bug."

"He did it, all right." The blacksmith nodded grimly. "Oh, there's no more bugs, I'll grant you that. But there's no more hall, neither, for his hocus-pocus collapsed it!"

"Worst of all," said another. "He's gone and took our milk."

"Your milk?" Gom was truly confused now. The young man called Mat hadn't been carrying anything when he ran from the village, except himself.

"It's like this," a wife said. "Farmer Marmot's cows have gone dry. Mat gave them a potion to bring their milk on again. One lick of that stuff and they jumped clear over the gate and took off we don't know where."

The crowd began to mutter once more.

"So now we've no milk or whey or cheese or cream—"

"And that's tantamount to stealing—"

"And the penalty for stealing is the whip!"

"Hey, hey," said Gom, thinking fast. "Aren't you all getting rather excited? Look, suppose the potion hasn't worked—and you have no way of knowing. In that case, there's still no milk, so it can't have been stolen. Now, suppose the potion has worked, and the cows are making milk again. In that case, Mat has done what you wanted, and far from stealing your milk supply, he's *restored* it, and it's the cows who've run off with it. But since the milk is really theirs in the first place, there's been no theft at all. Therefore, I'd say your accusations are unfounded. Understandable, but—"

"Enough." The blacksmith seized Gom and shook him until his teeth rattled. "Time's awasting. Let's get on."

Muttering, the crowd closed in, forming a tight circle about him.

Gom looked around. Far from talking them out of their anger, he'd only incensed them more.

The whip man stepped forward.

Gom turned to face him defiantly. As he did so, he

caught sight of Shadow at the edge of the crowd with his master.

The blacksmith roughly turned Gom's back to the whip, and Gom, his face set defiantly, clenched his teeth and braced himself for the blow.

Without warning, a huge black mass sprang into the circle, snarling and leaping about, snapping at everyone's feet.

Shadow!

There was instant pandemonium, the crowd breaking up and running off in all directions from the hound apparently gone mad.

"Go! Go! Quick!" Shadow urged Gom. "Now, while you can!"

Gom set off up the lane. "What about you!" he called back. Shadow was racing in crazy circles, emptying the last remnants off the green.

"I'll manage," the dog barked. "Good-bye. And good luck!"

"They'll kill you! Come on, come with me!" Gom shouted.

The dog stopped in his tracks, then suddenly, he raced up the lane to join Gom.

Together they ran, to the end of the lane, and onto the trail to Deeping Dale. A few folk started after them, but Gom and Shadow had too great a lead. They sprinted along until they were out of breath, and still kept going until they were heading down into Twisting Valley. Only when they were safely into that place did they stop to rest, off the trail a way amid tall grasses.

Shadow flopped down on his belly, his bony ribs heaving, his tongue lolling out. Gom lay back, listening to his own breath gradually slowing. Where was the foxy youth? he wondered. Mat, someone had called him. Gom hadn't seen sign of the lad, and he and Shadow had run fast enough, surely, to catch up with him. Maybe he'd kept clear of the trail for fear of being caught again. What a rascal he was, Gom thought. But he hadn't looked evil, or bad, not exactly.

As for Mat's supposed misdeeds . . . Gom leaned up on one elbow and plucked a blade of sweet grass. He could sympathize with the villagers for being duped once, or twice, maybe. But more than that? It served them right for letting the same fellow fool them over and over!

Half-smiling, Gom began to hum an old tune under his breath.

> Oh woe is me, for I am run out of town,
>   For letting my tongue run free . . .

He smiled to think of what mischief the wily Mat would have made among the gullible Clack folk before they ran him out, as no doubt they would have in the end.

Gom's smile faded. Pity they'd missed each other, he thought wistfully. Now there would have been a fine companion: obviously much traveled, with a fund of great stories to tell. And just as much misunderstood by normal folk it seemed, as Gom himself. But the lad couldn't be blamed for running off like that from those dreadful people.

Shadow began to whine.

"I'm afraid," the great dog said. "I have no master. What shall become of me?"

Gom reached out a hand and patted him.

"I don't know," he said. "But anything that happens to you from now on will be better than what went on back there." He sat up. "I haven't thanked you properly yet for what you did," he declared solemnly. "You're a very brave dog."

"Oh no I'm not." Shadow sat up too, panting in the heat. "Believe me, I'm not. I just don't know what came over me."

"You're altogether too modest," Gom insisted. "Listen: you sheltered me in your master's barn, risking a beating for letting a stranger onto the property. Then you did your mad dog act to save me. You could have been killed for that. You're a kind, brave creature, and I'm proud to have you for a friend."

"Really?" Shadow wagged his tail.

"Yes, indeed. You know, I was getting lonely, traveling alone. It's so good to have company."

They moved along at a steady pace until tiring at last, Gom stopped by a little water hole for elevenses. Unable to break the waybread, Gom gave Shadow one of his two remaining cakes to gnaw, then lay back under a clump of bushes, sheltering from the noonday heat.

Gnats played around his head, and somewhere close by a peeper sang a sleepy song. A bright blue butterfly fluttered past, lighted on a stand of creamy wild snapdragons. Gom wiped his forehead on his sleeve, conscious of his breath laboring in the humid heat. The air was dense and heavy down in the valleys, he thought, fanning his face with a broad dock leaf. He wondered how folk managed to stand it year after year.

Shadow, his jaws dripping from the water hole, flopped

down beside him. Reason told Gom that they should stay there while the sun passed overhead. But then he also felt that that was wasting time.

"Ten minutes," Gom said. "Then we must move on."

It was an effort. And not only because of the heat.

Twisting Valley was very well named, at least the twisting bit. Nowhere could one see more than a few hundred yards ahead. But "valley"? It was more like a gully, Gom soon found. The sides were steep, wild, and overgrown with hawthorn and honeysuckle, blocking the trail altogether in places.

Gom whistled under his breath as he went along in the afternoon sunshine, happy in Shadow's company, even though the hound would chase every rabbit and squirrel that he saw over Gom's objection.

Shadow, however, wasn't in the best of spirits. "I miss having a master," he said. "Someone to call me to heel, to tell me to go and to come. It doesn't feel right, running around loose like this."

Gom felt a little hurt. Oh? But I asked you not to go chasing my friends and you just didn't take any notice, he thought, though not wanting to argue, he didn't say that out loud.

"You'll get used to it," he remarked instead. "Soon you'll realize how to use your freedom, how lucky you are now not to have to come and go anymore at another's pleasure."

"You told me to follow you," the dog said, sounding a little sulky. "You should be my master now."

"Me?" Gom looked at the dog in surprise. "Oh no. I don't want to be anybody's master. You saved my skin, and for that you are my friend and equal."

Master indeed, Gom thought, much disturbed at the

idea. Yet seeing how miserable Shadow was with his new-found freedom, Gom made a real effort to humor him, until the dog got used to it. Time and again Gom recalled Shadow sternly from his forays into quail and rabbit territory on either side of the trail. But without success. Evidently recognizing Gom's halfheartedness, the hound didn't even pretend to obey.

Late in the afternoon, they stopped again to rest their legs. According to the map, the next village was three days away, in the lush green lands of Middle Vale. Gom rummaged in his pack for something to give Shadow. There wasn't much left, certainly for a dog.

"Don't worry," Shadow assured him, nosing his hand. "I'll forage." He ran off into the tangled scrub ignoring Gom's calls to come back.

Gom watched him go unhappily, not liking to think what Shadow would forage on. With a sigh, he lay back, locked his hands behind his head, and stared up at the clear afternoon sky. According to Carrick's map, it would take ten or so more days to reach the Lakes. And then?

He'd maybe find some of those inns Carrick had told him about and offer his services cutting wood, and doing other odd jobs about the place. And all the while he'd listen, and ask in ever so round about a way where a body might find one such as Harga.

As he lay there, daydreaming in the afternoon heat, he imagined he saw a black speck circling, way up high. He smiled, remembering Tak the raven.

The speck came lower and lower, growing bigger all the while.

Gom's smile froze.

That bird was huge, with wings bigger than any raven's. It couldn't be, Gom told himself, slowly sitting up, but even as he tried to get to his feet, it came at him—the skull-bird!

Gom rolled under a bush and lay, his blood racing. Katak come for him again! How?

The bird skimmed past with a whir of wings, then wheeled about to hover, looking down.

"Fool! You think to escape Katak's will? Think again, *little man*!"

Gom's middle went to jelly. Not the shapechanger, but Zamul! Ganash had personally escorted Zamul to the far side of the sound. "He'll not get out of there in a month of Sundays," the kundalara had assured Gom. What had gone wrong?

"I told you my master was going to give me magic of a different kind?" Zamul cried. "Well, he's given me the changing power, and here I am, in my master's own favorite shape, to get him back your rune!"

Banking sharply over the bush, Zamul thrust out his thick strong legs and, raking his talons across Gom's back, hauled him by his shirt from his shelter.

Dazed, Gom reached to cover the rune but Zamul clawed his hand away, and seized the stone.

A huge black shape sprang from the bushes and hurled itself at the hovering bird.

"Shadow!"

Released from Zamul's talons, Gom clutched the stone to him and crawled back to shelter. His back was afire, and his hand streamed blood.

Dog and bird were closely interlocked, a screaming, snarling mass of hair and blood and feather. Shadow's mouth closed on the bird's wing, but the bird, clawing at the dog's hindquarters, forced him to let it go. Shadow tried for the bird's throat only it was too quick. With a loud screech, it raked Shadow's side with its talons, laying the flesh open.

Shadow went down, struggled up, fell a second time to lie still.

"Shadow!" cried Gom, starting out from under the bush.

"The dog is dead, so now I'll have the rune, little man!" Exulting, Zamul fell upon him.

"What!" a new voice cried. "What in Ulm's name is going on!"

Gom caught a glimpse of a flashing knife blade and a shock of black curls, dark against the sun's rays.

A moment later there came a scream of human pain, and looking up, Gom saw Zamul kneeling on the grass, face contorted, blood running from a gashed shoulder, over his silver bracelet to splash his bright green breeches. The next instant, the image of the conjuror vanished and an injured skull-bird rose from the ground to flap clumsily away.

Had he imagined it? It had all happened so quickly. The ground heaved and tilted, came up to meet him with a roar. Through the noise there came another sound, a human voice.

"Good gracious—it's Master Gom!"

Carrick.

Chapter Fourteen

"**E**ASY NOW." Carrick bent down and slipped his arms under Gom. Then with a heave, he lifted Gom up, and strode off through the bushes.

"Wait!" Gom protested weakly. "Go look to the dog."

Zamul had said Shadow was dead, and he certainly seemed it, but he might just be alive still.

Carrick looked back. "The dog? It can wait." He strode on.

Gom twisted in the tinker's arms, trying to get down. "Carrick, we must go back. If he's alive, he's much worse off than I am."

"Maybe, but he's a dog, and you're a human, and there lies a world of difference," Carrick answered. "Ah, here we are."

Off the trail, only moments from where Gom had stopped to rest, a packhorse stood grazing, and various bundles lay scattered about in the long grass. Carrick laid Gom down carefully on a bright red blanket then set about producing a small iron pot, a bundle of clean white cloth, and a thick blue bottle stoppered with a stout cork.

"Turn over, Master Gom, if you can," Carrick said, kneeling beside him. "That's right. This will hurt. I'm sorry, but we must get you clean. First, let's have that shirt off you. And that stone, too," he added, as the rune came to light.

"No," Gom said quickly. "It's my lucky charm."

"And a right good one, too." Carrick nodded gravely. "It brought me along at the right moment."

Parting with the shirt wasn't too bad, but Gom cried out as Carrick dabbed his back.

"What are you using?" Gom said through his teeth.

"Only water," Carrick said, without stopping. "You've three very mean gouges, but not too deep. They'll mend. There," he went on. "Now they're cleaned off, we can put something on them to help them heal. Brace yourself, Master Gom. This stuff really stings."

Gom clamped his jaw tight against fresh pain as Carrick dabbed bright gold tincture from the blue bottle into his wounds.

"Liquid fire, they call it." Carrick grinned. "Don't know how the apothecaries make it, and heaven knows we professional travelers curse its sting often enough, but we wouldn't be without it. Hold on now. I'm going to bind you up a bit, and set one of my old shirts upon you."

Gom thought of Shadow, still lying in the heat among those bushes, dying, if not dead already, because there was no one to tend him.

"Carrick," Gom said urgently, "would you—"

"All in good time," the tinker said. "Can you ease up a bit?"

Beside himself, Gom suffered Carrick to sit him up and bind him with broad, clean cotton strips. Gom's back throbbed with pain. For all his efforts to avoid it, he thought, it seemed he'd had Mat's flogging after all.

The binding completed, the tinker slipped an oversized cotton shirt around Gom's shoulders and eased Gom's arms into the sleeves.

"Now," Carrick said. "Give us that hand."

"Please," Gom said, "my hand can wait. Please see Shadow now. He saved my life."

"He did?" Carrick took Gom's hand, turned it over. "Ummm," he said. "That's nasty. Only just missed the third tendon." He washed the gash, anointed it with the gold tincture too, and bound it.

"Strange," Carrick said as he worked. "How all this happened. Here I am, taking a rest, when I hear shouting, then a dog's snarl. Robbers, I thought. Setting upon some innocent traveler." He cocked an eye at Gom. "I get up, and run around the bushes, ready to take on a whole a gang of them and what do I find?" He held up three fingers in succession. "One lad, one dog, and a bird."

Gom watched him, tight-lipped, saying nothing.

Carrick tied up the binding around Gom's hand, set it on Gom's lap. "There you are, Master Gom. One hand, returned to owner. It'll soon mend, if you treat it right. As I was saying, there I was looking to see the source of those voices and I find but one boy."

Again Carrick waited, and again Gom stayed quiet. The peddler evidently suspected there was more to what happened than what he'd seen. And given the fact that Carrick had saved his life—and the rune—Gom knew that the tinker was due some sort of explanation. But he was too angry with Carrick to speak, and besides, what could he say?

"Of course, I could have been dreaming," Carrick continued, when still Gom didn't speak. "I could have imagined those voices shouting and all." The master tinker bundled up Gom's torn shirt and stowed it into one of the bags lying about. "But that bird was no dream, nor those injuries. That was some bird: big—and hideous, with its head looking like a skull, half-human. Where did it come from, Master Gom?"

Carrick was watching him closely.

Gom looked down. "Out of the clear blue sky," he muttered. Carrick apparently hadn't seen Zamul lose control of his bird shape. It had been quick. Again Gom wondered if he'd not imagined it, but then he remembered Zamul's boast . . . *he's given me the changing power* . . . Gom wondered whether he oughtn't to tell Carrick something of what had really happened, just in case the bird came back. Because something was altered. Zamul, for all his talk, had heretofore been squeamish about attacking a small, defenseless boy. Not so this new Zamul. The conjuror had swooped on him no less savagely than the original skull-bird, had laid open his back, would have killed him without a qualm. Gom sought the rune, held it tight, as though protecting it and seeking its protection in return. He'll not give you any more trouble, Ganash had said, and had truly believed it. Why not? The kundalara had not known of Zamul's new power to change shape, and with new cunning, Zamul had kept that knowledge from Ganash. But far from having to trudge long miles from the farther side of the sound to find Gom again, Zamul had flown swiftly in his powerful bird shape, and awaited his chance to strike.

Gom's mouth tightened. Ganash had called Katak an evil blight, and Gom had understood that from his own experience. But only now did he begin to see how evil. In such a short time Zamul had changed from a foolish, greedy man into a cold killer. Imagine such change spreading over the world!

"Funny." Carrick stood up. "I seem to remember Hort telling me as how he rescued you from something very similar up on the Bluff."

Gom kept his eyes on the ground.

"Oh well," the tinker said finally. "It's gone now. But we'll watch out for it, and spread the word along the trail. It looked big enough to take a full grown man, let alone a boy. And now," he said, "for that dog of yours."

He started back through the bushes the way they'd come.

"He's not mine," Gom called after him, but Carrick's words pleased him, all the same.

The moment Gom was alone, fresh pain swamped in, until it seemed that he was all back and the back was all pain.

Somewhere out there Zamul, though wounded, still waited. Gom thought of his earlier flight from the skull-bird through the pass, his fall from the Bluff. That time, which had been bad enough, he'd thought only of saving the rune. This was worse. For now Katak would be out not only to get back the rune, but to wreak vengeance on those who had shut him away. More: if Katak escaped his grotto, what calamity would then be loosed upon Ulm?

He wants power . . . over those who rule the people, to bend them to his will.

Whatever that was, it wasn't good. Gom shifted, wincing. So much, so much depended now on keeping the rune, handing it safely into his mother's keeping. How? How was such as he going to prevail over such remorseless will? He wondered, not for the first time, at his mother leaving such a valuable thing with him. He even, for a moment, regretted it himself, such a burden it was, to carry it around like this. Did Harga know what was going on? Surely, if she were as great as Ganash claimed. In that case—why didn't she just come out and claim it? It seemed to him that she should, for now not only his future, but that of the whole world seemed to depend on its safekeeping.

He sighed. Not knowing of Harga's purposes, he could only keep going as best he could. There was one comfort: Zamul wasn't all-powerful. He hadn't seen Carrick, had he? And however cruel and savage he had become he was obviously still as much a coward as ever, letting Carrick put him to flight. Small comfort: Gom was no nearer to solving the riddle and finding his mother. And with Zamul following, his chances seemed more remote than ever.

He sat miserably waiting for Carrick's return, oblivious to the sunlight, the rank stink of the undergrowth, the busy whine of insects around his head.

He nodded, and his chin sank onto his chest.

He dozed for a minute. Or two. Or three.

Gom's head snapped up at something: a slight movement, some faint noise nearby.

Straight across from him, Shadow was lying limp in the grass, Carrick bent over him, his arm going slowly up and down. Doing what? Something bright and sharp flashed in the man's hand. Gom shook his head, blinked, and focusing, saw stout black thread protruding from it.

The tinker was using a bodkin.

"Ah, you're awake." Carrick didn't turn his head, but continued to concentrate on his task. "I'm sewing up our friend's hide. Hole big as a kettle lid." The tinker's brown hands worked away, precise, sure, unhurried, cutting neat, tight stitches through Shadow's flesh.

Shadow lived!

On the grass beside the dog lay metal basins filled with various fluids, and a razor covered in soap and hair. Gom looked quickly to Shadow's side. Carrick had shaved it clean, exposing bluish skin.

Shadow lived. Gom's throat constricted. No thanks to him. That very morning, he'd urged his new acquaintance to leave his old life and come away with him. Anything's better than what you have, he'd said. And the dog had been almost killed.

The jagged line of black stitches slowly but surely replaced the gaping hole. His anger gone, Gom began to forgive Carrick's neglect of the dog. Perhaps Carrick had foreseen that tending Shadow would take much longer than fixing Gom, and for that reason had treated his human patient first.

"There." Carrick finished off the thread and trimmed the end with his knife. "He'll live, I think. But he's in bad condition. We'll have to carry him for a day or two. How are you feeling now?"

"Fine," Gom fibbed. "Carrick: if he lives, it's thanks to you. I'm sorry for being short. He's my friend, you see, and I owe him a great deal."

Carrick gravely heard him out.

"I understand, Master Gom. I'm sorry, too, for making you fret. But in my book, a man's a man, and a dog's a dog, and there's no doubt as to who comes first." He nodded down to the unconscious hound. "I never thought I'd be serving the like. Them and me, we don't see eye to eye. In fact, there's many a peddler and tinker in Ulm as carries evidence of snap-happy fangs."

He began to clear away his gear and stow it into one of the large bags lying around the horse's feet, thick canvas panniers that, when Carrick moved on, would hang at the beast's side.

"However, it's over," Carrick went on, kneeling over the pannier. "The cur will live, so you'll keep your friend. But say, I thought you'd be down in the lakelands long before now. How come you're still up here?"

Gom looked away. "I was delayed," he said.

"But you're still headed south?"

"Yes." Gom looked to Carrick in sudden hope. "Could we go together?"

Carrick smiled. "You stole my words, young one. You hungry?"

A moment ago, Gom would have said emphatically, no. But now he felt a small appetite coming upon him, in spite of Zamul, in spite of Shadow lying there badly injured, and in spite of his fear and pain. There he'd been, on the verge of certain death from that hated skullbird and now here he was, in the safe company of the very man he'd wished for.

He nodded.

"Good." Carrick closed the pannier and stood up. "First, I'll fetch your gear. Then we'll eat. Tell you what: I was going on for another hour or two, but we'll camp out here instead, and press on tomorrow. Then you can travel on Finnikin's back," he said, nodding to the packhorse behind them, "and Shadow can lie in one of the panniers. My, Master Gom." Carrick beamed down at him. "I'm that pleased to renew our acquaintance."

When Gom awoke the next morning, he felt stiff and bruised, but the pain in his back had eased some.

"It was the liquid fire," Carrick said, smiling. "And a young body bouncing back."

He bathed Gom's wounds and redressed them, then they had breakfast. Fresh oatcakes, and honey, and tea brewed over a little lamp. As they ate, Gom glanced to the sky, then to where Shadow lay, still sleeping.

"Let him," Carrick said. " 'Twill stand him in good stead."

When they'd finished eating, Carrick took out some dried beef and a large tin bowl, which he filled with water from a tin canteen.

"For that hound of yours when he awakes," he said, and went to load up the horse.

Shadow stirred, opened his eyes. "What happened?"

Gom bent over him. "Easy. You've a nasty wound," he said. "Here, here's water. Can you sit?"

Shadow struggled up shakily. Suddenly, he growled. "Who's he?"

The dog was eyeing Carrick.

"Carrick's a friend." Gom spoke softly, not wanting Carrick to hear him speaking in Shadow's tongue. "He saved us from that bird yesterday. In fact, he saved you twice over, for he stitched your side up good as new."

"He *what?*" Shadow twisted, craning to see, and yelped in pain.

Carrick looked around.

"Ah. The beast's awake, I see. Here," he said. "I've emptied one of the panniers. He'll fit in just fine. But first, let's take a look at him."

Carrick crossed over to where Shadow lay, and knelt down. Drawing his lips into a snarl, Shadow began to rise.

"That's enough," Carrick said sharply. "You want me to look at that side or not?"

Shadow subsided onto the ground and lay still while the tinker inspected his wound.

"It's seeping some." Carrick addressed Gom over the dog's head.

Gom watched for Shadow's reaction as Carrick dabbed the wounded side with liquid fire. To his surprise, Shadow only whimpered, twitched a little, but otherwise made no move.

To Gom's further surprise as Carrick restoppered the blue bottle, the hound reached out and licked the tinker's hand.

"Looks like he's taken to you," Gom observed enviously. Carrick, grunting, put the tincture away and set about preparing them all to leave. The dog, he saw, followed Carrick's every move, didn't complain as the tinker lifted him into the pannier. In silence, Gom suffered Carrick to help him up onto Finnikin's back, and stiffly settled himself sideways.

Carrick handed Gom the staff. "That's a fine piece you have there, Master Gom," he said. "I've never seen the like." He reached out and touched the little sparrow's head. "The carving's so fine that the creatures seem almost alive, particularly this little one."

Gom took it proudly. "My father made it," he said. "He was a fine woodcarver."

"That he was, and a fine father, too," Carrick added, "to have produced such a son as you. Gee up, Finnikin. We've lost time to recoup."

They made slow but steady progress that day, along
the narrow, twisting trail, Gom perched on Finnikin's
back, Shadow deeply asleep in his pannier, Carrick walking alongside, whistling tunelessly.

Gom looked upward uneasily, found the skies clear.
Zamul would be lying up somewhere, nursing his wounds.
But for how long? he wondered.

On either side, the steep banks of the valley shimmered
in the airless heat, and insects hummed among the bushes.

Gom held the staff absently, thinking how efficiently
Carrick had taken care of his two unexpected companions.
It seemed tinkers had to know much more than how to
mend pots. Gom pictured himself kneeling by Shadow's
side, sewing it up, applying remedies, and liked the idea.
He thought of the liquid fire. It was healing his back
like magic. Carrick hadn't made that. He'd gotten it
from—what was the word? An *apothecary*. Could that
mean *wizard?*

"Those apothecaries you mentioned yesterday," he asked.
"What do they do, Carrick?"

Carrick stopped his whistling. "Well, now, let's see:
they do pretty much the same as Mistress Gumby the
herb wife back in Green Vale, only being city men," he
said dryly, "they charge lots of money for what they do,
and grow rich and pompous in the doing. Why?"

Gom shrugged. "I just wondered." Apothecaries weren't
wizards, then, for wizards were secret, while those men
apparently lived highly public lives. But Harga knew all
about herbs and remedies. Wizards, then, were higher
than apothecaries, much higher, for they had to know
about more than herbs.

"Are you thinking to become an apothecary, Master

Gom?" The tinker smiled. "If so, 'tis an improvement on conjuring. But there's many things a lad can turn his hand to, if he wants a change from woodcutting. When you get down to the lakes, you'll see." The blue eyes regarded Gom keenly. "I don't see you as conjuror, nor do I see you growing fat on others folks's ills. You know, I'll be interested to see what you do opt for, in the end."

Gom listened, nodding. If Carrick thought him to be going down to the lakes to seek his fortune, let him. In fact, the more folk thought that, the better, when Gom began to ask questions. He smiled to himself. But when he started asking around after wizards, what would Carrick think then?

The next day, the trail emerged at last from the narrow confines of Twisting Valley, broadening out into Middle Vale, where the trail met the eastern bank of Long River, a broad, meandering watercourse flowing through Middle Vale, and on down Long Valley to the lakes.

As they went, Gom glanced up frequently for sign of the skull-bird. From time to time he did see distant specks circling up high, but they were too distant to identify.

They stopped that evening at Wellingford, a small village near the first river crossing. Gom looked around warily as they approached the inn, watching for Zamul in his human form. Was the conjuror already there, waiting? Gom decided to keep very close to Carrick. With his new brand of cunning, there was no telling what Zamul might do.

The tinker led Finnikin around to the stables, and delivered Shadow into the head groom's care.

"An old friend of mine," Carrick assured Gom. "He

guards my gear, so I don't have to unpack it and cart it all indoors. He'll take great good care of Shadow."

Gom, frowning, hoped so. All the way into the inn, and down to the inn parlor for supper, Gom looked about him for Zamul. So far, so good: no sign. Finally seated at table, Gom relaxed a little, enough to realize that he was very, very hungry.

Despite Gom's protests, Carrick dined him royally, and in addition told him many fine tales from his travels.

One thing the tinker couldn't stand, it seemed, was miserliness.

"It's one thing to be careful with one's purse, Gom, and I'm all for that, for a fool and his money are soon parted, as they say. But it's another for one man to cheat his fellow out of his due. Even then I can forgive it sometimes, for hunger can drive a body to extremes. It's the rich misers I'm talking of, the ones who try to cheat the honest traveling man for the sport of it—an occupational hazard of tinkers and peddlers and the like.

"There was once this old man who'd cheat me out of my proper price time and again until I got so resentful that I stopped visiting his house—a fine mansion, right in the middle of Hornholm. Well, he sent a fine carriage for me, with promises of payment to match. I mended his pots, got my fee. To my astonishment, he gave me two pennies extra for my trouble, so he said. I was just leaving, when he suddenly "remembered" that his wash copper needed mending.

"I looked at him and all his men standing around. It was clear there'd be no more payment, but if I refused— well, those men of his were big fellows, and too many for me. But I was determined he'd get no more than his due."

Gom leaned forward over the table. He always loved to see fair play. "How?"

The tinker took a draught of his ale, set down the mug.

"I mended it, a patch big as your thumbnail. But I fixed it so it would last for just two pennies' worth, which was until the first washload reached the boil."

"What happened?"

"They say he lost a load of his best holiday clothes. Serve him right, I say. But look at you," the tinker went on, "your head's fairly falling onto the table. To bed with you, for shame." Carrick stood up.

But Gom wasn't yet finished. Quickly, he drew out the map that Carrick had given him and spread it on the tablecloth.

"Show me," he said, "where we're going, and what we're going to see. There was so much, and I've forgotten."

Carrick sat down again, sighing good-naturedly. "Very quickly, then." He pointed out a little dot just south of Twisting Valley. "We are here. And this is where we're going." He traced a fine blue thread of water to an oval patch at its end.

"Langoth Lake," the tinker said. "And there along its western edge is Pen'langoth, the biggest city in all Ulm. That's where we're headed. You see that tiny mark just off the shore?"

Gom peered down. Yes, yes. A little dot just by Carrick's fingernail.

"That's Scandibar, the citadel where the lake lord lives with his family and all his fine councillors."

Lake lord. Gom stared at the dot, thinking of Ganash's words.

Katak . . . wants power . . . over those who rule the people . . . If Zamul ever managed to take back the rune, if Katak ever got out of his prison, the blight of his evil would spread over that whole region. *Lake lord.* Gom had thought of rulers as kings and queens, like the Queen of Quend whom Carrick had mentioned back in Green Vale. How important was this lake lord? he wondered.

"Does the lake lord wear a crown? What's he called?"

Carrick laughed. "One question at a time, young one. His name is Leochtor, Lord Leochtor. He doesn't like crowns. Or even the coronet he's supposed to wear. He's a proper, modest man. He dresses plain, keeping finery only for state affairs. He's a kind, just lord, who really seems to care for his folk." Carrick touched his chest. "Me, I bow to nobody, but if I had to, he'd be the one."

Leochtor sounded such a good man. Gom, listening earnestly, thought of the change for ill that could come upon the lake lord by Katak's hand, and shuddered. "Tell me about Pen'langoth," he said quickly. "What shall you do there?"

Carrick tapped the southwest tip of the lake. "There's where I always stay, at The Jolly Fisherman. It's away from the grand houses of the city, and close to the market where I set up stall. You'll like it. All the lake fishermen go there at night after the fleet's in. Now come," he said firmly, as Gom's eyes began to close. "Bed: we leave at dawn tomorrow."

Carrick took Gom up to a small, single chamber under the eaves. The bed was down soft, and the sheets were silky fine. Carrick is so kind, Gom thought, snuggling under the covers. This accommodation must have cost a pretty penny, and the man isn't rich. One day, Gom resolved, he'd have to find a way to repay his friend's generosity.

Gom half-waking, came up in the dark. What about Shadow lying in his stable stall? What if Zamul were about? Was the dog safe? Was the stable groom looking after him as promised? Quickly, Gom dressed and crept down the back stair, and out into the courtyard, looking about him all the time.

He slipped across the moonlit cobbles and into the dark of the stable doorway. A dim lantern shone down upon the groom's empty stool.

Gom frowned. Where was the man? And where was Shadow? He thought of calling the dog's name, but just then a horse snuffled, shifted in its sleep. Better not give himself away. He moved quietly down the stable, peering over the wickets into each stall in turn. Last but one, there was Shadow, on a pile of hay in the far corner.

"Shadow?" Relieved, Gom pushed open the wicket and went in.

As it swung to behind him a figure moved out from the back wall, a burly shape dressed in black shirt and bright green breeches. Zamul!

Gom turned to run back through the door, but the figure darted forward and caught him by the arm.

Chapter Fifteen

"**A**T HIM, Shadow!"

Gom's anguished cry cracked the night silence, bringing the entire stable awake. Horses snuffled, whuffled, neighed, then stamped and reared and kicked their stalls.

The hand tightened on Gom's arm. "Come out here and let's have a look at yer!" Before Gom could think, he was dragged out into the passageway, and under the dim lantern light.

Gom, struggling, pulled away to face his attacker, and halted in astonishment. Not Zamul after all! "Who— who are you?"

"The night watchman," the man said with obvious satisfaction. "Looking out for the likes of you."

The likes of him? What did that mean? "I'm a guest here," Gom protested. "This is my dog. I came to see how he was."

The man eyed Gom up and down. "And I'm the lake lord, a-sitting on my throne. You think I'm a fool? You're not the first to come in here looking for a horse to steal." The watchman seized Gom's arm and shook him roughly. "Come you on, young larrikin. You're going to see the master!"

Gom was marched, protesting all the while, out of the stables and across the inn yard. Lights popped up all over the house, and heads poked out of windows to see what all the fuss was. If he'd wanted to announce his presence in the inn, he couldn't have chosen a better way.

The innkeeper had only just gone to bed, and was not too glad at being rousted out again. It took one whole hour and Carrick to clear matters up and quiet things down.

Carrick uttered not one cross word about being woken up in the early hours by an angry host. All he said was, "Don't take it hard," as they went back upstairs. "You were only trying to be kind to that wretched animal of yours—even though," he added, "you waste your time. Still, no harm's come of it, save that you've now less than three hours' sleep left. We leave at dawn."

Soberly, Gom took off his clothes and climbed back into bed. No harm had come of the escapade, Carrick had said. Gom took comfort in that. In fact, he'd noticed particularly, none of the nightcapped heads peering out of doorways as he'd come back upstairs had looked remotely like Zamul. So he wasn't here, unless—sudden awful thought—he was disguised as one of them!

Gom turned over. What was he to do? Danger still stalked, but he couldn't stay by Carrick's side forever. Chastened by this last experience, Gom resolved to renew his watch, not only for skull-bird above, but for human conjuror below, in any shape or form.

And to find his mother, and quickly, before he lost the rune again!

The next day, they got in a good four hours' traveling before the sun rose high and hot. They followed the slow easy trail along the riverbank, taking their time. Gom's back was healing fast, so much so that in the afternoon, he forsook Finnikin and walked alongside Carrick, swinging his staff and looking about him all the while, covertly, so as not to provoke awkward questions. If Carrick did notice, he didn't say.

Shadow left his pannier in the cool of late afternoon for brief spells along the trail. The only trouble was that he would run off into the undergrowth in spite of Gom's anxious warnings. "You're not healed yet," Gom told him, going after him one time to bring him back. Neither did he want to let the dog out of his sight.

"I'll be fine," Shadow said. "It's good to be able to run about again, and I'm picking up so many interesting smells."

Gom was most unhappy about the dog's stubbornness, and he said as much to Carrick.

The next time Shadow ran off the trail, Carrick called him back.

"Here! Here, sir! To heel at once!"

The dog returned instantly, and from then on stayed by Carrick's feet.

Gom regarded Shadow with great resentment. How could he prefer a man who treated him like that to one who honored him as a friend?

For five days more they traveled thus, staying at little country inns at night, plodding beside the laden pack-horse during the slow hours. Each time they stopped, people brought their pots and pans for Carrick to mend, and Gom sat by him scrutinizing each strange face, while at the same time noticing how the tinker tapped his patches into place, until he knew the tools well enough to hand Carrick what he needed even before he asked.

And that amused Carrick, it seemed. "You want to be

a tinker, Master Gom? I'll take you as apprentice any day."

As they moved on, Gom glanced upward constantly, scanning the sky for Zamul, but saw no sign of the skull-bird. Now and then he'd put the rune to his ear, "listening" for warning vibrations. From time to time his heart would lurch as a traveler approached with pack-horse, or cart, or merely on foot. Most of them stopped to exchange friendly greetings with Carrick, and a little gossip. Gom looked them all over carefully, staying close by Carrick's elbow, staff at the ready, hand over the rune, to keep it from popping out through Carrick's big shirt neck. But as far as he could tell, those travelers were genuine enough, and after a brief nod to Gom, they went on their way.

Bit by bit, the narrow valley widened until Gom could no longer see its hill boundaries on either side. An impressive sight, but which left him feeling uneasily exposed.

Around midafternoon on the third day they reached a signpost inscribed in bold black letters that, of course, Gom couldn't read. Down the length of the post itself was inscribed what looked like a long, broad finger. And down its center a wavy thin line like a vein, complete with tributaries, ran down to the fingernail at its base.

Carrick pointed. "For us folks as can't read," he said. "The finger is Long Valley. The line is the river. And the nail is Langoth Lake. Those two words round the other side read 'Long Valley,' they tell me. There's no doubt us unlettered folk get better value for our money, wouldn't you say, Master Gom?" His glance was wry.

Gom nodded, returning the look. But Gom knew from

Carrick's gentle jest that the tinker minded not being able to read as much as he did. Perhaps, thought Gom, when he'd learned his letters from Harga, as surely he would, he could in turn pass the learning on to Carrick. Now wouldn't that be a splendid way to repay the man's great good kindness!

On the fourth day, Gom shed his bindings and enjoyed the cool of Carrick's loose shirt. Shadow's side also was improving rapidly and the hair was growing back over the jagged scar. Shadow began to worry the stitches, whining with discomfort. So that evening when they stopped for the night, Carrick cut them out and painted the scar with liquid fire.

"Looks well enough," the tinker told Gom. "Another week or two and his hair will have grown in. But he'll bear that mark for the rest of his life."

Near the end of the fifth day, they were toiling up a long, slow incline, rising above the sparkling river waters.

"Another minute," Carrick told Gom as they reached the crest, "and you'll have such a view. Whoa, Finnikin."

Gom stopped, looking down in delight at the country spread before him, in a vast wide arc. Through it, the glistening river curled down to a long oval lake on the horizon.

Lake Langoth. And there, around its eastern edge, Pen'langoth, the city. Gom gazed in wonder. A mass of rooftops, hundreds and hundreds of them, clustered along the lake shore. How could there be so many people in the world? Why, a body could lose himself in such a place! There, just off the mainland, exactly as Carrick had said, the lake lord's stone citadel jutted out of the calm blue water. Tiny flags flew from high twin turrets; and wooden drawbridges spanned the short distance to the shore.

The crescent harbor bristled with masts, and minute sailing boats scratched the lake's surface with fine white lines that feathered and vanished even as Gom watched them form.

"You're impressed, I see." Carrick shaded his eyes from the lengthening sunlight.

"Oh, yes," Gom replied, not taking his eyes off the city. "I've never seen the like. Is that the fishing fleet?"

"Aye. And just coming in, by the look of it. See the harbor there? That's Lakeside that I told you of. That's home, where they're headed. Tomorrow you shall watch them put in from the dock, if you've a mind. Back of it is the fish market, loaded with every kind of fish you can imagine! Come on, let's hurry," Carrick said. "Just talking about it makes me hungry for good fresh lake food again."

Gom pulled back, still gazing, rapt, at the sunny landscape, picturing the blight of Katak's evil crawling over it like a giant shadow, blocking out the light.

"Gom?" Carrick was waiting. But Gom was not yet ready to move on.

"Where's the regular market?" Where Carrick plied his trade.

"Ah," said Carrick. "I'm forgetting. You've never seen one before, have you?" Carrick pointed. "You see that bright patch next to the fish market, up from the shore? That's it."

Gom eyed the circular patch of bright colors amid the tight jumble of rooftops curiously, remembering Carrick telling him how the market was like the Green Vale fair, only so big that there was work for twenty tinkers all the year round.

Somewhere close to that place was The Jolly Fisherman. A crowded place, bustling with many strange faces. Come on, he told himself. You're seeing menace under every leaf and stone. As long as you're with Carrick, you're safe enough.

Gom hastened with Carrick down that last incline, until trail was suddenly road, wide enough to take traffic in both directions at once, and smooth as a floor. They passed houses, a few cottages at first, then growing bigger and more numerous until they were grander than any Gom had ever seen, grander than any of the inns they'd stayed in along the trail.

As they progressed through the city outskirts, traffic increased, mostly folk on horseback, and in strange enclosed carts like tiny wooden houses on wheels, with windows draped in curtains. Carriages, the tinker said, carrying gentlefolk. Gom shrank in close to Carrick's side.

Not so Shadow. He darted out into the middle of the road, starting a pair of horses, nearly ending up under carriage wheels.

"You, sir," Carrick called Shadow in sternly. "You'll stay close in here from now on unless you want to end up dead!"

Shadow barked his pleasure at Carrick's command, and went to heel. Gom turned away in disgust. Why, Shadow even preferred barking at Carrick to conversing in his own tongue with Gom, for he'd made no attempt all the way down Long Valley to talk with Gom alone. Oh well, Gom shrugged. He didn't want a lickey-lacky, but a friend, and Shadow evidently wasn't it.

Gom looked after the carriages curiously, wondering about the folk within them. He wasn't at all sure he'd like to travel that way, grand as it seemed. Being shut up like that would make him fidgety, and what if he wanted to stop to look at something along the way? Come to think, he much preferred to go as he was, on his own two feet.

The houses multiplied, closed ranks until they formed two solid phalanxes lining the road, huge houses, high as two, three huts piled atop one another!

The roadside was crowded now with passers-by on foot, different from the folk up north. These people were softer and pinker: smooth, well-scrubbed—and well fed, putting Gom in mind of Acorn. As for their clothes: Gom remembered Zamul's fancy jacket. They were brighter, finer, even the children's, and covered with elaborate braiding and shiny buttons of every size and color.

Some of the children made faces at him as they passed, and small wonder, Gom thought, becoming uncomfortably aware of his own derelict appearance: his ripped trousers, his dusty jacket, his worn-down boots. He glanced at his hands, grime-streaked from the day on the road, and realized that his face must look no better. Not surprising, either, he thought, suddenly enlightened, that the watchman back in Wellingford had considered him such a low fellow.

With mixed feelings, Gom finally turned off the main thoroughfare to follow Carrick past rows of tiny cottages toward the lake's edge. It was good to be away from all the staring faces, but the streets, narrow, and twisted, and ill-lit, afforded plenty of shelter for a would-be attacker.

"Here we are," Carrick said at last, to Gom's great relief.

They'd stopped short of the actual shore, halfway down a steep hill, in front of a large high building squatting in the midst of the cottages, a mother hen among her chicks.

The Jolly Fisherman, with its sign jutting out clearly over the inn's front doorway: the picture of a rotund fisherman, his legs kicking high in the air, one hand throwing a net, the other holding a frothing ale mug while miraculously not spilling a drop.

Gom kept close as Carrick unpacked his gear and handed over horse and dog to the stableboy's care. Then holding onto his own pack and staff, Gom hurried after the tinker into the inn.

It was big, and grand, much grander than the country inns, with great wooden beams and brass lanterns and windows everywhere.

Gom relaxed. It was open, and bright, and . . . safe, somehow.

A good place, Carrick said as they entered. As near to permanent home as he'd ever have. With as near to family as he'd ever have, the tinker added, presenting him to his hostess, Essie, a jolly widow.

She was a formidable woman. Her face was painted bright as a doll's, her shapely body was tightly encased in red silk, and she was hung all over with little glass beads that shook and sparkled with every move.

"Get that lamb upstairs, Carrick," Essie cried, throwing up her hands at Gom. "He looks dead on his feet, and in need of a good hot meal. And water. Go on, and I'll send the hip bath after him."

"You've landed on your feet," Carrick laughed, taking Gom up the winding stair to what he called his regular room: a wide attic chamber overlooking the lake. It was clean and plain, the furniture was big and solid, and a welcome fire already burned in the hearth. Nights were cold, down by the lakeside.

Gom ran to the window, but saw only a wide expanse of blackness with a lone light or two, from the odd night fisherman's boat out on the water.

"How do you mean, landed on my feet? What is a hip bath?" Gom asked, turning back to the room.

Before Carrick could answer, two men brought it in: a round tin tank deep enough for a full-grown man to sit in, with a high curved back to loll against. After the men, two chambermaids brought in large pails of steaming water, which they tipped into the bath.

"That's landing on your feet." Carrick nodded to the bath the moment he and Gom were alone. "Though I think you've done more than that, Master Gom. It's my judgment that you've been and gone and captured our Essie's heart. Most folks—including me, usually make do with that."

The tinker waved to a ewer of cold water standing on a chest by the wall.

"I don't like baths," Gom said. "Let's swap."

"Swap? 'Tis more than my life's worth." Carrick laughed. "I'm teasing you, lad. Jump in. 'Tis a treat fit enough for the lake lord himself, as you'll see. Here, I'm a-laying out a clean nightshirt on the bed for you to put on afterward, and a big dry towel. Take your time. I'm off for a mug of ale with Essie. After that, I'll bring us up some supper and see about getting an extra cot in here."

Carrick was leaving him alone? Gom was once again uneasy.

"While you're gone, should I bolt the door, Carrick?"

Carrick's eyes widened. "Eh? Whatever for?"

"Well." Gom cast about for a reason. "What if someone comes in whilst I'm in the bath?"

Carrick nodded. "Modest are you? No one will, I assure you. This attic floor is only for you and me and the inn folk." He smiled. "But if it makes you feel better, lad, by all means. Just don't fall asleep, though, and leave me locked out all night!" Laughing, Carrick went out.

Gom bolted the door behind him. Then, feeling better, he stripped off his clothes, and bending over, dabbled his fingers in the water. It was hot, though not overly. He slipped one foot into the bath. Mmmm: was good, he had to admit. He put the other foot in, then slowly lowered himself, savoring the feel of warm water sliding up to his waist, the gentle heat from the fire on the rest of him.

He leaned against the bath's high back, relaxing at last with a deep sigh of content. Carrick was right. The bath was fit for a lord. There were, he thought, recalling a lifetime of cold dips in the creek, cold washes in the bucket outside the hut door, baths . . . and baths.

When finally he climbed out to towel himself down, the water was almost cold, and his hands were wrinkled as wet washing—his fingers could scarce button up his clean nightshirt.

He smoothed back his wet hair and threw himself into a high wing chair beside the fire to wait for Carrick. His body hadn't felt so clean in a long while, and it tingled all over.

What more could he want? he thought, staring happily into the flames. Tonight he was going to eat a fine supper and sleep in a warm dry bed. And tomorrow he was going out with Carrick into the marketplace to begin his search for Harga in earnest.

When Gom awoke the next morning, Carrick was gone, and all his gear. The tinker's bed was made, and the hearth, swept. On the oval table in the middle of the room was set a wooden tray with oatcakes, an apple, and a mug of milk.

Gom threw his clothes on and ran to the door. There, he stopped, looking back into the room.

The message was perfectly clear. Carrick had let him sleep, and trusted Gom to eat his breakfast and find his own way to the tinker's market stall.

He ate up the contents of the breakfast tray standing by the window.

Below him the lake stretched into morning mist. Two large sailboats were putting out from the shore. He could quite plainly see the jumble of wooden stalls and pails and crates along the dockside that marked the fish market. Adjacent, and farther up from the shore, the brighter, gaudier stalls of the regular marketplace crowded a space big enough by the looks of it to lose the whole of Clack in. Gom peered down at the tiny canvas tops and banners and the masses of heads milling in between. He opened the window and leaned out for a better view, and the noise of the crowd and the shouts of merchants and artisans plying their trade surged up toward him.

". . . best cottons in all Ulm . . ."

". . . never see another bargain like this beautiful clay pot . . ."

". . . shoes mended while you wait . . ."

". . . your fortune told for a song . . ."

Gom gazed around at all the colors, trying to pick out

Carrick's green-and-white striped awning. But there were, he found, as many of those as of red and white, and blue and white, and yellow, and orange, and brown. If he wanted to find Carrick, he realized, he'd have to go and seek him.

Gom left the window, and, taking up his staff, made for the door. There, he paused, and on second thought, retrieved Stig's water bottle from his pack, filled it, and stowed it in his back pocket together with the map. Never know but he might be glad of it out there.

Now he went down the winding stairs to the main hallway that cut straight through the inn from front door to back. To Gom's right was the hot and noisy street, to the left was the inn yard, still shaded by high walls.

Gom turned left, to fetch Shadow from his stable stall.

He crossed the cool cobbled yard, to the stables opposite. Inside, the air was hot and moveless, and the smell of horse was strong. He stood for a moment, remembering the fuss in the stable at the first inn on the way, how he'd mistaken the watchman for Zamul. Shadow's stall, thought Gom, still smiling wryly at the memory of his embarrassment, was halfway down the passage, on the right.

Empty.

Of course. The dog would have gone with Carrick, Gom realized. Well, why should it matter to him? He left the stables, but instead of going back through the inn, he crossed the yard and went directly out into the street by the carriage entrance.

It was hot, crowded, and noisy. And over all was the strongest smell, fresh and dank at the same time. Gom wrinkled up his nose, sniffing.

"Fish! Fresh fish! Live crabs! Crayfish, alive-oh!" Cries

from the fish market, coming clean up from the water's edge.

Gom hurried down to the corner, and there the market was, right across the street, looking bigger and much more bewildering than it had from the attic window. How long would it take to find Carrick?

Crossing the cobbles, Gom dove into the crowd. He hadn't gone far before a large man pushed past, shoving Gom against a booth, jarring his ribs.

"Watch where you're a-goin'," the man snapped, and moved on, muttering angrily about folks minding other folks's toes.

Gom leaned against the booth, clutching his shirt neck close, chilled. What if that had been Zamul? Gom remembered the conjuror holding the woman's chain and she not having dreamed that he'd taken it from her. He began to wish he'd not jumped into the crowd so quickly. That he wore some other shirt than Carrick's with the oversized neck. Even that he'd left the rune behind.

Keeping the shirt neck tightly closed, Gom moved on, elbowing his way through the throng, seeking the sanctuary of Carrick's green and white awning, wishing that Carrick advertised his services as many of these others did, by touting loudly for custom.

All at once, Gom caught sight of a head of lank pale hair rearing higher than the rest. He stopped still, gazing at the long, thin, animated face, and the long, loose, animated arms, one hand holding high a big brown bottle, the sort that herb wives put their remedies in, the other hand pointing, gesticulating.

It was Mat, the youth from Bragget-on-the-Edge, whom he'd saved from a flogging.

". . . and I, Matamor Marplot, guarantee, gentlemen,"

Mat was shouting, so loudly that his face had turned pink. "Your hair will be as thick and bushy as when you were a lad!" Mat held the bottle higher, for all to see.

"How much did you say?" a gruff voice asked.

Mat turned toward the voice. "A shilling, dear sir." He fished a tiny silver coin from his own pocket and held it up. "One little shining shilling is all I ask for this wonderful elixir."

"Don't seem so much to ask," a man muttered, close by Gom. "Gimme one!" he called, and pushed his way to the front.

Smiling graciously, Mat stepped down from Gom's view.

"I'll try it. Might as well," came another voice. And soon there was a clamor for whatever Mat was selling. Gom considered pushing his way to the front to speak to Mat, but pulled back. The youth looked busy enough, and might not even remember him. Perhaps later, Gom thought. When the crowds had thinned a bit, he'd go back to see the lad then. Maybe Mat was staying hereabouts. In which case, Gom's spirits rose, he could introduce a new friend to Carrick and they could all sit together that evening in the inn.

He did wonder, as he pushed on, what the elixir was, and whether it was any better than the potions and remedies the lad had foisted on Bragget. Apothecary, Gom murmured to himself. Mat's acting the apothecary, without having had the training. Surely that could be quite dangerous.

He came across four other tinkers before he finally found Carrick. The man was sitting on his little stool under his awning, a pile of pots and pans already beside him waiting to be mended. The tinker's head was bent over a large iron skillet, which apparently belonged to the severe-looking wife standing beside him. Also beside him lolled Shadow, head on paws, eyes shut, tongue hanging out. Shadow's ribs, Gom noticed, were much fuller, and his coat was thicker over the starkness of the scar.

"Ah, Gom. Good morning." Carrick paused, looked up smiling, obviously glad to see him. The tinker dug in his pocket, drew out a handful of coins.

"Here. Enjoy yourself. Buy yourself a treat or two. Go on, Master Gom," he urged, as Gom drew back.

"But I've come to help you," Gom protested.

"Nonsense." Carrick pushed the money at him. "This is your first day. You can help me tomorrow, if you like."

Gom eyed the coins on Carrick's palm. His friend was so kind. But having sought and found the safety of Carrick's tent, he didn't want to go out again into those uncertain crowds. The tinker waited, hand outstretched. Come to think, Gom reasoned, if he continued to hide behind Carrick like this, how would he ever learn of Harga? He sighed, and thanking Carrick, took up the coins.

Carrick smartly poked the dog's side. "Up, Shadow, and go with Gom."

"No," Gom said quickly, not wanting unwilling company. "He'd much better stay out of harm's way, for his side still looks sore."

Before Carrick could argue, Gom left them both and pushed through the crowd, marveling at the number of booths and the variety of goods they displayed.

He stopped by one booth hung with shirts of all sizes and colors, fingered a blue one just his fit in fine crisp cotton, with shell buttons down the front and long sleeves that rolled up in hot weather. And a neck high enough to hide the rune. Slowly, he took out the money Carrick had given him.

He counted out the coins, then changed his mind. It didn't seem right, somehow, buying a shirt for himself with unearned money. He'd wait, for all his unease. He'd help Carrick tomorrow. Maybe after a week or two he'd have enough money of his own. Yet Carrick would be offended if he didn't get some small thing now.

He bought himself a sticky bun from a pastry stall and wandered on, to a table full of gleaming knives in fancy leather sheaths. Here was something else he needed. He selected one, balanced the blade on his palm. It was well made; solid, sharp, with a stout wooden handle. But the price! It was twice as much as Carrick had given Gom. And it was the cheapest!

Gom replaced it reluctantly. Too much, and hadn't he resolved to pay his own way?

He moved on again until, suddenly, he'd had enough. He looked around to take his bearings, intending to tell Carrick that he was going back to the inn for a rest. As he did so a gap formed in the crowd ahead and there was Zamul, staring straight at him.

The gap closed, then opened again.

The conjuror was gone.

Stiff with panic, Gom whirled about. Which way? Which way had Zamul moved? He turned about again. He must get back to Carrick, fast.

One hand tight about the staff, the other clutching the neck of his shirt over the rune, he struck out, pushing, shoving, poking folk's ribs and tripping them in his haste. Faster, he urged himself, expecting to feel Zamul's hand descend upon him at any moment.

He burst from the edge of the crowd and into the street. But which street? The inn street? No. That ran down to the lake, while this one lay parallel with the shore.

He glanced fearfully from right to left, feeling exposed. Trusting to his nose, Gom ran left, alongside the market-place until he reached the street corner and looked up the hill.

There! The inn sign stuck out quite clearly, swinging in the breeze. Gom crossed the street and ran up the steep slope, then through the inn porch, going from blinding sunlight into the gloom of the front hallway. He paused, blinking, until his eyes adjusted. To his right, Essie, in bright yellow dress and flowered apron, bustled about crowded parlor tables. Down the far end of the hall, the inn yard, now brilliant with sunshine, teemed with horses and wagons, and men passing and repassing the open back door.

Gom started up the stairs to Carrick's attic room. He'd just reached the first landing when he glanced up.

Descending toward him was the conjuror!

Gom turned and leapt down the staircase, two, three steps at a time, bumping into a chambermaid carrying up a pile of clean linen.

" 'ere 'ere, you young larrikin! Just look where you're going!"

"Sorry!" Gom called over his shoulder. Still looking back, he knocked into a cleaner coming up the staircase toting a mop and a full pail of water.

Gom ran, ignoring the angry calls at his back. He heard a clank, a curse. Zamul had found the bucket also.

Reaching the foot of the staircase, Gom looked about him, thinking fast. Where could he go now? Back into the crowded street? No. It would be so easy for Zamul to take him in that anonymous place, with no one to care.

On an impulse, Gom ran the other way, out into the inn yard to find it crammed with enormous wagons whose hooped covers arched over their tops like tents. A caravan, loaded and lined up ready to go.

Gom pressed himself against the inn wall.

Tall, fearsome men, in leather leggings and high-heeled shoes, leather gauntlets almost to the elbow, and broad-brimmed leather hats, were backing great packhorses into the wagons' shafts with a deal of cursing and hupping and clacking of hooves on the hard shiny cobbles. They looked quite different from the lakeside folk. Gom tried to guess what they could be. Not farmers, he was sure. Their bodies hadn't the stocky, muscular look of the farmers he knew. They were altogether different: lean, tall, hard. And their faces looked forbidding under the wide hat brims.

Every one of them carried a whip. Gom almost cried out as one cracked close by his ear.

Plucking up his courage, he crept around the courtyard periphery to the stables, and stood by the doorway, looking out.

There was no sign of Zamul in the courtyard. Had Gom managed to lose him? If so, now what? He turned about.

The stables seemed empty. The grooms were probably outside, helping the caravan on its way. Gom decided to hide in a pile of hay and wait for Carrick's return.

But at Shadow's stall Gom stopped in astonishment. The dog was lying in the far corner, and in a very sorry state.

Gom pushed open the stall wicket, and went in.

"So you came back, too." He crouched beside the dog. "Didn't I tell you that you'd have to go easy until your side—"

Gom slowly straightened up, his eyes on the hound's side. It was skinny still, just beginning to fill out, but— the hair grew thick and black and glossy all over, with *not a hint of a scar.*

Gom backed off, a step, two, his fist tight on the staff. "Shadow?"

With a vicious snarl, the figure leapt.

Gom raised the staff to defend himself, and lashed out. As stick struck home, the image of the dog shimmered in midair, dissolved, and began to reform in the shape of Zamul.

Seizing his chance, Gom ran out, down the empty passageway. He heard Zamul shout, the thud of the wicket swinging to, and heavy feet running down the passage after him.

Gom raced into the courtyard, took shelter behind one of the wagons, and peeped out. Zamul was standing in the stable doorway, gazing narrowly around.

Which way out?

Gom weighed his chances. He could never reach the inn door without being seen. But he might make it out to the street. He began to work his way around the carts, until, looking back, he saw the conjuror moving purposefully in his direction. Gom ran, in and out of the wagon line in crazy loops.

"Oy!" came a man's voice, harsh as the whip he cracked.

Gom scrambled up into one of the wagons and dropped the flap behind him. Light filtered through the canvas canopy—a mixed blessing, for while he could see in there, he would also be seen by anyone who chose to poke his head in through the flap. Gom crouched, breathless, among barrels, large wooden boxes, and half a dozen bulging sacks.

A hand seized the flap, shook it, and the voice came again.

"Here! What are you doing, skulking around our goods?"

Now Gom was really trapped. He waited for the flap to go up, for an arm to reach in to pull him out. To his surprise, another voice spoke up; a voice fawning and sly.

"I'm certainly not thinking to steal from the solahinn, honored sir. Only a fool would even think of it. I'm looking for my sister's boy. I don't suppose you've seen him? A squinty, little thing, a regular scruff, clothes all stained and torn."

"I've seen no boy. Try the stables. Now, out of the way, man, unless you want to get trampled underfoot."

The canopy flap jiggled smartly. Gom drew in his breath and braced himself, but the flap still didn't go up. The solahinn, as Zamul had called him, was only adjusting it. Gom sighed with relief. They didn't even suspect that he was in there. The solahinn had challenged Zamul, not Gom. And still the coward, apparently, the conjuror had retreated.

Another whipcrack, and a strident voice shouted something in a strange harsh tongue. An instant later, a crate slid into Gom, pinning him against a barrel as the wagon lurched into motion over the cobbles.

Gom heaved the crate aside, and moved free. Here was a pretty situation, he told himself. But never mind. It worked to his advantage. At least he'd get clear of Zamul. Once out of the inn yard, he'd simply climb from the cart and go to Carrick.

He listened, hearing outside street noises mingle with the rumble of wheels over rough paving. Market sounds, merchants calling out their wares. The sounds rose, then began to fade. Gom's wagon tilted as it pulled uphill now, away from the lake side.

Swaying and rocking on his heels with the bumping of the wagon, Gom moved to raise the flap. It wouldn't give. He tugged at it. Still it wouldn't budge. He set down the staff and using both hands now, pulled with all his might. The flap was sealed tight, from floor to roof.

Unbelieving, Gom worked his way around the wagon, crawling over and around the barrels and sacks and boxes. The canvas, tough as leather, was nailed down so tightly that not even a mouse could get in or out.

Gom sat down with a bump and covered his face in dismay. A refugee, a short-term stowaway in the sola-hinn's caravan: that's all he'd meant to be. But now, without intending it, he was their prisoner!

Chapter Sixteen

CREAKING and grinding, the wagon wheels rolled on. The air beneath the canvas grew hot and close. Sweat started from Gom's skin, ran down his chest and back. His shirt clung in damp patches, and his hair stuck to his brow.

He sat against a barrel for a while, bouncing and swaying at every lurch. Where was he going—and with whom? The minutes passed. How long had he been in that closed and stuffy space? It seemed like hours. They surely, he thought, must have long left Pen'langoth behind by now. And also Zamul, he reminded himself, trying to cheer himself a little.

He foraged for Stig's water bottle, glad now at his forethought, and was just taking a tepid sip when a sudden really big lurch sent water spattering onto the wagon floor. Gom wiped his mouth, and restoppered the bottle. Another, and a crate slid toward him. He dodged clear and crouched by the canvas.

They were going sharply down.

The wagon rolled, tilted, righted itself and Gom heard the swish of water under the wagon chassis. Were they crossing a ford? Gom braced himself on all fours as it stopped abruptly, went sprawling as it jerked on again amid shouts and whipcracks.

Gom stayed down, listening to water rushing under him.

Another lurch, and the wagon climbed again. A wave of heat swept through him, making him feel dizzy. He crawled back among the assorted cargo and sat down, wiping his face on his sleeve. It was past elevenses, and the fullness from the sticky bun was long gone. On a sudden thought, he jumped up and tried a barrel lid. It was clamped tight. He put his ear to it. Liquid of some kind swished inside it. Ale? If so, it was of no use to him, for he couldn't get at it. He tried the others. The same. The crates were also sealed down, with nails. The sacks looked more promising, being fastened only with knotted twine. He opened one and found dried peas inside.

Hungry as he was, however, he took only a handful. One had to be careful not to eat too many dried peas at once for they swelled in one's middle and made one quite ill. He chewed them slowly, carefully, wondering where he was. The caravan had obviously just forded a river. Long River? If so, then they were headed east. Worse and worse!

He took the map from his pocket, spread it out in the filtered sunlight. Yes, they could have reached only Long River this soon. They were going east, then, just as he'd thought. Beyond the river's eastern banks a line of hills marked Long Valley's nether boundary. Beyond those hills stretched a vast tract of open land unmarked by any trail or city, or town, or even village.

He looked at the name of that tract, the letters strung out so widely from end to end that Gom could put his finger in between each of them. Two words again, short. The beginning of the second one looked like a bird in flight. He folded the map, wishing once more that he could read. They couldn't be going far without road or trail to travel on. Not in these wagons. Gom took comfort from that.

Some comfort! They'd already gone far enough for him. And when those men opened up the wagon, they were sure to find him. He thought of their cruel faces. What would they think when they saw him in there hiding amongst their precious cargo? They'd been short enough with Zamul, and he only walking around outside the wagons. What would they do to him when they found him stowed away right inside one?

Dried peas also made one very thirsty, and a little sick, he reminded himself, beginning to feel the after-effect of his makeshift meal. He took another sip of water, let it trickle slowly down his throat.

He had to think of some excuse. But what? Zamul had told the men that he was looking for his runaway nephew. Gom stuck out his chin and patted his chest. "At your service, dear sirs," he mimicked Zamul's fawning tone. "One nephew, going for his life!"

Where was the conjuror now? Gom wondered. He tried to put himself in Zamul's place, in that crowded yard, looking for a boy who'd suddenly vanished like one of his own magic trifles. Had the man assumed that he'd managed to slip from the yard and back to Carrick? In that case he'd be hanging about Carrick's stall, or lurking in the inn, waiting for Gom to reappear.

On the other hand, he might have guessed that Gom had taken refuge in one of the wagons. In this case, Gom realized with a jolt, the man was even now perhaps circling above in high, wide sweeps, tracking the caravan to its journey's end.

His mouth suddenly gone dry again, Gom took another

drink, thinking how he was in trouble whichever way. And with no escape that he could see.

Gom stoppered the water bottle, put it away, and as he did so, his hand nudged his seed box.

He drew it out, opened the lid. His box of tiny treasures. Much had happened since he'd put the seeds in it. Then he'd never even heard the name, Ulm, and Katak had been but a bad waking dream.

And here he was, so busy scrambling from minute to minute to stay alive, to hold onto his mother's rune, to keep Katak from getting free again. He thought of his vision in the bear cave, when the sparrow had come to life to give him the riddle. Riddle! So much was happening now he scarce had a moment even to think of it. He was certainly no closer to solving it.

From Air and Earth comes seed . . .

He jiggled the box gently. "Tell me," he whispered to the tiny germs of life, "what is the secret?"

The wagon bumped violently, bouncing Gom's hand. A few of the seeds fell onto the wagon floor and lodged into cracks, out of sight forever. Sighing, Gom put the rest away and leaned back.

Oh, what a clumsy failure he was.

He took up the staff absently, twirled it between his palms. The sparrow's head, moving to and fro with the motion of his hands, seemed to deny his words, which made him smile suddenly in spite of everything. "You don't think I'm a failure, then?" he whispered, and almost laughed aloud as the bird still shook her head. "Maybe you're right," he conceded, his smile lingering.

Come to think, he'd managed to cope with some bad surprises. Katak, and Zamul. So far. But now?

His smile fading, he laid aside the staff.

He couldn't think anymore. The air was pressing in upon him, and his head had begun to throb. He closed his eyes. Oh, for one, just one breath of cool, fresh air . . .

Loud sounds brought him to his senses, many hooves thudding toward the caravan. Gom opened his eyes, finding it almost dark now under the canopy.

He scrambled to his feet, and felt around the edges of the canvas trying to prise it open just enough to see what was happening, but it still held as tightly as ever. If only he had not forgotten his knife! If only he could have bought one at the fair! He pressed his ear against the canvas.

Presently, there came a distant shout, which was answered from the caravan. The wagons rumbled and creaked to a halt.

Zamul? He shook his head. That one was too much a coward to take on a single solahinn, let alone a whole caravan. And . . . he heard now the sound of galloping hooves, not of one horse, but several.

The galloping horses drew closer, and suddenly they were all about the wagons, in and out, calling loudly. Was it raiders? If so, then he was in double jeopardy! Gom foraged around, retrieved the staff from among the sacks and crates, and faced the canopy entrance, looking as brave as he could.

There came a shout of sudden laughter, and voices exchanging loud greetings. More laughter, then a whip cracked, the caravan moved on, faster now, surrounded by the riders.

Gom relaxed. Not a robbery, but a meeting of fellows.

A mounted party come to escort their fresh provisions, bought at the Pen'langoth market. Did that mean that they'd almost arrived?

Gom glanced up at the darkened canopy. They were well beyond the hills, and traveling still, and therefore miles from Pen'langoth, much farther than he thought they'd go.

If they had reached the end of the journey, what then? Would the men eat straightaway, or would they first unload the wagons? Gom's lips tightened grimly. If they unloaded first, then he was truly sunk.

An hour later, the caravan slowed again, and this time, amid more shouts and whip cracks, the wagon creaked to a final halt.

He heard the sounds of the horses being freed from their halters, and their tired heavy feet backing off, then the moment he'd been dreading, the sound of the canvas being untied.

He got up stiffly, pins and needles starting in his legs, and limped over to the far end of the wagon. There, he crouched behind the barrels and bales and waited, his eyes on the canvas flap.

The flap moved, and a cool fresh breeze riffled over him, smelling of earth and sweet, damp grass. Gom tensed, waiting for someone to climb up into the wagon. But at a sudden shout, the men went away.

Gom waited for a minute or two, but they didn't come back. Crickets chirped, a horse stamped, and somewhere in the distance, a small wild thing chittered.

Cautiously, he crawled to the edge of the wagon and peered out.

Under a full moon the hooped carts looked like ghostly

giant mushrooms on the flat, grassy ground. Nearby, the carthorses, tethered to stakes, stood grazing. Beyond them, a pack of riding horses wandered freely. Gom jumped from the wagon and crept out under the shelter of its shadow. No sign of any bird, but . . . He stood quite still for a minute, on the edge of darkness, eyeing the horses warily, minded how Zamul had almost gotten the better of him by taking Shadow's shape. The horses gave him barely a glance.

Gom breathed out, and looked more widely about him. At his right reared a high stockade. At his left clustered tents of plain brown canvas, and over all wafted the delicious smell of cooking. Cooking! Come to think, Gom was very hungry.

Gom crept toward the smell.

Beyond the tents was a huge bonfire around which were gathered at least a hundred men, all with the same kind of hats and leggings and boots, and fierce, forbidding faces.

It was easy to see why they'd left the wagons so suddenly. They were eating noisily from tin plates, mounds of food, constantly replenished from a huge pot suspended over the fire. Gom licked his lips. They were drinking, too, from tall tin cups, which they filled to overflowing from a barrel in their midst.

Suddenly one of them stood up, raised his cup and cried out,

"Dahai Solahinn! Hah dahnai gho dey nah! Hai-tah! Hai-tah!"

The rest raised their cups, too, and yelled the same thing: a frightening sound, and not reassuring. Gom blocked his ears to lessen it. Pride was in those voices, and ruthlessness. What did the words mean?

One of the men struck up a chord on a dark wooden instrument with a long straight neck and many shining strings. Then he began to play a fast tune amid clapping and slapping and clanking of cups. Faster and faster went the man's fingers, and the men began to sway in time with the music.

Two of the men set aside their plates and, linking elbows, began to dance with great vigor, leaping, twirling, and kicking like fierce horses.

In spite of his fear, Gom's heart uplifted at seeing such wonderful movement, such strength and savage grace.

The men sat again to loud applause, and took up their cups. At that, the leader stood, raised his cup on high, and repeated his call. A loud chord from the strings, and the men began chanting:

> Dey solahinn; hai-tah! hai-tah!
> Dahbai bey Vargue; hai-tah! hai-tah!
> Tey bai hinnay; hai-tah! hai-tah! hai-tah!
> Roh dai lahn-ney; hai-tah! hai-tah!
> Hah dahnai gho dey nah!
> Ma-lah bahn na-mah chai nah!
> Lahn dai gho,
> Sola rho.
> Hinn-eh, hinn-eh, hata-lahdin hey,
> Vah gadohr! hai-tah! hai-tah!
> Vah ramohr! hai-tah! hai-tah!
> Hai-tah! hai-tah! hai-tah! hai-tah!

On the last shout the men stood and clashed their cups together.

Gom stood entranced. The music was crude, the words were incomprehensible, but the total effect was compelling.

The sound of strings struck again, a fresh tune, even

more frenzied and loud, and the men began to talk and laugh over the noise. Gom stirred himself. What was he doing there? He must go, while he could.

He moved quietly around the tents, away from the light and the warmth and the wonderful smell of food, hunger gnawing at his belly. He passed the giant wagons, and walked on toward the high stockade. If he were right, he was somewhere east of Lake Langoth—whether south or north of the lake city, he had no way of knowing. But if he moved back westward, he'd have to pass through the eastern hillrange he'd seen on the map, then come to Long River. From there he could surely ask his way back to Pen'langoth and Lakeside.

He looked up, found the twin stars, and took his bearings. Westward lay around the other side of the stockade.

He struck out by the high fence, the sounds from the fireside growing fainter. The stockade was big as a fair-sized field. He was pondering its purpose when something kicked the other side of the fence, making him jump.

He stopped still, scarcely breathing.

The kick came again, and this time, a horse's quiet whuffle.

"Who's there?" the question came.

Gom looked up the stockade fence. Too high to see over, too sheer to climb, and those spikes atop didn't look very hospitable. He moved on a way, found a hole big enough to see through. Inside stood a knot of horses, tall, proud colts with a wild look. Why, Gom would bet no one had ever ridden those backs. So what were they doing in there?

By the fence stood the colt who must have kicked it. Taking a quick breath, Gom called. "Gom Gobblechuck of Windy Mountain greets you, and bids you good evening."

The colt whinnied in surprise, moved to where Gom's face was outlined in his peephole, summoning some of his fellows over as he came.

"I thought I heard somebody out there." It put its nose to the hole. "You greet us in our own tongue!"

Gom tossed his head and blew through his lips. "Only just," he said. "I learned a word or two from our farm horses back home."

"Farm horses? What do you mean?" asked another colt, a bright red roan.

"They're like those packhorses over there," Gom pointed to the bulky figures grazing in their wide open space, forgetting that the horses could see neither through, nor over, the fence. "Like those, they work for men, pulling loads, and plows, and haywagons, and the like."

"Ah! This is another of those hated humans who sell us into slavery," the first colt snorted angrily. "If we could only get at him!"

The colts, advancing, began to kick against the stockade fence.

Stung, Gom whinnied in protest.

"I don't sell, or buy, horses," he cried. "I'm a woodcutter by trade. Why, my father and I even pulled our own cart for ourselves. As for me, I don't hold with anybody owning anybody, not at all."

The colts stopped, surprised.

"Oh, really?" asked a black and brown and white piebald. "So what are you doing here, if not looking for a horse?"

Gom peered about him. He should be going on his

way. Every moment he spent in that solahinn camp was dangerous. And for all he knew Zamul might still be by in some guise or other, waiting for him to emerge onto the wide plain. But he just couldn't walk out on his new acquaintances. Putting his face back to the hole, he told them how he'd been running from someone, how he'd hidden in the solahinn wagon. How he'd just climbed out, and was about to make off home again.

"Fortunate," the roan called out bitterly. "That you go while we stay."

A huge colt moved up through the cluster. Gom gazed at it in awe. It was totally black save for a gleaming silver ringmark on the brow, and stood a full hand above the others, even the roan.

"Why do you talk to such a one?" the black colt demanded of the others. "Humans are beneath contempt."

"He sounds friendly," the roan said. "And he speaks our tongue."

"Ah! Will that set us free? Leave him. You demean yourselves by stooping to speak with the like."

Stoop, indeed! "I'm as good as you," Gom snorted indignantly. "And I've done you no harm. Who are these solahinn, that they shut you up in there?"

"They are horse traders. They chase us wild ones from one end of the High Vargue to the other," the piebald explained. "They take and break us, then sell us to the highest bidder."

"That's terrible," Gom cried. "Why do you stand for it?"

"We have no choice," the roan said. "When our time comes, we're caught by cunning maneuvers and sent from these our beloved plains forever."

"Bah!" The black colt neighed loudly, pawing the

ground. "Only if you allow it. They'll never send me from these plains!"

"Ah, you talk like that tonight," a gray colt answered. "But tomorrow, when they crack their whips, you'll sing a different tune. Think yourself lucky. Your future's assured. At least you know where you're going."

"Lucky?" The black colt reared fiercely, showing the whites of his eyes. "If that be luck, then keep it!" With a kick of his hind hooves, the stallion-to-be moved away around to the stockade's far side.

Gom started back a little, yet sensing fear behind the bravado. "What magnificence," he murmured. "What pride. No insult intended to the rest of you," he added hastily, realizing that he'd spoken out loud.

"None taken," said the roan. "It doesn't take much of an eye to see that he's no ordinary horse. Stormfleet, we call him. He's a cito, as you can tell from his ringmark."

Gom could tell nothing of the sort, for he'd never heard the word. "Pardon me? What's a cito?"

"This lad certainly has led a sheltered life," the piebald snickered. "Surely citos are legendary throughout Ulm."

"They happen once in a thousand years," the roan explained kindly. "They live so long we have never counted their years. Stormfleet will outlive us and our children for many generations."

Gom thanked the roan, grateful for the courteous reply.

The piebald tossed his mane. "So here we are, caught in the traps set for Stormfleet. And unless you want to be caught, too, I advise you to be moving on without delay. You're lucky the guards haven't found you already."

Guards? Gom looked around nervously.

"Thanks for the warning," he said. But danger or no, he couldn't leave without a last word from the cito.

Gom worked his way around the fence until he reached the place where Stormfleet stood, and put his face to the nearest peephole. Oh, what a magnificent creature he was. Proud, independent. Fierce.

What a friend that horse would make!

"What I hear is disgusting!" Gom cried. "The solahinn are a disgrace. I tell you, I wish I could do something to help you!"

Stormfleet's head snapped up. "A human's word is cheap. Go, and thank your stars that this fence parts us, or you'd not stay in one piece."

"Not fair!" Gom answered him. "I wish you only great good."

"You're a human," the horse retorted. "There's scarce one alive I'd not wish grave harm."

The colt moved away.

Gom stood watching him, his face to the hole. "Cheap, eh?" he muttered. Well, they'd see about that! He'd find the gate to this place and open it and let them all out. He moved around the fence perimeter, until he was almost in view of the wagons again. It had to have a gate, he told himself. A couple of steps more, and there it was.

It was stout and heavy, simply a movable section of the fence on great iron hinges. And it was secured with a thick iron bar.

He set aside the staff, put his hands to the bar and tried to lift it. It gave a little, then stuck. Hold on, Gom muttered. Another minute and he'd have it.

He braced himself for another heave, but at that moment, a harsh voice rang out.

"Kahaganai! Dagadah ak hanai?"

Chapter Seventeen

BONY FINGERS dug into Gom's shoulder and whipped him around.

"Who are you? Where have you come from, boy?" the man asked, this time in the common tongue.

Gom swallowed hard. The excuse that he'd rehearsed back in the wagon didn't sound so good now.

The man raised a gauntleted hand and shook his whip at Gom.

"Can't find your tongue, boy? Then I'll find it for you. Come." Gom grabbed his staff as the solahinn dragged him from the stockade, past the wagons and tents, to the men around the fire.

At Gom's approach, the music and the talking stopped, and all eyes were on him. His captor spoke, pointed his whip at Gom. At the man's words, a murmur went through the gathering. No doubt the solahinn was telling his fellows how he'd found Gom.

One of the men stood up, waved at Gom, speaking rapidly.

Gom's captor looked down at him. "Hundro there is our chief wagoneer. He says he saw you in Pen'langoth this afternoon, sneaking around the caravan."

"I—" Gom began.

The solahinn shook out his whip and cracked it. "The truth, boy!"

"M-my uncle is a cruel man," he said, shamefully

conscious of the break in his voice. "He hates me, and beats me. I couldn't stand it any longer. This afternoon, I ran. I hid in the inn yard, but he found me." He looked around in sudden hope. "One of you saw him chase me from the stables?"

No one spoke.

Gom went on. "So I climbed into a wagon, only for a minute, mind. The next thing I know, I can't get out, and now here I am." He tried to look sorrowful rather than afraid, putting to good use the wobble in his voice. "My mother—she'll be going out of her mind, wondering where I am. If you could just tell me which way to go, I'll be off home at once."

Another spoke up, a slower voice, more wordy, but sounding just as harsh and unfriendly. Gom watched him intently. His witness?

Gom's captor glared down at him. "Does your uncle wear a black shirt and bright green britches?"

"Yes, yes," Gom said, nodding in relief. But to his dismay, the man shook him angrily.

"You take us for complete fools? That rogue, whom one of my men caught skulking around the wagons, is a common juggler, or conjuror, as he calls himself." The man laid his hand on Gom's staff. "I wouldn't be surprised if this were not a stick for juggling and trickery. It looks fancy enough," he said, and made to seize it.

But tightening his grip on the staff, Gom pulled back. "Indeed not!" he cried. "This was made by my father, and let any man here speak ill of him!"

The man looked startled for a moment, then, laughing, let his hand fall.

"Our boy has more grit in him than his uncle, eh?"

Amid a general murmur, the solahinn went on. " 'Tis lucky for us that you don't defend your—*uncle* so fiercely. The man's a thief and a rogue. We've brushed with him before, over the matter of a horse." The man stopped laughing abruptly, and bending down, thrust his face close to Gom's. "Now you may be his nephew as you claim, but more likely you lie. I say you're his agent, sent to see if we've caught our prize." He straightened up. "Don't look so shocked. It's no secret that a cito's in the offing. You can't deny it."

"But I can," Gom protested. "I swear that until I came here, I'd never even heard of the word!"

"Oh?" Gom's captor cocked an eyebrow. "So who told you now?"

Gom groaned inwardly. What had he done! How could he possibly tell those men that he'd learned it from the horses in the stockade?

"I, er, overheard it," he said.

"You overheard it, eh?" The solahinn leader looked around to the gathering. "So this enterprising lad speaks our language after all." The man rapped out a question to Gom in the solahinn tongue. Naturally, Gom didn't understand a word.

"You see?" the leader cried triumphantly. "Another lie!"

He eyed Gom in such a way that made Gom's knees go weak. "Let me tell you how I found this liar: he was so intent on getting back to his mother that he was standing outside the stockade gate, both hands on the bar, trying to lift it. And when I asked him what he was at, he couldn't find a word to say."

The men were silent.

"Perhaps," the man went on, "he thought to take a certain horse to ride. One that would get him home in no time at all!"

This brought scattered laughter.

"Come," the man said to Gom, speaking now in mock deference. "It's clear that we deal not with the lying, sniveling boy that we see, but with a very talented accomplice to that scoundrel, Zamul. We must have ourselves a conference here."

The man seized Gom's staff now, and pulled him none too gently toward the bonfire.

Gom eyed the leaping flames, his throat dry. What were they going to do to him? He looked around, seeking escape, but saw only tall figures crowding in on every hand.

To Gom's relief, the man merely thrust him to the ground beside the fire, threw the staff down after him, and bowed in mock courtesy. "Allow me to introduce myself properly: Jofor, chieftain of the solahinn, at your service."

Gom reached for the staff, drew it in beside him. Then, looking up, he forced himself to face the ring of hostile whips around him. "Gom Gobblechuck of Windy Mountain," he replied, his knuckles white upon the staff. But he didn't say anything about being at anybody's service.

"I see. Well, Gom Gobblechuck, you sit there while we decide what to do with you." Jofor called one of the men to watch him, and went to speak with several of his fellows farther around the fire.

Gom sat looking into the flames, thinking. There was luck for you! Jofor thought him a spy. A spy for Zamul, come to help steal the cito. A horse thief, caught red-handed. They'd surely punish him.

His flesh crawled. He could almost feel the whips lashing his skin, his poor back, only just healed. Why, they might even kill him.

He felt for the rune, found it lying outside his shirt in full view. But would that matter? Those men clearly measured wealth and power in terms of horses, not small black stones scratched with strange markings. No, only those who knew would recognize such a thing, and covet it. Men like Zamul.

He slipped it back under his shirt anyway, and gazed upward to the moonlit sky. At least for the moment he was clear of that one. At least the rune was safe, even if he was in danger of his life.

He straightened his legs out in front of him, rubbing his knees. Still a bit sore from the long hours shut up in the wagon. Pulling on his staff, he first knelt, then stood up warily, his eye on his guard's whip, and shifted from one leg to the other, to ease them. At that moment, Jofor rose from his conference and walked back to him.

"You like to dance, I see." Jofor turned with a laugh to his men. "Music! Where's Chodur?"

"Here!" The musician appeared before them, his stringed box hanging at his chest.

Jofor smiled coldly. "You like to dance, Gom Gobblechuck of Windy Mountain? Then you shall dance for us."

Gom stared up at him aghast. "Dance? I don't know how."

"Dance, I said." Jofor cracked his whip, making Gom jump. Chodur struck a loud chord.

Gom's mind raced frantically. He couldn't dance! He'd never joined in the dancing back in Clack, fearful of his feet going the wrong way, unwilling to look foolish in front of the townsfolk. Besides, his knees were stiff, and his legs ached. No, he couldn't, wouldn't dance.

Jofor cracked his whip again, curling it past Gom's ankles. Gom stepped onto his left foot, back onto his right.

"Knees up," Jofor said. *Crack.* "Quick, or I'll help you." *Crack.*

Gom stepped sideways again, onto his left foot, did a little hop, then halfheartedly, went back onto his right. Chodur began a slow, clumsy tune in a shambling bear's gait. Laughter rippled around the firelit circle.

Gom's rage surged. He saw a small gap, a dark space leading away from the fire. He turned and ran. A moment later sharp pain cut his ankles, jerking his feet from under him. He fell headlong, face down in the dirt, the staff flying from his hand.

"The next time," Jofor said, unwinding his whip from around Gom's ankles, "you'll bleed. Now, *dance!*"

Gom danced, shuffling around in a slow circle, first on one foot, then the other, slide, hup, slide, hup. His face grew hot with humiliation.

"Faster," Jofor said, and at a signal several of the onlookers also took up their whips, and, forming a ring around Gom, began to snap at his legs. Gom dodged out of range of one whip only to whirl within range of another. The men around the fire began to clap, first in slow rhythm, then faster, driving Chodur's fingers, the pace of the whips.

Gom leapt and spun and twisted, his stiffness, his cramp now forgotten in his desire to avoid that cutting leather. His heart banged against his ribs, his throat was hot and dry. And his fury was almost unbearable. Such hateful, cruel folk. How long, how long, before they let him stop? The firelight blurred, the darkness wheeled about his head. Gom slipped, fell, and amid loud applause, lay at Jofor's feet.

They picked him up, set him down by the fire and handed him a plate.

"Eat," Jofor said. "Then we talk."

Gom thrust the plate aside, tipping the food out. He couldn't eat. He felt sick, and he'd starve, he told himself, before he ate with them. What he wouldn't give to pay them back!

Someone began the loud chant he'd heard earlier. The rest joined in, their voices at this range overwhelming.

Gom listened, staring stiffly into the fire.

"You like our song?" Jofor was back.

Gom shrugged. "How can I? I don't understand a word."

"Then we must accommodate our guest," Jofor said to the assembly. "Let us sing it again, in the common tongue." And oh, the pride with which he spat out the last two words.

The men began again, familiar words mouthed in harsh, flat accents to that strange chant. In spite of his anger, Gom found himself caught up in the words.

Solahinn we, hai-tah! hai-tah!
Of the High Vargue, hai-tah! hai-tah!
Ever we ride, hai-tah! hai-tah! hai-tah!
This ground so wide, hai-tah! hai-tah!
Masters of these flat lands,
Culling with our tireless hands
Great wild herds,
Beasts of the plains:
Riding, riding, in pursuit abiding;
Ours to take, hai-tah! hai-tah!

Ours to break, hai-tah! hai-tah!
Hai-tah! hai-tah! hai-tah! hai-tah!

On the last shout, Jofor stood, hauled Gom to his feet. "Time for business. You want a horse, you shall have a horse. Come." He walked Gom back toward the stockade, the rest following.

Jofor halted them by the gate. "In here as you know," Jofor said, "are horses fresh caught. Pick one, ride it around the stockade, and it's yours."

Chapter Eighteen

"**W**ELL?" Jofor demanded, hoisting him up level with the top of the fence.

Gom looked out over the bright moonlit compound. "It's too dark to see. Maybe tomorrow—"

Jofor shook him impatiently. "Now. Tonight. Over the fence with you."

Over those sharp pointed stakes? Not that he wanted to go in at all. There were at least thirty enraged colts down there! Catching sight of the two heads peeping over the fence in the bright moonlight, one of the horses pawed the ground, sending clods of earth thudding against the barricade.

Gom played for time. "My staff, I left it by the fire."

Jofor's eyebrows came up. "Staff?" He turned to the man beside him. "Fetch our guest his little stick," he said, then shouted after the man: "He mustn't think us thieves."

Gom's face grew warm. Jofor couldn't wait for the show to begin. He looked along the fence, at the men waiting with Jofor to see him trampled underfoot. Anger rekindled within him. What wouldn't he give to disappoint them!

Maybe—Gom's eyes narrowed—maybe he could. He remembered a day long ago when his brother Horvin, the one who'd snatched the rune and come to grief, had bargained with Gom for a little green tree frog in a frog jumping contest. Against unfair odds Gom had won that frog squarely from under his brother's nose. For how was Horvin to know that Gom could speak with the frog and work out a joint strategy to beat Horvin's cheating?

Could he manage the like here?

The question was, which colt to choose. The roan had been the most kind. One quiet word in its ear, if he could find it, and they'd both go free. Jofor wouldn't mind losing one horse. And yet . . . it didn't seem fair to leave the rest behind.

Gom looked to the cito standing in the middle, apart from the rest. There was a leader! If he could ride Storm-fleet, then they all had a chance. If. It was a risk, even to approach him. *Think yourself lucky this fence parts us . . . or you'd not stay in one piece.*

Gom bit his lip. The rune was the thing. He must get it out of there.

Still. He pointed over the fence.

"I choose the cito," he said. "That is, if our agreement holds."

A spontaneous shout of laughter sent the horses inside rearing and neighing and kicking up their heels.

Jofor waved his men to silence. "Indeed it does, boy. We solahinn are men of our word."

The staff arrived. Jofor thrust it into Gom's hand, then hitched him up and over the spikes, to let him fall face down into churned up earth. After a moment, Gom stood painfully, retrieved his staff, and dusted himself off, glancing around the moonlit fence at the broad-brimmed hats outlining its top, the avid faces watching him.

The cito, he'd said, and Jofor had confidently agreed. Jofor: a cold, callous man, who'd carelessly traded the priceless cito, not expecting Gom to survive his ordeal.

Gom, face set, staff raised defensively, worked his way around the inside perimeter. The colts looked huge from this side of the fence. How, Gom wondered, was he ever going to reach Stormfleet without being trampled?

One of the colts noticed him.

Gom froze. It was not one of those he'd spoken with.

The colt shied, stepped toward him. Gom snorted and blew out his cheeks. "Hold: I'm a friend."

It was not enough.

The colt reared, neighing loudly at seeing a hated human so near. Then it bore down on him, picking up other colts with it. At the last minute, Gom spun aside, and the colts rammed the fence.

"You're going the wrong way!" Jofor shouted from the gate. "That's not how to catch a cito, boy!"

Gom thought fast. The rune: could it help him? Laughter mixed with jeers as Gom fled across the churning compound floor to the other side, his mind working frantically, his eyes seeking Stormfleet. No time. No time for magic now.

As the colts wheeled to charge again, Gom glimpsed the black shape in their midst, silver ringmark shining.

"Stormfleet!" he called, but the colts were on him. A flying hoof caught Gom on the shoulder, knocking him to the ground. Another hit him and pain flashed in his arm. He tucked in his head and rolled and the colts grazed past to crash once more into the stockade fence.

As Gom rolled, his head hit a small rock jutting from the churned up earth. Dazed, he wiped his face on the back of his hand, brought it away smeared in blood. He sat up, his breath coming short and sharp, listening.

Silence, now.

Gom looked up.

Sighting Stormfleet in the middle of the compound, he scrambled up and zigzagged toward him rabbit-fashion as the others came about.

"Stormfleet! It's me, Gom!"

The cito reared, teetered on his hind legs, towering over him.

Gom raised the staff to ward him off. "They caught me trying to open the gate," he cried out. "They've thrown me in here to die."

"So you say."

Gom thumped the staff on the ground. "I mean it!"

"The little one speaks true!" The roan pushed through the crowd. "I heard him at the gate, trying to lift the bar," he went on, and turned to those behind him. "If I'd known who it was, I'd never have let you charge."

The cito's hooves came down beside Gom. "What if I believe you?"

"Listen: let me on your back, ride me around this place and we can go, they promised." Gom glanced to the rest. "You can get out too, if you're quick."

Jofor's voice came from the perimeter. "Hey! You there?" When Gom didn't answer, the men around the fence began to mutter.

"Quick," Gom urged Stormfleet. "Before it's too late!"

Stormfleet eyed him sideways. "Why should you help me?"

"Why shouldn't I?" Gom retorted, and added, "I'm helping myself too."

From atop the fence, Jofor's voice came again. "Boy?"

All went still.

"Maybe he's hurt," a man called. "Shall we take a look?"

"Not yet," came Jofor's reply. "Come on. The show's over."

"Wait!" Gom cried out to them, then quietly, "Stormfleet?"

The cito looked down, as though weighing him. Then knelt, touching his proud head to the dirt. Gom climbed the colt's back with dignity, but as they straightened up, he almost lost it. He'd never dreamed he'd be so high!

The other colts dropped back now, fully revealing horse and rider, and at once there came a loud gasp from around the stockade.

Gom raised his staff, his "little stick" as Jofor had called it. From her high perch the sparrow faced Jofor, her tiny seed eyes gleaming. Gom's heart swelled.

"Forward!" he whuffled. A couple of steps, and Gom grabbed for the colt's mane with his free hand, feeling the powerful shoulders moving under him. The cito's back was broad and round and slippery. Gom was no rider. The slightest jar one way would have him off, he realized, and hoped the men did not.

Stormfleet walked slowly around the compound, Gom his staff held high ceremonially, the other colts falling in behind, circling the fence in full procession. Easing into the cito's gait, Gom passed under Jofor's incredulous gaze, feeling good with his victory—so good in fact, that he took the horses around a second, then a third, time. At the end of the final lap, Gom signaled those following with the staff, and tugging on Stormfleet's mane, drew up before Jofor.

Out of the silence, there came a single cheer, then two, then a spattering of men waved their hats, applauding.

A spattering, no more. Jofor, and those around him were scowling.

"Behold, Jofor of the solahinn," Gom called loudly, taking in with a sweep of his staff the men ringing the fence. "This cito I chose. I rode him not once, but three times around the stockade. This makes him mine, as you promised. Now honor your word and open the gate."

A murmur ran around the fence. Jofor muttered at the men beside him.

Lifting his head, he called out across the stockade.

"There's evil afoot here," he said. "First that great bird of ill omen follows our caravan all the way from Pen'langoth, and now, this." He waved a hand at Gom. "This can be no real boy!" he cried. "But some necromancer's figment, a cunning ruse to steal the cito!"

Gom, dismayed at Jofor's news, nevertheless held his ground.

"Indeed I am a boy, and real enough!" he called back. "I'm the plain son of a woodcutter. And see—these are real bruises that I'll have by the morrow, and this is real blood!" He wiped his forehead and held up his palm.

Jofor, his face stony, didn't reply.

Gom didn't like the look of him. Would the man refuse to let them go?

"You said that the solahinn were men of their word, Jofor. The gate, if you please."

The men began to mutter. One of them shouted something across the compound. Then another. And another.

Jofor looked sternly from them to Gom, then spoke with those around him. "Very well," he said at last. He cracked his whip and snapped out a command. Men jumped down out of sight and Gom heard the heavy iron bar being raised.

Gom breathed in relief. "You see?" he told Stormfleet.

"Don't trust him," the cito answered. "Don't trust any

of them. They have great cunning. They'll be sure to try and stop us."

Gom didn't doubt it. He looked around at the colts. "In that case," he said, "when the gate opens, let's have your fiercest stampede ever. We'll overrun them first, then scatter."

Quickly, Gom slung the staff at his back, freeing his other hand to keep himself from falling. Even as he did this, the gate began to open slowly, almost reluctantly, with a creak and a groan.

There was a moment's stillness then the colts charged through, scattering men and whips in all directions. Braced as he was, Gom was all but thrown. He dug his fingers into the cito's mane and desperately hung on. He had a fleeting glimpse of Jofor's shocked face, heard his shout.

"To horse! They're stampeding!"

"And I'm falling!" Gom cried desperately, feeling the great back slipping from under him.

"Come up!" Stormfleet called. "Ease up toward my neck, then use your knees! Lean down, down! Hold onto my mane, that's right. Now draw your elbows in either side!"

They thundered on through the camp, past the tents, past the bonfire, Gom sliding and bouncing around. One mistake and he'd go under the threshing hooves. Then the horses would go free and he'd be left for Jofor. He squeezed his knees into Stormfleet's flanks, and, winding strands of wiry mane around his hands, he laid his cheek on the cito's neck and clung.

They galloped on, raising great noise and dust until, clear of the camp, Gom lifted his head a fraction to call out.

"Scatter now! Go! Good speed, and good luck!"

With neighs of thanks, the colts sped away in all directions. A few minutes later Gom and Stormfleet were galloping over an empty plain.

After the briefest time, Gom begged Stormfleet to stop. His fingers were numb and his knees were giving out under him. He was losing the horse's rhythm, and at any moment he was going to fall.

"I can't," Stormfleet called back. "I'll change my gait. That'll help. How's this? The men call it 'rack.' "

Without slackening pace the rhythm changed to a smoother one that was at least bearable.

The sky began to lighten in the east behind them, a dull red glow, sure sign of bad weather. Under that ominous dawn light, Gom saw a vast expanse of knee-high waving grasses. Gom looked from side to side apprehensively. Zamul was not far away, he could almost sense him. But Zamul or no, he'd reached his limit.

"Slow!" Gom cried again, and this time he meant it. "I'm falling off!"

Stormfleet slowed to a canter, then a trot, then a walk. "There's a spring just ahead," he said. "We can stop for a brief time. But then we must press on, for the solahinn surely follow us."

Not just the solahinn, Gom thought grimly, scanning the skies, the wide spaces around them. He let go of Stormfleet's mane, rubbed his face, his numb knuckles, feeling warmth and life return. A few moments, no more, and he'd be able to go on.

Stormfleet whinnied softly, tossed his mane. "Ah, the spring, Master Gom."

Ahead, an isolated clump of nubby bushes sprouted

from a dip in the level grassland. Gom eyed them anxiously, thinking of Zamul.

At that moment some inner sense caused him to glance up.

Way above him, was a speck, and even as he watched, it came closer, circling down through the sun's red glow. Gom's heart jumped.

"Stormfleet! My enemy approaches. He will kill me if he can."

Stormfleet looked around. "Where? I see no rider."

"Not the solahinn, Stormfleet. He flies above us. Go!"

The cito broke into a full gallop. Gom clung, not daring to look up for fear of falling. His whole body was wound up tight. At every moment, he expected to feel the bird's wings brush his head, the fearful talons rake his back.

Wind's sudden draft was all the warning they had as the attacker swooped. Gom ducked as, with a loud cry, the bird swerved past.

"Faster, Stormfleet!" Gom sobbed. They raced on, Gom lying along the cito's back, his hands tight-laced into Stormfleet's mane.

The bird came down again, and this time, with unerring accuracy, its beak snatched the thong and pulled. The thin leather bit into Gom's throat, and snapped.

"No!" Gom cried out in anguish as the great skull-bird soared up into the red sky, tiny stone on broken thong dangling from the hooked claws.

"Stop, Stormfleet, stop!"

As Stormfleet slowed sharply, Gom's gaze followed the spiraling bird, such rage and sorrow as he'd never known ripping through him. He thought of Katak, in his dark prison, awaiting sure release. Of gentle Ganash who would pay the price. Of the peaceful lakelands, and other places he'd not yet seen, the gray blight of evil spread over them, killing joy and light. And he himself, the rune's keeper, ruined, his quest come to naught. Oh, Mother, Mother, he cried inwardly, I've failed you!

His rage, his anguish surged. "No!" he screamed after the ascending bird, and wished for wings.

Zamul must not have that stone!

Banking lazily on the air currents, the great bird prepared to fly away. But at the height of the turn, its shape began to shimmer in the sun's low rays.

Gom's mouth opened in horror. The bird shape was dissolving. For one instant, the figure of Zamul hung suspended, spread-eagled, black against the dull red sky. Then with a very loud and human cry, the figure began to fall.

Stormfleet whinnied and stamped and tossed his mane in exultation, but Gom hid his face.

There came a short, sharp scream, then a thud, which Gom all but felt up on Stormfleet's back.

Then silence.

Some way ahead on the flat wide plain lay a huddled shape dressed in black and green.

Gom slid off Stormfleet's back and moved slowly forward.

"Stay where you are," Stormfleet cautioned him. "It may be a trap. The ways of men are endlessly cunning."

"He's dead, I know it," Gom said in a low voice. "He took something from me. I have to go get it back." He moved on toward the body of Zamul. What would he find when he reached it?

Stormfleet went before him, snuffling cautiously, then suddenly dipping his head, the cito plucked something from the ground, something that glistened as it dangled from his mouth.

Gom ran forward.

The rune! He took the stone, clutched it to him. Saved! And with it, Ganash, and the lake lord, and all those other people out there, and Katak would stay in his grotto.

He rubbed its markings, remembering Horvin. The day his brother had snatched it from him, he hadn't run three yards with it before he'd fallen, and the rune, flying from his hand, had landed back at Gom's feet. When Zamul had first stolen the rune, it had been quiescent. Not so now. Alive, it had once again flown back to Gom. Gom squeezed the rune tight, felt a faint vibration.

His rune, that had hung about his neck for all his life! No, not his rune, he corrected himself soberly. His mother's magic stone, which he must still deliver into her hands.

But, he looked down. What to do with poor Zamul?

Stormfleet pawed the ground restlessly. "Come. The solahinn haven't let us off this easily."

"But I can't leave—" Gom began.

"Just exactly what do you propose to do, Master Gom? Bury the creature? With what?" Stormfleet trotted up to Zamul's body, and around it, and came back again. "Don't even go near that thing," he said. "It's not a sight for you. Leave him to the solahinn. Give them something to think about. Come," he urged. "Quickly, quickly." He trotted over to the water.

Gom stood uncertainly. Leave Zamul to the solahinn? That was an idea. What would they think when they sighted the body of the man whom they thought to be

Gom's master, and Gom riding away on their priceless cito?

He quickly knotted the thong and slipped the rune back on. He ran to the water hole, drank, and sluiced the blood off him, stinging the grazes on his head and hands. Then he washed the rune, too, of the conjuror's touch. The image of Zamul changing shape wouldn't go away. What a horrible way to die!

Zamul had obviously lost control again, just as he'd done before, first back up north, when Carrick wounded him. Then in the stables only yesterday, when Gom had struck him with the staff. Changing shape and holding it must take great energy and much concentration, Gom thought. The gift of magic was not without its price. He sighed heavily.

Stormfleet nuzzled his shoulder. "Time to move on," he said. "You're not still moping over that human, are you?" The cito shook his mane. "You know, I'm beginning to think there's some truth in what that Jofor said. You can be no common human boy, as you claim, not with that creature after you. And grieving over that scum? Who are you, anyway?"

Gom looked up, surprised. "Why, I'm as I said: a woodcutter's son, from Windy Mountain, which is back of nowhere. My father, rest his soul, was but a plain man of the earth."

"Maybe," Stormfleet said. "And maybe you think that truly. But earth breeds earth, and there's more to you than that. Master Gom, a seed's true nature will out in the end, and reveal its source, grass and tree and horse—and even human. So who's your dam?"

Gom gazed at Stormfleet in wonder. "My mother is Harga," he said. "Harga the Brown."

"Aha!" Stormfleet tossed his mane triumphantly. "There you are. I knew it! No earth child is she, but the greatest—" He broke off, his nose snuffling the air, his ears twitching.

Gom was too dazed to notice. "You know Harga? What do you know, Stormfleet!"

Stormfleet neighed urgently. "No time! Up, Master Gom! We must ride!" The cito knelt.

Gom looked around, saw nothing but empty plain.

Wind blew about his head.

The beast speaks true, Gom Gobblechuck. Go with him! I cannot help you, for riders come from all directions. Speed, and the cito's cunning is your only chance against them!

Gom scrambled onto Stormfleet's back, and they set off at a gallop, westward, away from the sun, in the direction of Long Valley. Suddenly, Stormfleet checked and reared, nearly toppling Gom from his perch. Straight ahead, a solid line of riders came over the horizon, approaching fast.

Stormfleet wheeled about and set off north. But riders came from that way, too. They looked east, then south. On every hand, just as Wind had warned Gom, riders advanced through the waving grasses.

Gom held tight, feeling the fear rising through both of them as Stormfleet turned and turned about.

The riders neared.

Stormfleet stopped still. "We'll let them come close, then make a break for it. It's our best chance!" he neighed.

Some chance, thought Gom, looked at the advancing ring of riders. And at the same time thinking that Stormfleet was every bit as stubborn as he.

Stormfleet turned slowly about, watching the riders close in. Gom could make out their hats flapping back in the wind. There came a faint triumphant shout, then two, then more.

"Hai-tah! Hai-tah! Dahai-kah!"

Gom watched them helplessly. He was so close to success, with Zamul gone now. And he'd even begun to solve the riddle.

My father was but a plain man of the earth . . . Who is your dam . . . Harga, Harga the Brown . . .

"From Air and Earth comes seed . . ."

Could he yet solve it, get them out of there? Panic sped his thought, sharpened his mind. He remembered his vision back in the cave, of the sparrow and the bear. Air and Earth, sparrow and bear—Harga and Stig! And if they were the Air and the Earth, then—with a shock, the truth burst upon him.

I, he breathed. *I myself am the seed!*

The horsemen closed in so near that Gom could see Jofor leading, hear his harsh cries over the rest. A whip cracked, sending Stormfleet rearing again.

In the stockade there'd been no time for magic. But here? He closed his hand about his mother's stone. In the deep cave under Great Krugk, his will had worked the rune's power—by Harga's wish, for sure.

Would she help now?

As Jofor's whip curled out toward him, with one hand clutching Stormfleet's mane, the other, the rune, Gom drew his mind to a single point.

Mother! he urged with his whole thought. *As I'm the seed, so hear me! Help me now!*

The whip snicked past his ear, but he never felt it, for in that same moment the horsemen, the wide dawn sky and the waving plains vanished like smoke, and he with the cito were engulfed in a whirl of sound and light.

Chapter Nineteen

MOTIONLESS at the center of the rushing, roaring vortex, Gom clung to Stormfleet's mane, one hand still locked about his mother's stone. He closed his eyes, tried to calm his pounding heart. Don't panic, he told himself. Don't be afraid. This must be Harga's doing. She'd heard him, and was answering with powerful magic.

The sound of the wind rose in pitch. Light exploded against his eyelids. He squeezed them tighter shut, thinking, Stormfleet must be terrified.

"Don't worry! We're safe!" Gom yelled in Stormfleet's ear. His voice sounded tiny, thin. If the cito heard it, he didn't answer. They hung in space, fused together like a wooden carving, the noisy whirlwind turning about them, until Gom's head filled with images of frantic trees, and flashing silver leaves.

All at once, the vortex slowed, the soundpitch fell, and the light faded.

But the trees remained, towering about him, slowly straightening and settling back their branches in the aftermath. They were real!

Gom gazed at them in awe.

Their ancient mossy trunks and limbs were looped with hairy creepers thick as his arm. Letting go of Stormfleet's mane, he reached out, felt rough, cool bark and moss soft as a mouse's ear.

Gom let out a deep breath, his heart filling with admiration. "I was born in a wood, I was raised in a wood, and I've seen woods a-plenty on my travels, but I've never seen your like," he declared. "You must be the greatest wood in all Ulm."

A gentle wind touched his face, lifting the leaves above his head with a soft, soothing sound. Not the Wind he knew, but a gentle, dreamy cousin.

Gom looked down, saw his other hand still stiff about his mother's rune. One by one, he relaxed his fingers, lifting them from the little stone until it fell against him, dangling from its crudely knotted thong. Soon, any moment now, he'd lift it from around his neck for the last time. Unconsciously, he laid his palm across his chest against his coming loss.

Stormfleet stirred under him. "What happened? Where is this?"

Gom shook his head. "I don't know. His voice was hushed. "I think—I think my mother brought us here." He peered through the dim trees, waiting for Harga to emerge. She was very near, he felt it. "Mother!" he called. "Mother, I'm here!"

The call rang through the greenwood.

Here . . . ere . . . ere . . .

But Harga didn't come.

With a sigh, Gom turned back to the cito. "Stormfleet, what do you know of my mother?"

"Not a deal. All wizards are secretive folk. And she's of the Brown Order, the most secretive of all, for those folk work alone." Stormfleet gently butted Gom's shoulder. "Had I dreamed you were her son, I'd have taken to you sooner. Save present company, she's the only human I'd tolerate."

"Why?"

"She's friend to all creatures, and she speaks all tongues. Of course," he went on, "I can see your connection now, for no one else in all Ulm knows the languages of beasts!"

"You didn't know that she had a son?"

Stormfleet blew out his cheeks. "No, no more does anyone else. Harga dropped from sight a good while back. They say she was caught up in some high wizardry east of the Vargue, where no man goes."

East of the Vargue? If Gom remembered rightly, the High Vargue had stretched to the very edge of Carrick's map. He tried to make sense of what Stormfleet was saying, but was too hungry to think.

Gom looked around at the trees, the creepers, the knee-high ferns they were standing in. Nothing here to eat. They'd have to forage.

"Come, Stormfleet." Gom strode toward a gap in the trees.

Stormfleet raised his head, sniffed the air cautiously, then followed.

They had not gone above three dozen paces when gloom exploded into brilliant sunshine. Before them was a small bright clearing, thick-carpeted with tender grass and, glory, dark wineberries, round, yellow breadberries, and plump strawberries bright as rubies in the light; clumps of cob blooms, ripe brown nuts already crowding the high spiked stems, and golden grapes on vines. To wash all this down? At the clearing's edge, a spring splashed over pebbles. Gom gazed wide-eyed at this summer feast—nay, *banquet*. A gift from Harga, for sure.

But where was the giver?

He frowned faintly. Of course. He'd still not solved the riddle. But not long now, he thought excitedly. Not once he had food inside him to fortify his thinking . . .

Gom plucked and ate until he could eat no more. Then, while Stormfleet nibbled on, he sat and leaned against a tree. There, with the sense of Harga strong and warm about him, he turned his mind back to the puzzle.

From Air and Earth comes seed . . . That first line he now knew. Air was Harga, Earth was Stig, and he was the seed sprung from the two.

By Fire and Water is tempered . . .

Fire and Water? Hmm. Gom pursed his mouth. Two opposing elements. One destroyed life, the other nurtured it. But back home on Windy Mountain, Pinkle the black-smith had needed both to strengthen iron into steel.

Exclaiming softly, Gom sat up. By fire and water he'd conquered Katak, and he'd danced to the fire of the whip on the plain—and thus had his "path of experience" strengthened him!

In Wood is kernel's secret essence known,
And purpose comes to light.

Wood.

He reached for the staff and looked the sparrow in the eye, the little bird who'd spoken with his mother's voice.

"Is it you?" he whispered. "Are you the Wood?" He'd thought so since the night in the cave. But he could be wrong. Come to think, the sparrow had said *in* wood. Not *from* or *by* wood.

He set the staff down, leaned back again, thinking of when he'd chopped Hort's wood. The axe, cleaving the weathered bark, had exposed the bright, the hidden grain, the inner stuff. *The secret essence?*

Maybe, but of a thing full grown.

If he read the riddle right, then he, Gom, possessed some secret essence. An essence with a purpose important enough for Harga to risk her precious rune, her own son's life to have him find her.

In Wood is secret essence known . . . He gazed into the trees . . . and came up slowly.

The answer was all around him: this was a wood. And he was in it! Right here he was about to discover his own secret essence. And his purpose!

Stormfleet trotted over to stand by him.

"Master Gom: if your mother brought us here, where is she?"

Gom turned from his thought with an effort. "Don't know," he said. "But she's close."

"Then why doesn't she come?"

"She—gave me a task. It's not yet done. She won't come until then."

"What sort of task?"

Gom remembered Ganash's warning. "I can't say."

"You'll finish it here?"

"Any minute now."

"Is there any way that I can help you along?"

Gom shook his head. "Thank you, but the answer's here," he said, and laid a finger on his brow.

A cool breeze blew over them, setting the vines swaying. Gom looked up, glimpsed stars twinkling in an evening sky. The day gone by already?

Darkness fell, the moon, edging into view, flooded the space with light.

Gom gazed around at the majestic trees, thinking of Stig in a rush of longing. He began to hum quietly to himself, then to sing.

> On the day my father died,
> I raised up on high—

Stormfleet snuffled softly. Still singing, Gom glanced up to find the horse standing alert, ears pricked, looking out into the darkness. Gom followed his direction, saw nothing but wide mossy trunks, and creeper, and—the strangest creatures he'd ever seen: part man, part bear, tall and shaggy, and crowned with antlers like a stag's.

Gom faltered, then stopped altogether. The creatures ceased swaying, yet stayed put, their eyes fixed on him. So well did they merge with the trees now that Gom wouldn't have seen them had he not known they were there. What were they doing, standing like that, staring at him? Why, Gom's face grew warm. They were waiting for him to go on singing.

"It's all right—I think," Gom murmured to Stormfleet. Clearing his throat, he began his song anew.

> On the day my father died,
> I raised up on high his cairn of stone;
> And left behind my homely mountainside,
> For to roam about the world alone.
>
> Now I must seek and I must find
> The riddle's hidden key:
> The treasure locked within my mind,
> To bring my mother to me.

In spite of his reassurance, Gom noticed, Stormfleet didn't move, but remained watchful until he was satisfied for himself that all was well. Not until Gom finished his quest song did the cito finally stir, and bend his head once more to his grazing.

The strange creatures remained, waiting.

For more? Gom sang on, songs that his father had taught him. He began a woodchopping song, then remembering where he was, hastily dropped that for another celebrating the coming of summer.

The creatures stood throughout, swaying as if in ecstasy, until Gom had sung all he knew three times around. Then, in Stig's honor, he repeated his quest song, adding more verses, turning the tune's sad overtones into a hearty ballad of his travels, finishing on a happy note just as Stig would have wanted, for his father had been such a cheerful soul.

The last notes faded, and so did the mysterious visitors, without sign or word. Gom ran to the edge of the clearing, to where the creatures had stood, found no sign that they'd ever been there.

He took off the rune and held it up to the moonlight. Harga's rune. And yet in a way his, too, having worn it so long. And hadn't he worked magic with it? He sighed. Harga's magic, not his.

He gazed out into the darkness. The idea of making magic intrigued him. It also made him smile. He, a woodcutter's son, making magic? There I go again, he told himself. Am I not also Harga's son?

Like her, he knew the tongues of beasts. He'd also bet he'd gotten his gift of waking dreams from her.

He paced about the clearing. Power, inherited from Harga . . . He stopped still. His "secret essence"! As his mother was a wizard, so would he be, his mother's son!

He paced again, this knowledge raw upon him, until it stretched a little, softened, settled about his shoulders more comfortably.

Of course, he should have guessed it sooner. It was so obvious now. But what of his purpose? Not simply, to make his own magic one day. No. There must be more to the riddle's mystery than that. What? Gom put his hands to his head, in a fever now.

"You look tired," Stormfleet whickered, looking up. "Try to rest."

Rest? With his mind a vortex? Gom lowered his hands. Stormfleet was right. He was past thinking. He stroked the cito's neck, bade him good night, and lay down. Maybe tomorrow, he thought, and closed his eyes.

But sleep didn't come easily. Over and over the question turned on its axis, around and around, for hours. To what purpose . . . purpose . . . purpose . . .

He galloped across the plain, Stormfleet moving swiftly under him. But ever ahead the gray cloud crawled, blocking the sun. "Faster, Stormfleet!" Gom cried. "Katak spreads his blight!" The horse's hooves flew over the grasses, but fast as they flew, the cloud flew faster.

Gom glanced up.

Overhead, a wide dark shape flew with powerful wingbeats, and, even as Gom looked, it swooped, straight for the rune.

Gom closed his hand about the stone and lashed out with the staff.

The dark form twisted, fell. And as it fell, the ground opened to receive it. Then Katak's cry rose from the depths.

"You have overcome . . ."

". . . the world's dark doom this day!" cried Ganash, suddenly appearing, but Katak's fading shout prevailed:

". . . yet you have not destroyed me . . ."

The sun was just up when Gom awoke, his dream strong upon him.

"Mother," he said drowsily. "At last I know."

Far from ending, it was only just beginning, his purpose, his task. When or where it would lead, he could not even venture to guess. But at the mere thought of it, a faint spark of excitement kindled within him. He got up, stretched, and looked about the clearing to find Stormfleet already awake, grazing at its far side.

Not ready yet for morning talk, Gom walked to the spring where, kneeling, he drank deeply, then dunked his head.

The icy water hurt his very bone. He came up spluttering and shivering, but wide awake now.

A warning snort from Stormfleet brought Gom upright, turned him from the water's edge. He held still, not daring to breathe. From the middle of the clearing, a small brown figure raised her outspread arms toward him.

"Gom?"

He swallowed. "Mother?"

At his voice, she moved to meet him, broke into a run.

"Gom! My dear, dear son!" she said.

The Balladeer's Song

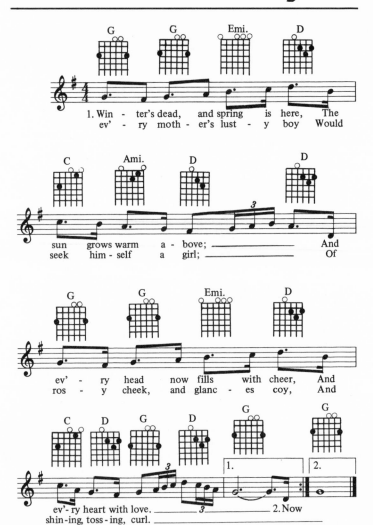

Mudge's Song

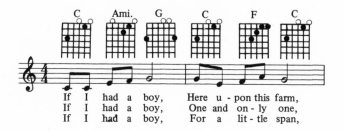

If   I   had   a   boy,   Here   u - pon this farm,
If   I   had   a   boy,   One   and   on - ly   one,
If   I   had   a   boy,   For   a   lit - tle   span,

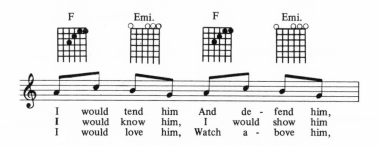

I   would   tend   him   And   de -   fend   him,
I   would   know   him,   I   would   show   him
I   would   love   him,   Watch   a -   bove   him,

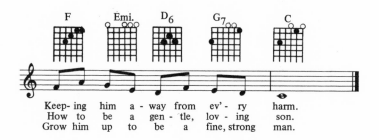

Keep- ing   him   a - way   from   ev' - ry   harm.
How   to   be   a   gen - tle,   lov - ing   son.
Grow   him   up   to   be   a   fine, strong   man.

Chant of the Solahinn

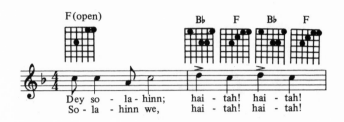

Dey so - la - hinn; hai - tah! hai - tah!
So - la - hinn we, hai - tah! hai - tah!

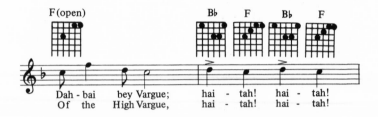

Dah - bai bey Vargue; hai - tah! hai - tah!
Of the High Vargue, hai - tah! hai - tah!

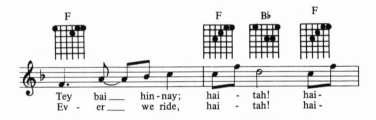

Tey bai___ hin - nay; hai - tah! hai -
Ev - er___ we ride, hai - tah! hai -

tah! hai - tah! Roh dai lahn - ney;
tah! hai - tah! This ground so wide,

Gom's Quest Song

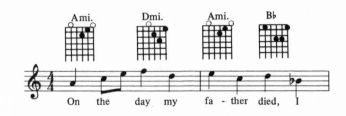

On the day my fa - ther died, I

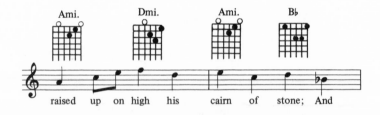

raised up on high his cairn of stone; And

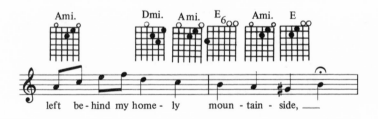

left be - hind my home - ly moun - tain - side, ___

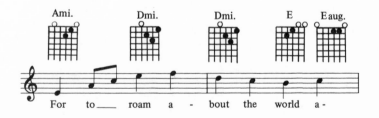

For to ___ roam a - bout the world a -

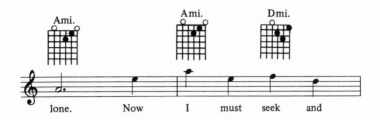

lone.   Now   I   must   seek   and

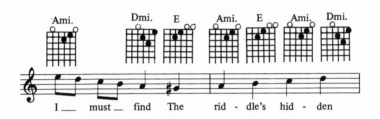

I __   must __   find   The   rid - dle's   hid - den

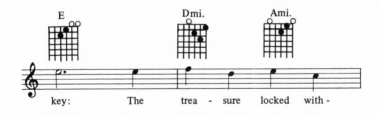

key: The   trea - sure   locked   with -

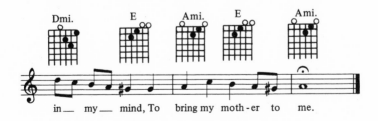

in __ my __ mind, To   bring my   moth - er   to   me.

Grace Chetwin

has been thinking about Gom Gobblechuck and his history for a long time. After graduating from Southampton University in England, she moved to New Zealand where she married Paddy Roberts. During the busy time after their daughters were born, she taught school and also formed her own dance company. Later her family settled on Long Island, New York, the setting for her first two suspense fantasies, *On All Hallow's Eve* and *Out of the Dark World*. Through it all, she continued to be fascinated with thoughts of what had happened to Gom in the land of Ulm. Then she began to write the TALES OF GOM. The first, *Gom on Windy Mountain*, is the prequel to a trilogy that will include *The Riddle and the Rune*, *The Crystal Stair*, and *The Starstone*.

4283

PLEASE SHARE YOUR
ON THIS

COMMENT:

COMMENT:

COMMENT:

COMMENT:

COMMENT:

COMMENT:

COMMENT:

COMMENT:

COMMENT:

COMMENT:

COMMENT:

COMMENT:

COMMENT:

COMMENT:

G-4